D1008929

Praise for Wayfarers of Fate

[*Wayfarers of Fate*] is vital to our understanding of the world we live in today. It portrays the conflict of values and the suffering brought about through war.

Dr Jules Vautrot, Prof. Emeritus, Chico State University

Wayfarers [is a] fine work. I'm pleased it's printed. The distortions of the Spanish War will be long in correcting. Your book is very helpful to that end.

Archbishop Edwin O'Brien, Head, Catholic Military Services and Bishop of Baltimore

Beautiful echoes of living and breathing the stark and mystical atmosphere of [Spain]. [He] creates very likeable characters, endearing to the reader; one's heart is wrenched at what they endure – the heartache and torture.

Andrew Armstrong, Library Director, Christendom College

This is one of the greatest anti-war … novels of all time.

The Challenge Magazine

I really enjoyed the book, having studied in Spain in the 1960s.

Father Anthony Bannon, Legionaries of Christ

I enjoyed the book very much.

John Moorehouse, *Catholic Men's Quarterly*

Marvellous reading, wonderful, a gem.

Roberta Whitney, St. Mary's, Kansas

Wayfarers of Fate is a cult favourite [in America]. The anti-communist, pro-Catholic approach and today's war on terror spark interest in the book.

Press Enterprise

Author and renowned TV/radio star touches the hearts of many with his novel.

Empire Radio News

As new as tomorrow's paper and as old as time. Sensitive. Explosive. Should be read by millions. It has the stamp of greatness.

Independent Journal

The basic theme so vividly depicted in *Wayfarers of Fate* ... rings true today ... I thank John Steinbacher, through his epic novel, for instilling in me a greater sense of urgency and motivating me all the more to speed up my quest to help remove these self-destructive diabolical forces within man before it's too late.

Alfred Barrios, PhD, Self-programmed Control Center

John Steinbacher is able to lift you up to an emotional peak, until you think you can't stand it, and then he brings you smashing back down again.

Gary Allen, author, *Western Islands Press*

[*Wayfarers*] captures the chaos, horrors and desolation of war. The characters are graphically tragic and the story a human tragedy. [The] descriptive narrative is all too real. [The] passion and devotion register vividly.

Patricia Harding, literary critic

WAYFARERS OF FATE

A Novel of the Spanish Civil War

John Steinbacher

ATHENA PRESS
LONDON

ISBN 10-digit: 1 84748 088 8
ISBN 13-digit: 978 1 84748 088 0

First Published 2006 by
Dorrance Publishing Co., Inc.
Pittsburgh, PA, USA

This Edition Published 2008 by
ATHENA PRESS
Queen's House, 2 Holly Road
Twickenham TW1 4EG
United Kingdom

Printed for Athena Press

In fond memory of Frances Marion, the legendary Oscar-winning MGM screenwriter, for her advice and encouragement in the writing of this book.

Also by John Steinbacher

Bitter Harvest

The Child Seducers

The Conspirators: Men Against God

It Comes Up Murder

Robert Francis Kennedy: the man, the mysticism, the murder (with Walter Winchell)

Distant Running

The Seven Deadly Sins and why we love them

Four Women Against Cancer – Foreword

An Inward Stillness and an Inward Healing: An anthology of lectures on emotions, stress and cancer, presented at conferences of the Cancer Federation, Inc., with case histories

Against all Odds: the Cancer Federation's triumphant history

Human Sexuality (contributed one chapter)

Prize Essays and Other Writings

John Steinbacher has also contributed many articles to *Classic Images* and *Films of the Golden Age* magazines. CD versions are also available of some of his books, including *The Child Seducers* read by John Carradine.

All flesh is as grass, and all the glory of man as the flower of the grass. The grass withereth and the flower fadeth away; but the Word of the Lord liveth for ever.

The Letter of Peter

Author's Note

The year of our Lord 1936 was a fateful time in the history of the world. The sand in the hourglass of International Communism was running low. Now the moment had come towards which they had lived and worked. A nation was locked in the throes of civil war and the testament of Lenin was at stake; for the first time communism's teachings would be put to the initial stern test outside the land that had spawned it.

Both Russia and Germany used the Spanish Civil War to perfect the murderous weaponry they would employ in World War II, but it was International Communism that stood to gain the most. Even the horrors unleashed by Hitler would not have as permanent an effect on our world.

In the wide sweep of history there had been no challenge to the Western way of life equal to the dark, ever-encroaching shadow of International Communism. The shadow permeated all areas of life, persuading, wooing, winning, losing, but always moving relentlessly forward towards the goal of world revolution.

Though this novel is set in the turbulent days of the Spanish Civil War, the author has not sought to write a war story in the usual sense of that term. The fighting, the battles, the struggle are all secondary to the more important fact of the struggle within the soul of a young man. The war years serve merely as a focal point, a point of emphasis for the ceaseless warfare between the many creeds of the modern day.

This story has been repeated endlessly, even in our own time, and the future holds for the Western world many more years of incessant struggle against diabolical forces that threaten to undermine the fabric of our civilisation. To understand the Spanish Civil War is to better understand the forces involved in today's worldwide war on terror.

This book is basically true. Names of principal characters have been changed to fit the demands of literary necessity.

The Gathering Storm

Let no man think lightly of evil, saying in his heart it will not come unto me.

By the falling of water drops the water pot is filled. The fool becomes full of evil, even if he gather it little by little.

The 'Dhammapada' of Buddha

Madrid, 1934

Juan Avila started the car, marvelling at the sound of power beneath the hood. 'I don't think anyone could catch us on the road, by the sound of this motor,' he said.

Pepe laughed shortly and flashed his companion a knowing glance. 'I suppose you're nervous. They always are – the first time.'

'Well, you have to admit it's a dangerous thing. I feel rather like Columbus must have as he set sail for China from the coast of Spain.' Juan resented the man's thinly veiled disdain.

'When you've made as many trips as I,' said Pepe, 'you'll find they're much like a drug. The dreams of one drown the memories of the others. Then there's always the thrill of pitting your strength alone, in the dark, against the bloodhounds of the capitalists.'

Nearing the spot, Juan glanced about apprehensively. Not a car was in sight. The shadow of two pedestrians loomed briefly under a flickering lamp. The crack of a nightwatchman's stick, tapping the doors of his allotted shops was the only sound that broke the stillness of the sleeping street.

Pepe swore a great oath. 'By all the powers of Satan,' he hissed, 'we have a couple of Civil Guards in that doorway yonder. I wonder why?'

The very name of that foreboding presence sent a chill

through Juan's being. Could an eavesdropper have overheard their plans? No, that was impossible. It must be mere coincidence.

There was now but a hundred feet to go. Pepe felt about on the floor of the car. His teeth flashed in a tense grin. As he sat erect again a hand grenade was clenched tightly in his fingers. Removing the pin, Pepe swung the door wide, stepping out on to the running board. Hanging on with his left hand, his right arm described a wide arc as he adroitly threw the bomb.

An inferno broke loose. First, the tinkling of glass as the missile tore through. Then, a second later, a roar that echoed and re-echoed around the deserted street, shaking the adjacent buildings. A wide sheet of flame shot through the broken window, illuminating with dazzling brilliance every detail of the surrounding houses. Windows shot open, as if by magic, and heads appeared, nightcapped and tousled. Worst of all, black-caped figures, with gleaming rifles and patent leather, flat-backed hats, heralded the approach of the mobile brigade of the feared Civil Guard.

The car leapt forward as Juan floored the accelerator. Up the hill towards Olavide he went, gaining by seconds: fifty, sixty, seventy. Shots ripped and tore around him. He heard, next to him, a sharp cough, followed by a low, gurgling sound. He was, by this time, far too immersed in his driving to pay any attention to what was going on. Then, just as he appeared to be free from danger, a bullet ploughed into the front tyre.

With a screaming of wheels on pavement, the vehicle careened wildly around. Juan knew in a flash that a crash was inevitable. By sheer force of will he guided the lunging vehicle into one of the many narrow side streets. Jamming on the brakes, he half-capsized with a rending roar into a wall that surrounded the house beside him.

Still acting on instinct, Juan limped from the car and doubled back on his trail, stumbling along the narrow sidewalk, falling at last, gasping and weak from his exertions, into a darkened doorway. He did so not a moment too soon, for Civil Guards were everywhere.

Juan hugged the cold stones in a sudden paroxysm of fear; but luck was with him. After what must have been hours, he dared to lift his head and peer around, noting that he had escaped with nothing more serious than an unaccountable lump on his forehead. No visible scratches or cuts, though broken glass was strewn all over the street. He breathed an audible sigh of relief.

The blushing light of early dawn was sending its rosy appeal into the black night, as if forgiving the hatred of man and seeking to tell the peace and poetry of nature. Sore in every muscle, Juan eased himself erect and made his way wearily towards the Metro station of Fuencarral, hoping he would be taken for what he was supposed to be, a hiker preparing a trip to the mountains. Yes, he had planned the whole thing well, even to the proper garb. He smiled grimly. Too bad about Pepe. Dead, probably, but better off than in the hands of the Civil Guard.

A little tavern was open on a side street as he neared the Glorieta de Bilbao. They were serving *churros*, those crisp-fried morning delicacies so loved by the Spanish people.

With a stifled yawn, the sleepy woman behind the counter stared at him. 'Young man,' she said, 'you're up early. You must have heard all the shooting; but that's so common these days that it would be more surprising not to hear it in some parts of Madrid.'

'The shooting?' Juan glanced suspiciously at the woman. 'No, I've heard nothing that sounded like shooting.'

I must stay calm, he thought. *Under all conditions, I must remain calm.*

She shrugged her shoulders in disbelief. 'You must sleep very soundly then, young man.'

'Have you a telephone?' he asked.

'Yes, of course. However, it's a public one and you'll have to pay.'

The sleepy voice of his brother, Pedro, droned in his ear. 'Yes, this is Pedro. Oh, Juan. Well, what've you been up to now, brainy one?'

Juan lowered his voice to a whisper. 'I'm in grave danger. You've got to come, and at once. You must get me out of this.'

Shortly thereafter a taxi stopped before the entrance of the Metro station. Juan was all but thrown into the rear seat by his brother.

15

'Say nothing now, you fool,' Pedro said. 'Do you want the driver to broadcast the news, mass organiser – or something?'

He barked to the driver. 'To the Estación del Norte, and hurry! We must make the seven o'clock train.'

As they wheeled rapidly away from the sidewalk, Juan slumped down in the corner. The silence was heavy and oppressive. Pedro was angry, that much at least was clear. And Juan remembered other days. Days when that same sort of slowly kindled fury would be written on an older face, a face that was not unlike the one before him – the face of his dead father. And his father's words sounded again in his ears.

It had been one of his regular nights at the Party meeting. Juan had been detained somewhat later than usual. As he stepped quickly towards the doorway of his house, the dim glow from the street lamp had illumined his face for an instant. Dark eyes and curly black hair crowned a lofty forehead, features calculated by nature to seduce just about anyone. This was coupled with a body athletically slim and tall, a figure of graceful poise.

Carefully Juan had inserted his key into the ancient lock. With a dull creaking the door had swung open to reveal the familiar form of his father, his face pale with anger.

'Well, young man,' he said, 'what is the meaning of all this?'

'The meaning?' Juan's slim figure had tautened perceptibly. 'I have none to offer. I was detained by my professor of physics and that is all.'

Don Juan Avila's eyes had flashed, the blood rushing into his face. 'How dare you speak to your father in that tone of voice? To your room, young man, before I lose my composure. We'll talk on the morrow.'

When Juan entered his room that night, Pedro had whispered sharply, 'Juan, is that you?'

'Who else?'

'Well, eat your food, brainy one. You'll find it under your bed as usual on nights like this. Tomorrow you'll find a mighty storm brewing.'

Pedro Avila. Juan could not avoid smiling at the resemblance between the father and his younger brother. The same heavy, broad forehead; the deep-set, grey eyes, staring unblinkingly and fearlessly at life. A stubborn face, no doubt, and yet a face of great calm. Juan was forced always to admit, though often begrudgingly, that his brother inspired great confidence and trust in all those who knew him.

'Storms have blown over this house before, my brother,' said Juan, 'and we are not carried away as yet. Bigger storms must come one day. Then the small buffetings of these family quarrels will be as a breeze in the midst of a hurricane.'

'Words, words. All I ever hear from you are words,' his brother had replied. 'So far I see little action of any kind, only words that buffet my eardrums. Why can't you be sensible, Juan? Take things as they come. When you're older there will be plenty of time for opinions. Now you'll always be on the losing side. Father's fully aware of all your little confabulations, though I doubt if he senses exactly where your road is leading you. You're supposed to be the brainy one of this family, and yet I fail to see where those brains of yours are taking you, for you're always in trouble of one kind or another. Of course I'll never say a word about it, but if Father knew that you were a spokesman for a student group that seems to be of the slightly abnormal way of thinking, to express it politely, he'd have a seizure, and Mother would be prostrate. If that ever happens, I'll break your damned neck. No one has any right to trouble a household with these infernal hodgepodge ideas.'

Juan had flared back. 'You can't understand, nor will you ever be able to understand. As long as you get three meals a day, can go to school and come back with your stupid grades, you're content. You remind me of a dumb ox.'

'An ox, am I? Well, just remember brainy brother; bulls die in the ring with all measure of man-made unpleasantness to accompany them to their death. The oxen lead them to the ring, and then go back to the fields that await them.'

Pedro's heavy hand on his arm aroused Juan from his reverie. The voices, the words, the memories faded away. Stark reality flooded in once again.

They had reached the station, and Juan saw, with a visible shudder, the stalwart forms of the inevitable Civil Guards, accompanied by a solitary plain-clothes man. They were asking for documents, and searching all who passed with rough but methodical hands.

Hiding behind the hefty form of his brother, Juan heard Pedro reply to the demands of the guard. 'Certainly, at seven o'clock in the morning, going up to the mountains for some hiking; we have brought along our baptismal papers and our records of grades in school.'

The guards sidled closer. 'You seem very jaunty this morning. Perhaps you'd enjoy cooling your heels until tonight?'

'My brother meant no offence,' said Juan. 'It's just that we want to reach the mountains before the better part of the day has passed.'

For an instant the spokesman for the duo of guards looked full into Juan's face. He began to speak – hesitated, and then signalled them on with an imperious wave of his arm. 'Damned hoodlums,' he mumbled noisily. 'They think they run the whole city.'

As Pedro shouldered his way resolutely through the thinning crowd, Juan felt like a baggage cart as he trundled along in the rear. *Don't look back,* he thought. *The worst thing you can do is to look back.*

Seated at last in the almost empty second-class carriage, Juan leaned back and released a pent-up sigh. He was disgruntled to hear his brother growl angrily in return, 'Save your breath. If you let out so much air you'll never breathe again. Keep something inside, and take whatever comes. I don't know what you're up to these days, brainy one, but whatever it is, I'll wager it's not healthy for either of us. Have you thought of the mess you're going to cause?'

'Mess?' Juan turned to him and flashed a grim smile. 'I'm sure I don't know what you mean, brother.'

'Oh, don't you?' Pedro clenched his great hands. 'Strange that you never know anything about it, and yet you're always willing to be a participant. What's worse, I think you're not only a participant but a leader. Well, understand this much. I've no use for the creed you seem to espouse so highly. I wouldn't have come this time, save that Mother insisted I help you out again. I know little enough about your creed, thank God, but I do know enough about it to know that it can lead only to the grave.'

'Don't all creeds?'

'Don't they do what?'

Juan laughed shortly, and threw his cap into the air. 'Why, lead to the grave, of course.'

'That may be,' returned Pedro, 'but some faster than others. By the looks of you, I'd say that you've already been seeing the spirits from another world. Don't tell me you've been reading books all night. They say there are many ghosts up in the valley of Fuenfria. Since that's where we're heading, perhaps it's as well that you've already been initiated into their company.'

Juan squirmed under the cold shower of Pedro's biting sarcasm but he knew he would have to bear it for a time. He sensed nothing but calamity ahead.

'By the way,' Pedro continued, 'I might tell you now that we are going to climb up the *Siete Picos* today. I want your face blistered by the sun, else you'll never prove to a soul that you've been out of Madrid at all.'

With a groan, Juan flashed his brother a pleading glance. 'I doubt if I'll make it, but I'll try. After all, I'm slightly more than out of condition, and I haven't slept in forty-eight hours.'

'You bet you'll try. You'll try about twelve hours of it at least. If you're so out of training that you can't make it, I'll carry you up the slope.'

'Aren't you the noble one?' Juan was growing tired of Pedro's insistent needling. 'I can still out-walk you, even if I haven't slept for two days.'

The family was having lunch around the table. Juan, with his peeling nose and lobster-coloured face, was every inch the mountain hiker. He was so bone weary he could scarcely move. Even his neck throbbed and ached. The unaccustomed exertion of the strenuous climb, coupled with the mental and emotional tumult of the preceding hours, had rendered him virtually speechless from fatigue.

His two young sisters, seemingly oblivious of any uneasiness in the room, were chattering softly together. Pedro was tense and nervous, expecting the inevitable. The front pages of all the Madrid newspapers had carried the news. Civil Guards had overtaken the bullet-riddled car, and had discovered a critically injured anarchist. Word had it that his recovery was assured, though he had not regained consciousness at last report.

The doorbell rang. Juan stared at his brother, and in his eyes was a mute appeal. Once again, insistently, the bell rang out. Pedro's chair rasped against the floor. Without a word he arose and walked along the passage towards the door.

'Does Juan Avila live here?' came the loud query.

The reply was evasive. 'Perhaps. Who are you? What do you want him for?'

'I'd say everything speaks for itself. Suffice to say that we should enjoy his company today.'

Juan struggled to his feet. He turned his eyes away from his mother's accusing glance. Kissing her lightly upon the cheek, he walked firmly to the door. She said not a word, yet her eyes held a world of soundless terror – Delores, of the once beautiful face, now drawn and grey. Lines of sorrow and bitterness pulled down the corners of the once gay mouth. Juan remembered, in his childhood days, that stately figure, with great eyes dreaming of flowers and poetry. Those same eyes had dulled now under the passage of time. He had always known that she longed to stroll with the crowds that thronged the streets below; yet she had been the wife of the *Apoderado* of the Duque del Bosque, and seldom appeared, even now, in public, for it was not proper. Her entire life had been centred about her husband and her children. To church on Sundays, to rosary services on Fridays, and perhaps to the theatre on Thursdays – if her husband could be inveigled into taking her. Aside from this, the weary days passed endlessly, with only the time-consuming sewing and household tasks to enliven her life.

At last the open door, and Juan came face to face with those he had sensed he would meet. Two Civil Guards and a plain-clothes man. He was relieved to see that they were not the trio of the station encounter. Now he felt the shame of rough hands pushing him unceremoniously on to the floor of the police wagon, where he found, to his instant surprise, other members of his anarchist youth centre. One of the unfortunates had a welt across his mouth, and a cut on his forehead oozed drops of bright, shiny blood. Juan felt suddenly ill. It was evident that the man had been badly beaten.

Already a group of idlers formed about the police wagon, overflowing from the sidewalk into the street, the usual curiosity seekers that form anywhere in Madrid, though the street may have been deserted but seconds before.

And as the vehicle rumbled away over the rough street, Juan was reminded of that other long-ago revolution and of the tumbrils clattering over the ancient cobblestones of Paris.

He was in a dark room, with little ventilation and no comforts; but he was not thinking of physical pain or discomfort. As the natural leader of the group, none of whom had accompanied him on his unfortunate mission, he quickly seized the initiative and thought only of his possible defence.

'Comrades,' he said, looking steadily at each in turn, 'come to the centre of the room.'

Once he had them there, he whispered, 'Talk in as low a tone as possible, and as near the centre of the room as you can. The walls have ears – mechanical ears. We must all say that we know one another from the reunions, for that we can't deny. We've had no activity in subversive campaigning, nor in any political plots. I've been a spokesman for political reunions and that's all. Then too, I went to the mountains for a few days with my brother for a holiday. I was overtired from my work.'

Minutes after, all was still. The door was shoved violently open by a thundering captain of the guard. 'In the Devil's own name,' he roared, 'who's responsible for putting these hooligans together in one cage? I'll know who's responsible for this stupid blunder, for by all the saints, it'll probably cost me my place. I'll be removed to some crazy provincial village.' He paused to take note of the cell, singling out Juan's jaunty and assured air as the butt of his wrath. 'You there – everything is peaceful, I take it? Well, my fine friend, I'll say that everything's not so peaceful as you might think.' He turned to the cowering guard and continued in the same vein. 'And you, my loyal stalwart, don't you know that a hornet's nest has been let loose? With all the shooting and whatnot, there's been more harm done than with the actual bomb itself. Everything happens to me.' He shook his head in woeful disbelief.

Juan could not help smiling at how small coincidences could make or unmake, could create or destroy a life.

He was left alone for two days and nights. Not a word was he allowed to speak, and from the guards he received only curses and abuse. Was not he one of those responsible for the killing of so many policemen? He was alone, with time to think. It was a time to plan and scheme – and a time to remember.

He remembered his father's words on the occasion of his seventeenth birthday. In the darkness of the filthy cell the voice sounded strangely clear.

'Juan, my son. I've made great sacrifices that I've not mentioned heretofore. Nonetheless, you're coming to the age when you must be told the facts. You've been to school to acquire knowledge. It's well and good that this should be so. But no man can propound knowledge until he has digested whatever he has obtained in his youth. You have to understand this thing. You cannot pass judgment about a series of events and lives that you have never had the slightest opportunity to observe. I don't know where your footsteps have taken you, my son, nor into what books of philosophy you've dipped, but I do know that those same books construe cases to prove their point. Their suppositions may be all wrong from the outset. They've taught you well, or ill, whichever you prefer, and I can only pray that one day you will see the folly of your ways. I've long since despaired of changing you by any other means. My son, I hope you will always remember to say your prayers, even as I remember to say mine. You're still very young, and have only a short time to look back upon. Still, as the years toll on, your memory will recall little coincidences, small items strewn along the pathway of your life. These things will cause you to pause and reflect. In any case, prayer is a good custom. It makes you forget your person, if only for a little time.'

In the darkened cell, Juan sought to remember the prayers of his youth. But they were gone now – all gone – even as his faith was gone, not to be regained.

A sound at the cell door aroused him from his thoughts. To

his surprise, the dark-clothed figure of the Duque del Bosque, his dead father's employer, blocked the view into the dark passageway. His first instinct upon seeing the dignified form in the doorway was to run. He wanted to flee anywhere to escape the accusing face that bent over him.

'Well, you've found the trouble you've looked for these past years. Your mother, I might say, is in a terrible state. Your brother behaves as if all the demons of hell had broken loose inside him. He would like to get his hands on you first of all. Then he would like to murder the Civil Guards and, worst of all, he wants to blow up all the centres of anarchist youth. You, at least, are safe for the moment, thank God. As I say, your mother is prostrate. Your sisters don't seem to know what is happening, and you, my fine friend, are in a most precarious position. Your happy little adventure of the other evening is considered a direct blow at the state, and in these troubled times such actions are not being passed over lightly. No, you're in a bad position.' He shook his head and stared moodily at Juan.

Hanging his head and avoiding the man's piercing glance, Juan bit his lip and remained silent. Why had the Duque come here – to this place where only rats and darkness were at home? He wished, above all else, that the man would leave.

The Duque was old-fashioned in his ways, and Juan sensed instinctively what was passing through the man's mind. His long life had been straight-laced and strict, lacking in humour. The face, with its thin, aquiline nose, the dark, deep-set eyes, high forehead, and slightly sensuous mouth, revealed him to be an innate artist, one who considers all things, be they animate or inanimate, distinct works of art. Polished in manner, a trifle cynical, he was accustomed to wealth in such degree that it no longer remained a thing of importance to him. Since the ninth century, when his mighty-limbed ancestor had hacked and hewn his way through Saracen hordes to save his king's banner, wealth and ownership had been an integral part of his family's tradition. And yet Juan was certain, in this moment, that the Duque's bond of friendship with his dead father had been great and to men such as these friendship was a chain impossible to break.

He heard, as from a great distance, the man's voice, tired and old. 'If you've not forgotten your prayers, my fighting friend, you'd better pray hard. There's only a slim chance of getting you out of a twenty-year sentence in Rio de Oro, which would mean your end long before that. Don't say a thing to anyone, and in answer to their every question say only that I'm taking care of your defence. Under no circumstances speak to another prisoner. He might be, and in all probability will be, an informer. Don't write or scribble a thing. That I should live to see the day when the son of my dear friend, Don Juan Avila, may his soul be at rest, is locked up in a dungeon like a common criminal! You should be thoroughly ashamed. But words sound futile in the face of reality. I'll try to secure your release, though I wonder why I should, since it appears you'll only get involved in more of these crazy escapades. I don't wish to have anything to do with the ideals of that Party you so foolishly seem to espouse.'

In all this time Juan had not uttered a word. Now his thoughts flew backwards, even as the footsteps of the Duque were fading away down the long corridor. The old man was right, in part at least. Yet if this same man had been forced, by circumstances, into different surroundings, both social and economic, his frame of mind would have been entirely different. How true was the ancient proverb, 'the scene takes the colour of the glass we look through.' Juan smiled at the analogy. This man of royal blood had been favoured by destiny. His parents had showered upon him the gifts and possessions of his every whim and fancy. He had doubtless been an apt student, but he had never known a moment of difficulty in pursuing his activities. He had never known the problems of debt and credit, of fighting against the odds between income and outgo. Juan remembered his garden, filled with flowers that served to pacify a turbulent day. He had strolled there many times when his father was still alive, and the fragrance of the flowers seemed even stronger in memory.

Shrugging his shoulders, he turned away from the barred door, and threw himself down upon the narrow cot. But sleep would not come. If the Duque had been born in between poverty of all kinds, both physical and spiritual, and had been forced to fight his way through life with all the burdens of lack and need, with the hatred of unfulfilled desire burning in his breast, and with the thwarting bitterness of striving for impossible aims, then his outlook would have been considerably altered. The absence of schooling of a proper nature warped and hindered the best of brains. In the balance of Juan's brooding thoughts, in the darkness of the lonely cell, the weight fell once again towards the needy masses. If the organisations of this present world had produced two antagonistic forces, then there must be a form, a philosophy or a political creed that would serve to span this ever-widening gulf.

Voices in the Wind

When a man allows himself to be guided by passion, his conduct
will be wrong. This is true whether the passion be fear or love or
sorrow or distress. The ambition and wickedness of one man can
reduce the whole State to rebellious disorder, for such is the
nature of influence.

The Ta Hsio of Tsang

Juan was sent to the general prison next to the Monclo, the red-
brick building known as the Carcel Modelo. There he was put
into one of the cells with two other men, one a cheap racketeer,
the other held on a burglary charge. He remembered the counsel
of the Duque; so, although it was sometimes difficult, he held his
peace, save to conduct the inevitable niceties.

These were sullen days, darkened by the depersonalising of a
grey mass of convicts, who day in and day out, hour after hour,
knew what they were going to do at exactly the same hour, the next
day, the next week, the next month, and so on until the end of their
terms. Juan would stare at them as they queued in front of their
cells, going out in pairs along the rail-floored corridors, down the
clanking iron stairs. All were dressed in identical grey, with their
funny cylindrical caps, their corresponding numbers on jacket and
cap. On they would march to their positions in the great courtyard.
'Left face!' would thunder from the loudspeakers: new alignments
for different jobs, different teams, some to the pantry, some to the
bakeries, others to the workhouses. All to some job that did not
attract their attention, for each was thinking of his own particular
grievance. Some went with remorse; many in hatred; a few with
forgiveness; others with thoughts of revenge.

It was a murky day in February when Juan's name and number
were called out over the loudspeaker. Four months had passed.

He walked down to the long hall where guests were received, his heart pounding wildly, his pulse racing. As he was led into one of the conversation booths, the guard growled roughly as he pushed him forward, 'There's your family! It's better than you deserve, you damned anarchist. You and your kind are responsible for the death of my brother up in Oviedo.'

Delores, his mother, stood there with trembling lips, dressed in her accustomed black. His sisters, who were startling replicas of their mother, kept twisting and turning limp white handkerchiefs in their small hands. Pedro stared at him in abject disgust. The Duque looked solemn.

It's the end, he thought. *They've come to tell me that their appeals were useless.*

A grille between them forbade contact. Delores, as usual, said nothing in the way of condemnation, only inquiring as to his well-being. She had brought him a packet, and it was being thoroughly examined by the guards. Not much, she reminded him, only some tortillas, a little ham, and some chorizo sausage. She complained that her bottle of wine had been confiscated at the gate.

'My guards will be merry this night,' he said without humour.

The Duque interrupted sharply. 'You've plenty of influence behind you. Everybody's trying to help, and I think you'll be freed. You've not been recognised as the driver of the cab, although one Civil Guardsman claims he saw you leaving on the train the morning of the incident. But the other guard is not sure, and your brother's alibi has come to be our greatest boon. The judges are my friends.'

'The judges are my friends.' The words sounded through Juan's brain like the tolling of a bell. If he had been an unknown somebody, a stern judge would have sentenced him to twenty years' hard labour. He breathed easily, and was surprised to note that his heart had ceased its pounding. Nothing would happen, or he might get six months' confinement for having belonged to an illegal organisation.

Five months later a pale and reedy Juan appeared at the family home. During his confinement, Juan's dreams and thoughts had become so intermingled as to be inseparable, one from the other.

This was his punishment for doing the thing he knew with all his being was the right thing. Some day his chance would come. Everywhere about him, even on this day of freedom, he could see the drab figures of necessity, the majority desperately striving to outdo the minority. Was it possible that wherever he went, whatever life he touched, be it in the country or the city, he would always encounter these drab figures? One day he would gather about him those who seemed most in need of spiritual support. He would regain his confidence, talk to the people around him in his infectious and emotional way, and win them over to his ideas. This was his dedication.

But bygones were forgotten in action, and several days later saw the brothers racing up the hill of the Calle Luchana to board the tram that was provided for the students of their school in the distant Cuatro Caminos. They were barely able to catch it. Juan, being the faster, scrambled aboard after one prodigious bound. Hanging on precariously with one hand, he stretched out the other to his labouring brother. Pedro grasped the proffered hand and was yanked bodily inwards.

'You're too fat,' observed Juan with a wry smile.

'Perhaps I am at that,' responded Pedro.

They were hailed by the usual crowd of noisy students. In the front of the vehicle were congregated all the seniors studying business administration. These were Juan's classmates, and he joined them amidst a chorus of shouted greetings.

'Well, Juan Avila, I thought the Civil Guards had done away with you by now.'

'Not quite.' He grinned. 'They did their noblest, however.'

'Well,' the unseen conversationalist echoed from a packed mass of students, 'you were never one to run from a fight, I'll say that much for you.'

Juan did not reply. As the tram heaved and bucked along, he relapsed into moody silence. *How singular the way action unites and custom separates,* he thought, *and all in short spaces of time. A few seconds ago, Pedro and I were running to achieve a goal, which was nothing but an old, broken-down train. Minutes later it's as though we lived in separate worlds. Pedro in his world of undergraduate students, and I in my own little world.*

The great, red-brick school building looked like a monstrous beehive. Thousands of beings – small and fat, thin and tall, tall and fat, thin and small – entered and disappeared, to come out again sometime later, noisier than before. Their suppressed feelings overflowed in the winding street, not unlike clouds of smoke coming forth from a chimney, billowing in a forever expanding radius until they finally disappear into the distance. The day was cold, and the building held little warmth.

In time the recreation period arrived amidst an overflowing torrent of relief. It was noon. Still the sun had been unable to penetrate the gripping hand of frost. An inch-thick coating of ice lay on the smallest puddles. The trees were motionless in the paralysing grip of cold. Sparrows hopped about on hardened feet with ruffled feathers, trying vainly to find something to eat on the hard ground.

Behind the iron railings that separated the poor students from the rich, blued hands ringed the bars. Faces that were already old in youth hissed and booed at the sons of the capitalists, those who had the more luxurious grounds, the better clothes. A football came soaring over the railing. Caught by a member of the hissing, booing group, the ball was quickly ripped to pieces by a knife. The football players became enraged at the interruption of their game. Stones began to fall in the midst of the shabbily dressed students.

A running figure interposed itself between the barrier and the stone-throwers. Springing upon the wall of masonry, he hung on the fence. Alone and undaunted, he faced the belligerence of his fellow students.

'One moment,' came like a clarion from the flashing-eyed youth. 'Listen to me. You're showing yourselves to be nothing but a lot of cowardly knaves. If you had to sweep those classrooms yonder, as those working students do, and clean the latrines every day, how would you feel? We complain about the food – and yet we have some. We complain about our petty difficulties – and yet we have some levity. We can raise a protest – and they cannot. You are driven to school in cars – they walk several miles to their houses. They see the food that we get – and they taste the food they eat. We have good, strong clothes, boots, and woollen socks to keep out the cold. What do they have? They have canvas *alpargatas*, and broken clothes that are so threadbare that they're torn in more than one place. You know me. I'm Juan Avila. Thanks to the generosity of the Duque del Bosque, I am one of you, but being one of you, I take their side in shame for your cowardly actions.'

Voices had been rising all the while. Now one of his fellows called out, 'Oh, close your mouth, Avila, before somebody closes it for you.'

The rumble of voices became more ominous. Juan raised a clenched fist in the air and thundered above the rising sound. 'Yes, I understand their hate! I know what's in their hearts! So would you, you milk-fed pigs, if you thought about it for even one instant. But no – you are too full of yourselves. Let us rejoin this fight without fences or walls when we leave school. Then let the better man prove himself, and you who have cried the loudest and thrown the biggest stones will meet your match.'

Black-robed figures began to appear in the doorways. There was a mad scamper. Where before passion had sprouted, now there was only the cloak of silence, and the fleeting form of a youthful runner.

The word passed from class to class, from room to room. Little balls of paper, carrying messages, were dropped carelessly in front of another member of a class, as, silent and with crossed arms, the students streamed by each other in double file. A wink of an eye, a barely perceptible raising of an eyebrow: the message was understood. A great bell tolled discordantly across the gloomy passageways, the endless classrooms, and the vast halls. The beehive opened its doors and the milling, shouting, throbbing mass poured forth under a leaden sky.

Gradually the moving throng dispersed. Two silent groups faced each other. One was well dressed and the other not; yet the faces had the same desire, the same expression, whether they were of one unit or of the other: hard mouths, fanatical eyes, flushed cheeks.

Around the campfires, in bygone days, warriors had danced, jumped and shouted, proclaiming to the world their courage and their fearlessness, vowing to overcome the enemy. Then, donning war masks, and painting their faces to achieve hideous expressions, with loud cries and shouts, wielding their clubs and axes, they had entered into battle. They had striven for victory over the enemy because of their right and the other's wrong, or because of their might and the other's weakness.

Now was the instant of waiting, the mustering of courage. No matter how well linked the chain of remembrance may be for youth, still, to launch an attack, to fulfil the grievance that memories retained, a desperate act must strike the spark to ignite the powder of conflict.

Juan's voice lilted up in its vibrant baritone. 'Weren't you brave in throwing stones and insulting those behind bars who could not defend themselves? What are you waiting for? Are you hoping the police will come, so you won't have to exert your well-fed selves?'

The most resolute stepped forward, still with slight hesitation. Action is difficult when things are unorganised, when the coldness of time has smothered the hot flame of argument.

Now there came a chance word. Perhaps it was an insult, a movement, or yet fear, which is the leader of all unpremeditated things. Two were fighting, then four. A second later, everybody was lashing out. Pent-up passions exploded; not passions of today, or of yesterday, or even of creed. Behind them lay pure hate, unfathomable and strange. Hate, the fire of destiny that blazes over even the most profoundly quiet of men, leaving after it the charred remains of something that was, and shall be no more. Men came running down the street to join the fray. These, too, were men who dreamed of success, men who were dressed in the clothing of need, for it was a workers' quarter. A shrill whistle announced the arrival of the police.

In the surging, throbbing throng, two groups were slowly but inexorably coming together. They were like the centres of light from which rays spring and are dispersed. Here a kick; there a blow, followed by a curse and a sigh; pulling, hugging, and squeezing, falling and rising again.

Sweating and panting, unforgiving and unbeaten, Juan and Pedro's eyes met. Perhaps remembrance of their mother's tender embrace in their childhood poured oil on the troubled waters.

From the greatest fear, laughter often is derived. So, from the primordial reactions of battle, these brothers found themselves united in the courage of fight, the cruelty of blows.

Already the navy blue of uniforms could be seen among the struggling belligerents. The fear of parents, the ridicule of friends, the possible detention by the police broke up the locked combatants. Running down the narrow street that bordered the garden of the school, Juan and Pedro sped into the coming night, nor did they stop until they had reached the fence of the Hippodrome, a good mile or more away.

Panting and out of breath, Pedro leaned against the fence. 'What the hell's the use of it all?' he asked aloud.

'I sometimes wish I knew,' said Juan. 'But I will say this much: I couldn't stand those stupid fools who aren't worth the price of a bag of peanuts throwing stones at those miserable boys on the other side of the fence. I notice, though, that as usual we came out on opposite sides. I suppose I should be used to it by now.'

'After all, my idealistic friend,' said Pedro, still gasping for breath, 'we are fortunate that the Duque has seen fit to pay our tuition; else we would be on the other side of the fence, too, if we were there at all. Besides, their tuition is paid as well as ours, and when all is said and done, through the payments that we make, they will be able to receive their baccalaureate, and perhaps will be able to acquire a career through which they can emerge from their poverty.'

'Big words,' grumbled Juan, 'but hardly realistic. You will never in a million years be able to understand that it is to the masses of the rejected that we owe our allegiance, and not to the favoured few. The Duque may think he's being kind by helping us attend school, but it's not really kindness at all. He merely feels that he is repaying father for all the miserable years of low salaries and substandard living that he endured before he died. He's trying to pacify his conscience.'

Pedro chuckled. 'Juan, you're hopeless. You can always think of more ways to talk yourself out of a corner.'

'And you,' returned Juan, 'are always saying that you dislike contentions, and yet I am nearly ready to swear that you are sorry when it's all over.'

They were nearing a tram. As they climbed stiffly aboard, the conductor gave them a glance of appraisal. 'Well, my boys, have bandits fallen upon you?' He looked back at his passengers and raised his voice. 'Perhaps you were in that little skirmish at Cuatro Caminos.'

Without a word, the two bedraggled passengers flung themselves off on to the sidewalk as the tram was getting under way.

'This will never do,' said Juan. 'We must try to clean ourselves up a bit. Your sweater is torn. Perhaps you can knot a few threads and make it look reasonably decent. When we reach the first fountain, we'll wash our faces and clean ourselves up.'

'As I recall it,' returned Pedro, 'there is a fountain just around the corner in the Calle Martinez Campos.'

Thunder on the Horizon

Though I speak with the tongues of men and of angels, and have
not charity, I am become as sounding brass, or a tinkling cymbal.

The Letter to the Corinthians

When the brothers reached their house, darkness had fallen, and a
stormy greeting awaited them. Dona Delores swayed into battle
like a true ship of the line.

'Such a disgrace,' she cried. 'And you, Juan, just out of prison.
What's to become of us? Father Ramon told me all about it, so
you need not make up any false tales. Throw those atrocious
clothes in that basket in the corner. To bed with the both of you!'

'Mother,' admonished Juan, 'with all due respect, I am nineteen years of age. You know that I have to go to the mechanical
studies class tonight. I've already lost out a great deal.'

'You've lost out all right,' she said, 'and in more ways than you
may think. If the school should ever learn of your days in prison,
you would no longer be a student there. Fortunately we have
managed to cover that up, so far, but you do little to make things
easy.'

'Don't you realise,' said Juan, 'that I'm not leaving to have a
good time. I don't mind going without dinner, if that's your wish,
but each day that I lose means more points against me. I may have
an honest chance to secure a scholarship, and I must present my
homework punctually, or else not at all.'

Delores sighed and seated herself in the great oak chair,
despair in her eyes. 'Juan, my son,' she said, 'there's not a soul
more solicitous of your welfare than I. Your father too, when he
lived, sought only to further your welfare. But life isn't what you
seem to think it is in your youth. Every man must learn one thing,
whether he be porter or king, and that's to control himself and
learn to subdue his whims for the improvement of others. You're

not alone in this world, Juan. You seem always to be courting success, and that's a most dangerous thing, for you may never attain it. I fear that you think that life would stop then and there but life doesn't stop with such things. Somehow I have failed.'

'No, Mother,' Juan protested, 'you haven't failed. Perhaps it isn't something that can be said in so many words.'

'Yes, I've failed all right – and your father has failed. But if there is still a God in heaven, and I believe there is, He will one day show you the way. I've seen many people come and go. Those who flash in a day go out in a day. You will stay here this night, and without dinner, as I said. If you will act like a child, you must be treated as one. That was a foolish thing you did this afternoon. You acted well in stopping the stoning, but you also instigated the riot that followed, and that wasn't good at all. The Duque told me all about it, so don't bother to deny it. You must have known that Pedro would be in that fight, and on the other side. My son, I cannot permit you to turn against those who are closest to you. When all others will have deserted you, we will still stand beside you – at least in our prayers.'

Pedro had retreated to his room long since, and Juan found him now, lying on the bed. His hands laced behind his head, he was a picture of vast contentment.

The same Pedro, thought Juan, *unconcerned as ever with the problems that torture my soul.* And then he said aloud, 'Can't you even worry about losing your dinner?'

A broad smile lit Pedro's face. 'What's done is done. What has to come will come. So why should I worry about it?'

Quickly Juan gathered his books together, and started for the door. He had to get to his classes. This ridiculous detention was of no importance, anyway. Bigger things were astir on the night wind.

The brisk air cooled his face and brought the embers of his passion down to lines of thought. 'She's right,' he said, and did not realise he had spoken aloud until a passing figure stopped for an instant and stared at him in surprise. He had to get out of this rut. If he didn't succeed, another generation would fail, even as countless others had failed. Why was it that when he sought to improve things he was branded as fractious and uncontrolled? He wondered if it was possible that in the legends of history each step had been carefully planned beforehand. The idea was absurd. Only the drive and push of people, going against wind and current and ostracised by society, pursued by the will of kings and the arm of the law, escaped the steps over which the common herd had passed.

It was eleven o'clock when Juan left the school. No young people stormed and shouted as they left this shadowed doorway. The night air was bitter cold, and he shivered as he turned up the collar of his coat. Juan reflected that the attitude of the students who attended the night school differed immensely from that of his contemporaries in the day school. The urge to acquire knowledge and to take on those elements of culture that are necessary in shaping plans for the future was apparent here.

He had noticed, with some chagrin, that he had been unable to give as good an account of himself in fights as he had in the past. Juan was still considered one of the most dangerous opponents in school, but he knew that it was due more to his unbounded energy and lack of fear than his physical prowess. Yet fear had haunted him more than once in the weeks and months that had passed. Fear had shadowed him down the streets and had followed him into the prison, to make itself felt in the stillness of night when the world seemed to pause for an instant in its endless rotation.

Perhaps some training in a gymnasium would be a tonic to enliven his courage that, at times, seemed to falter. And so his footsteps took him this night to the municipal gymnasium, where he requested permission to become a member. He was welcomed with eagerness, since he was a student and appeared to be alert and interested in the sights about him. And about him were the young men who frequent night gymnasiums: wrestlers, would-be boxers, bouncers of dives and dens, all mingled together with the open-faced sons of workingmen, who themselves had come from work, hoping to earn extra money by playing in small-time professional football.

Wherever he went Juan found the same story of need. It had become his basic impression of life. Now he found himself dreaming of quixotic adventures. Perhaps he would be like that fictional hero, tilting at windmills, and mistaking flocks of sheep for battling armies. He smiled at the idea.

A thickset ex-pugilist shouldered his way through the sweating forms. 'Your name is Juan Avila, as I see by your signature on our registration card.'

'That's correct.' Juan eyed him suspiciously.

'Well, I'm Fernando Arias, the instructor. What sport are you most interested in?'

'Boxing,' said Juan.

'Did you bring any clothes along?'

'No.'

'Well, before you begin, you'd better get that face in order. It looks to me as if you've already been doing some fighting. Or am I too bold? In any case, come along with me and let me have a look at you.'

They entered a dingy office, ill lit and stuffy. Photographs of moustachioed, heavily muscled men glared vacantly from yellowed frames.

'Let's have a look. Take off your clothes.'

Juan winced but obeyed dutifully, while the man looked him over as if he were examining a dray horse.

'Yes,' He prodded at Juan's biceps, 'you have possibilities. You've a good frame, but you're too skinny. Do you smoke?'

'No.'

'Ever been drunk?'

Colouring, Juan shook his head in wordless denial.

'I won't ask about women,' grinned the trainer. 'In any case I suppose you're the good-boy type. Well, all the better, for boxing is a rough game, especially for the purposes that you have in mind. And I think I judge you fairly.' The shrewd, gimlet-like eyes hooked on to Juan's face.

'You know a great deal, apparently,' said Juan.

'I know only what I'm supposed to know,' interposed the man coldly. 'Remember, the fee's payable in advance. If not, there's no boxing. Bring along a towel, some trunks, soap, and a pair of *alpargatas*. That's all you'll need for the present. Well, be off with you,' and he waved him out of the door. 'I'm in a great hurry to attend to my work.'

Juan left the place a bit crestfallen. He had expected to find a different atmosphere, and the sight of the half-naked forms around him did little to enliven his mood. This would be no easy thing.

He crossed the street and walked quickly away into the darkness. A familiar building brought him up short: the house of the Duque del Bosque. He had not realised he had walked so far. Built in the early sixteenth century, its walls were of granite, and the balconies were of iron – iron and granite – symbols of past ages, of history and tradition. The buildings roundabout seemed flimsy by comparison, for, though they looked down upon the twin-storey house, it was not perceptibly shortened. It took two modern floors to equal one of the old. Geometrically designed, its proportions were its chief ornaments, only the patterns about the doorway and windows mellowing the heaviness of its lines. Great eaves overlapped the straight facade. For hundreds of years this building had stood through wind, rain, snow and heat. For hundreds of years more it would stand – unless man should bring it down. Juan looked at it and frowned. In that place was the man who stood for everything that he detested. It was the symbol of a way of life that soon would be no more. One day this great mansion would be levelled to the earth, and with it would fall all of the death and disease that haunted his land.

Flickering gas lamps dotted the street. His footsteps took him to the Plaza Mayor, largest of its day and the most wondrous. From its balconies, kings had seen the populace manifest itself in joy, in anger, and in hate. Bullfights had been staged in the massive surroundings. Playwrights had occasioned fame in its storied setting. Duels had sprung from the shadowed arches. Bandits and robbers had invaded through the maze of caves that at one time wound their tortuous passage underneath the great Moorish wall that had surrounded the mighty castle of Magerit. Houses had sprung up on those walls, had surrounded and eaten into them, until not a vestige was left, save for a great tower enclosed in a cheap, shoddy tenement house on the Calle de la Escalinata. This was Madrid – his Madrid. And some day this great city would be a place where poverty and sorrow would be forgotten in the joyous rush of freedom. He would plan and study and work. He would train and scheme and remember. One day he would be ready to lead this city into the great new world that waited only for the proper time.

At last, weary from the unaccustomed exertions of the day, he boarded a tram on the Puerta del Sol for his house in the distant Calle Luchana.

That night his sleep was troubled. In his dreams processions of figures were fleeing down darkened streets, while cars, without shape or substance, wove through the elusive forms. They appeared and disappeared like an anchor chain slipping into the sea, the first distorted links fading into unknown depths. Hands grew from a point to awesome size; size and dimensions shifted about. Creatures of the subconscious leapt into vivid reality with forms and characters, disappearing once again into misty wraiths.

When Juan woke, he found remembrance weighing heavily upon a troubled mind and a weary body. How could he clear the confusion and doubt from his mind? Perhaps if he rode into the country, away from the din and the tumult, he could find a moment of peace.

Pedro decided, of a sudden, that he, too, would like to ride that day. Juan shrugged his shoulders. Why argue about it? In any case his brother would not be dissuaded.

It was a stormy day. The clouds swept by as if in a hurry to get somewhere. Wind whipped around the flanks of the horses, making them shy and restless.

Down the Cuesta de San Vicente they trotted. Up that historical hill had stormed the Almoravides in their fervent desire to reconquer the castle of Magerit that had fallen into the hands of the Christians. Their might had failed, and even today the slaughterhouse of their ill-starred campaign is called El Campo del Moro, the field of the Moor. The legends of Madrid were about them now, their ghost-like forms wreathing into patterns of remembrance.

There was the nook, captured by walls of sandstone, where great poplars shaded the soil that later on, in spring, would be carpeted with flowers. In that place, Luis Candelas had held his rendezvous with veiled ladies of Madrid who had succumbed to his valour as noble bandit and despoiler of the rich. He had become the protector of the poor.

Now the two young men stepped up their pace to the tireless short gallop of the true Spanish horse. The wind had melted away, and they rode with ease towards the palace of the still-distant Pardo.

'Pedro, you've forgotten how to ride,' called Juan.

His brother flashed him a slow smile in return. 'I can still out-ride and out-run you any day of the week.'

'Follow me, then.' And Juan's mare leapt forward. He had the sensation of being left behind. Larks rose about him, singing noisily as they flew upwards, fluttering, poised on the air, venting the message of their song far and near.

The thundering hoof beats drummed into his being. Now he was the master of his destiny, breasting the storms of time. He felt as if the wings of Hermes were magically lifting him.

At last they reached the Puente de la Reina, where the queen had stopped so many times that the place took her name. Juan reined in his horse, for an unexpected sight greeted his eyes.

A group of people, carefree and happy, were out on a holiday lark. Guitars were being strummed, and the lilting song of the gay *jota* came through the clean air like a message of frank gaiety and human friendliness.

'What is it?' Pedro had reined up beside him, his horse champing impatiently to be off and away once again.

'I'm not sure. It looks like a party of people on an outing in the country. They're not country people, of that I'm certain.'

'Well, what are we waiting for? Let's ride over and have a look.'

'Why not,' said Juan but Pedro already had trotted his horse forward.

The things of nature were around them. Farther back, Juan could see the evidence of man's neglect: the sturdy, scrubby oaks, thorny bush, the rolling and sandy hills, here and there dotted with stones; poplars, chestnuts, and eucalyptuses were dwindling away. Pardo and the Zarzuela, its strange cliffs and precipices seeming, for no apparent reason, to end each hill or knoll, then, breaking down in steps towards the dry, sandy riverbed – hunting site for kings. Deer, boar, rabbits, and partridges teemed and multiplied. Overhead the hawk spiralled endlessly, looking eagerly for its hapless prey. Higher up in heaven's vault, the great golden eagle glared down, searching for nobler victims. Beyond, were the rolling hills, and the upheaval of mighty mountains. Passes were there that had echoed with cries of battle, in the surge of Europe's invaders. Now those invaders had gone, yet the mighty boulders remained, looking down with a forbidding stare at the pilgrimage of man. Juan breathed deeply of the crisp air. This was Spain. This was his land. And he remembered the day when it seemed as if Fate had turned over another leaf in the book of life. Again he saw the long lines of serious-faced people and the black-veiled ladies. In a room turned into a chapel lay the body of his father in a great, mahogany box, the white hands clasping a heavy silver cross. That once stern face had held, in death, the placidity of the oblivion of thought and trouble.

There had come the long, endless walk behind the swaying, horse-drawn hearse, and the lining up, as, one by one, young and old had walked by, mumbling incoherent phrases of comfort. There had been the thronged cemetery – city of the dead – where man's craft endeavours to hold the memories of those who have gone. Husky, brutal-faced men had lowered that closed coffin into the yawning grave, a shower of pebbles following in its wake and rattling gloomily upon the closed lid.

Even now Juan bit his lip and blinked his eyes savagely. Those gravediggers had been talking among themselves. The one to his right had smelt of liquor, and looked askance at the priest who had come as if to hurry the procedure. The man had winked an eye at the workman before him, with the unmistakable inference that money was involved in the proceedings. Was not this coffin of richest mahogany? So there it was again. Men, sunk down to the lowest pit of shame because of that invisible yoke, money – greed and lust, imprisoning the human being. Rage was in his heart, and the rest of the proceedings had passed him by without reason or thought. He still could hear the thump of the spades full of earth falling upon that which had been his father. Perhaps if his father had been able to secure the best physician in the city he might have been saved. If he had not been forced to work like a dog all of his life so the Duque could fulfil all his fancies and whims, he would not have had the heart attack that resulted in his untimely death. And there were all those ghoulish creatures that had surrounded the pomp and vanity of his social caste. They had been there, and why? To fill their purses with their evil gain.

'My, the young man looks extremely serious for such a beautiful day.' The voice, soft and low, laughed merrily in his ear. 'Come down from that horse, and let us have a look at you.'

The clouds in his mind seemed suddenly to flee away. He was staring down into the face of a girl who must have been created by the gods. She was dressed in a close-fitting jersey and grey flannel pants, strong walking shoes, with a black narrow belt encompassing her trim waist. Her platinum hair was cropped short, almost like a boy's, yet with all her masculine attire she remained singularly soft and feminine, exuding grace with every movement of her lithe body.

Her eyes are grey, he mused. *Like windows of a Viennese palace that reflect the Danube on a summer day.* Juan smiled at his wandering imagination.

A matter of minutes, and he found himself in the midst of the small group of people. The girl stood back, smiling at him in a most disarming way. An older man, dressed in sombre black, caught the direction of Juan's glance.

'You like her, young man,' he observed. 'Well, perhaps you will have a chance to become better acquainted.'

'Really?' Juan was nonplussed. 'How is this?'

'I'm always interested in young men, and you and your friend here look like you could take care of yourselves. They call me Ricardo, by the way. I presume you're from Madrid.'

Why did these people want to know about him? Who were they? And this beautiful girl – she wasn't Spanish, of that he was sure. German? Perhaps, though she spoke fluent Spanish.

'I'm Juan Avila,' he said, 'and this is my brother, Pedro.'

'Your brother is suspicious, I see,' replied the man, 'and you are puzzled. Well, perhaps we'll be able to clear this mystery up for you some day. For now, suffice to say that this girl you seem to find so enchanting, as we all do, is Hilda Krantz. She's a comrade we esteem highly. We're most interested in her becoming well acquainted with the Spanish people. Any courtesies you might extend her in the days ahead will be most appreciated. And for now, we must bid you goodbye, but we shall meet again, when it is time.'

Pedro was clearly angry during the long ride back to the city. For a good half of the distance he said nothing, then blurted, 'So you found that girl attractive? Well, I don't like it. I don't like any of it. Why did he imply that he and that girl would see us again? It's not good, I tell you. I didn't like the look on that man's face. He's not to be trusted.'

'Ah, you talk big words, but you don't know what you say,' returned Juan. 'I'll admit that I can't understand this puzzle either, but the chance to meet that girl again is inviting enough.'

'It smells of death,' said Pedro. 'I still don't like it.'

Juan laughed. 'Pedro, my brother, you've a vivid imagination. Perhaps this is the very opportunity I've sought. Who knows? Fate has strange ways of dealing with men.'

'Yes,' agreed Pedro, 'and Fate has stranger ways of dealing men out of the game.'

'For such a prize,' declared Juan, 'I would gladly take the risk.'

Day of Decision

In all your work, one straight course pursue, and upright aim.
Have powers of goodness, possessing few desires.
Such men shall soon be asked by others to instruct.

                              The Miao Fa Lien Hua Ching

A few evenings later, Juan gathered his savings together and left
the night school. Around the corner of Areneros he walked, his
hands in the pockets of his raincoat and his hat shielding his face.
The gas lamps that were scattered infrequently, flickered dimly
over the black mirror of the street. It had been raining heavily,
and every now and again gusty squalls pushed the low dark clouds
across the face of the moon.

He turned into the maze of the narrow, crooked streets that
lay in the shadow of the broad Princessa. These streets were all
that remained of the old village that had lain just outside Madrid,
corresponding to dusty, ancient cattle-ways. Grey crumbling walls
were transformed into yellow patterns and figured mosaics. From
these same windows, the good neighbours had seen flourish and
die – before that great, surging city that absorbed, surrounded and
moved relentlessly onward – the beautiful gardens and orchards
that once had belonged to the nunneries and convents, the
fabulous households of bygone days.

At last he saw the municipal gymnasium and made his way
towards the ornate entrance.

A familiar voice fell on his ears as he reached the inside of the
vast building. It seemed to echo around him in the gloom, dimly,
like a film that remains out of focus. Then, with a start, the voice
became clear, and he remembered the man in black.

'Comrades,' came the words, 'the time has come for the proletariat of the world to take a stand. We must stand together against
the group that, although in the minority, is so firmly entrenched

in society's organisation that it holds not only the spoils, but also the keys to the spoils. Why should we, the ones that work and make it possible for that minority to live, be subjected to such a yoke, placed upon us by the police and the armed forces? After all, those same police and armed forces are under the control and subject to the direction of that minority.'

A chorus of deep-toned assent echoed through the corridor. Juan's control was fast disappearing. His hands clenched until the nails dug into his palms. His whole body grew taut and tense. This was the answer. Here was the way he had searched for so long. In front of him he saw, as if the building itself had disappeared, a red horizon from which flames and explosions burst, and people scurried from left to right without direction or thought. Panic was their only guide. Civil war!

'I knew you would come.' The voice was behind him now, strong and assured.

Juan whirled about to find his acquaintance, still dressed in funereal black.

'Yes,' the man continued, 'I knew you would come tonight.'

'You seem to know a great deal,' said Juan. 'And I have a great many questions that have plagued me of late.'

'Questions? We have plenty of time for questions,' said the man. 'And there is time for much more.'

'I came here to enrol in my first boxing class,' said Juan. 'That's all.'

'Yes, I know. But I also knew that you would be here this night, and so I arranged this little meeting so that you could become acquainted with some of our friends. Friends, my boy, are most important in any movement. And we are your friends.'

'What of the girl?' questioned Juan.

'Hilda? Oh, she's in good hands and will see you when it is convenient.' He suddenly lowered his voice as if in deepest confidence. 'You can be of help to us in this matter. Hilda is anxious to learn a great deal about Spain. She has a deep love for the Spanish people, and only a true son of Spain can teach her its lore.'

Juan smiled grimly. 'The lore of Spain, my friend, is not learned in a day. We are an ancient people, and age has mellowed our outlook on life.'

'An astute observation,' said the man. 'By the way, I am known as Ricardo by those who are considered my friends. And, now that the formalities have been set aside, my car awaits us. I should enjoy the privilege of escorting you to another meeting of even greater significance.'

'But how can I go with a perfect stranger?' said Juan. 'How do I know that you won't hit me on the head and throw me into a ditch?'

Ricardo smiled and crossed his long arms. His cavernous face seemed more funereal than ever. 'My friend,' he said, 'you don't know these things. But nothing has ever been accomplished in this world without a certain amount of risk. In this case, I can guarantee that the rewards are sufficiently high.'

'And what,' said Juan, 'are these rewards?'

'The rewards, my sceptical friend, are power such as you never dreamed possible. You're a man, and no longer a boy. I know that you regret being treated as a child by your family. First there was your father, a great man in his own way, doubtless. He sought to rule you by thundering forth his law in his own inimitable fashion. On the other hand, your mother,' he raised his hand as if to fend off Juan's protests, 'has tried to hold on to you with eager hands. Yet, long since, you have escaped from that maternal embrace, at least in your heart. You owe a certain allegiance to the Duque del Bosque, but I say to you that the tiger cannot lie down with the lamb.' He paused and looked long and searchingly into Juan's dark eyes. 'What will be your answer, my comrade? There can only be one road for you. If you turn back from that road it can only mean spiritual and moral defeat for you. Come – walk with us down this road together. It will be a glorious journey and Spain, the land you love, will be the better for your having done so.'

Juan felt as if he would burst. How had this man known the innermost secrets of his heart? As if the dawn were driving away the blackness of night, he saw, in ever-closer terms, the light shining in the darkness of his soul.

And so the days fled away, filled with new and conflicting ideas, overflowing with the strange new wonder of first love.

★

Juan went with Hilda, one golden, sun-drenched day, to see the old University of Alcala de Henares, one of the world's first seats of higher learning.

For the first time he began to wonder if, perhaps, he was being used by this girl but, in the long slide that he had begun since first they met, momentum was gaining over reason.

Hand in hand they entered the Posada del Estudiante, and the glory of past ages held them in its breathless spell.

'Oh,' Hilda breathed, and tightened her fingers. She glanced at him, her slightly moistened lips parted in expectation. Her grey eyes glowed with a new fire, as the golden streams of light filtered down from the windows far overhead.

'Do you like it, Hilda?' He turned to face her, holding both her hands in his. 'I do so want you to like my Spain.'

'Oh yes, Juan. Words can't say how much.'

'Look well, my dear, for behind each of these columns,' he released her hand and gestured with his expressive fingers, 'are the whispers of the students and the learned men of the past.'

'I can almost hear them,' she returned.

'Yes, when the heart's in tune, they say you can hear them,' he continued in the same vein. 'People used to come to this place from all over the world to hear the words of Garcilaso de la Vega, the great philosopher. Cervantes used to tell his gaping students of his unbelievable adventures in trying to save other slaves who had been imprisoned along the Barbary Coast, even as he.'

'Yes, go on.'

He smiled into her eyes. 'Of course, I could go on all day. It was here that Cardinal Cisneros thundered at quavering youth with the stern foreboding of his iron character… But perhaps it's better to leave something to the imagination.'

The silver hair glinted in the light. Hilda nodded and gazed rapturously about the time-hallowed place. Overhead, the beautifully carved ceiling of Mudejer style ringed the scene with its glowing brown ornaments, a suspicion of green lurking in its octagonal depths. On one side was the oaken pulpit. A carved, heavy staircase mounted upward. Tradition seeped out from every nook and cranny.

'I know so little about you, Hilda,' he said, as they left the elusive ghosts of bygone days.

She shielded her eyes as the sun hit them with brutal force. 'What's there to know?'

'Oh Hilda,' he stopped and took her hand in his. 'I want to know all there is. I want to know that I can trust you, that I can hold you in my arms and know you're truly mine.'

'Juan, you came into my life only a short time ago, and yet I feel that I've known you always. There's really not much to tell. Some day I will be able to tell you the whole story, but for now I can only tell you this much: I used to wait to board the *Strassenbahn* that headed along the border of the Rhine. As I waited, sometimes for a great length of time, I used to look across the little garden that separated the street, with its stony bulwarks, from that great river. I could see the bustle of tugs, ploughing up and down, bearing their burdens through the water. And I remember that the rowing clubhouses were closed, and the paint was peeling from their sides, with their doors nailed shut. On the far side of the Rhine were the grey houses where the poorer tenants lived, and behind it all were the factory chimneys.'

'And where was this?' he asked.

'Oh,' she smiled, 'I forgot to say. It was Düsseldorf, and it was in those terrible days of the depression. I remember that I used to sit in a corner of the tram so that I could watch without being observed. You see, my darling, faces were always interesting to me. I remember the thickset workmen, with their vacant stares. Their eyes meant nothing whatsoever, for they never reacted to impressions of colour or shape or form.'

'They're alike the world over,' said Juan. 'Physical exhaustion overcomes thought.'

'Yes. And then there was the housewife. Oh, I enjoyed watching the housewife, with her big, black satchel resting on her more than ample lap.' She laughed in amused remembrance. 'But it really wasn't funny, I suppose. That bag usually had far greater filling capacity than ever was used. Then there were the poor roughened hands, the shoes cracking where feet, in interminable fight against time, beat out their endless drudgery.'

He stared at her in surprise. 'You sound almost as though you were making a speech. I'm not a heathen, you know. You don't have to convert me to your point of view. Remember I'm a Communist, too.'

'I'm sorry.' She sighed and seated herself under a vast poplar tree. 'The shade feels wonderful. Here, sit down.' And she patted the ground beside her. 'It's just that I remember the colour. Everything seemed to be grey in Düsseldorf. The sky was grey. The buildings were grey. The clothes were grey. Even the people looked grey.'

Juan grunted in approval. 'Yes, the gay Rhineland of old: things are not so gay any more, and I'm not so sure that the *rindfleisch* pot bubbles quite so merrily as in the past.'

'Oh, things are much better now,' she said. 'But they were hard when I was growing up. I always wanted to live and act in colour, above all that sordid grey. And how could this be done? How could the daughter of a man who was so drunk, most of the time, that he lived only in his world of memories, ever accomplish such a thing? Well, it wasn't easy.' She lay back, and crossed her long legs, staring interestedly up at the blue sky framed in the aura of green leaves. 'No, it wasn't easy.'

'Yes,' Juan agreed, 'the curse of Versailles was hanging heavy over Europe in those days. Sometimes it seems as if that name were only made to breed hate. The last French kings were torn apart by the mobs of Paris because of it. Bismarck crashed his iron fist against mutilated France, and Germany smouldered in hate and ruin.'

Hilda crossed her arms behind her head, and smiled broadly. 'Now, who's making a speech? But of course you're right. I remember my poor old father talking about the time when, in his youth, the people would lock arms and sing to the music of a waltz at the slightest possible motive. The good beer and the Rhine wine flowed in those days.' She lapsed into silence.

Juan turned and looked at her. He could see her now as a beautiful, desirable woman, yet there must have been no gayness in that flawless face in her girlhood. There must have been no smile in the beautiful grey eyes, only the stern tragedy of making both ends meet, subduing and conquering the poetry of faith.

The big clock in the dining room was chiming the hour of twelve when Juan crept in. Removing his shoes, he stole softly into bed. As he rolled over to turn out the small night lamp, he met the steady gaze of his brother.

'You keep strange hours, brother, for an ambitious student.'

'I was detained by a professor.'

Pedro sat erect and glared at him. 'Don't bother to lie to me. You haven't attended a class in over a month. We got the report this evening from the school.'

'Oh?' Juan tried to sound casual. 'I didn't think I was that popular around there.'

'You must think you're a demigod or something,' said Pedro, running his great hands through his thick hair. 'Frankly, I think you're a damn fool!'

Juan had been lolling comfortably in the bed. Now he threw the quilt aside and sprang to his feet, his face darkening with anger. 'Are you insinuating that I'm unable to take care of myself? I can still handle you any day of the week.'

Looking curiously at his brother, Pedro replied, 'I'm not insinuating anything, but I am telling you: I know what you're up to. You're not content with bombing innocent people's stores. No, now you have to join the Communists in the open.'

Their voices had been rising all the while. Now Delores' footsteps sounded in the corridor.

Juan dropped back down upon the bed. 'Oh, go to hell!' he said. 'You're so set and narrow-minded that it's impossible to reason with you.'

Delores, her hair askew, opened the door without knocking and strode into the room.

'I won't have these arguments where the girls can hear them,' she said. 'You sound like two teamsters who've sold each other a bad mule. Certainly you don't sound like the two little boys who were once so happy playing together. Oh, this town has ruined us all, I'm afraid.' She dabbed at her eyes with trembling fingers.

'It's not this town, Mother,' said Pedro. 'Rather, say that it's our philosopher friend here, who thinks everyone's narrow-minded but himself. Such a sad state of affairs!'

'And you, Juan.' Delores turned to him and fixed her dark

eyes upon his flushed face. 'I don't know what you've gotten yourself into, but I'm beginning to suspect the worst.'

Juan sighed, but made no reply. He was thinking of a girl with eyes of grey, the sun in her hair and a smile on her lips.

A Trembling in the Earth

Prepare war, stir up the mighty men. Let all the men of war draw near, let them come up. Beat your ploughshares into swords, and your pruning hooks into spears; let the weak say, 'I am a mighty warrior.'

The Book of Joel

Juan stood in a corner of the gymnasium, watching with avid interest the swirl of planned confusion about him. In a far corner the usual bevy of heavy-muscled wrestlers tried out on each other the various holds. In the centre was a training ring for the boxers. Distributed over the remainder of the place, like groups of marionettes, were bouncing, skipping, lunging, jumping figures. Some wore tight-fitting black pants and woollen sweaters. Others wore shorts. Everyone moved as if they were automatons. Some were a bit too thin-featured to be healthy, although, by their muscular development, one would consider them strong. Here and there was a battered, broken face and the dazed expression of the man on the tragic downward trail of the unsuccessful pugilist. Other faces could be seen: hard and cruel, bad men and youths, the bouncers and the strong-armed men of the various organisations, people whose only goal was to better their physical conditions so that they might harm more effectively, hurt and destroy.

A voice at his elbow, and a quizzical face came into view. 'Well, you seem very interested in all the proceedings?'

'I am,' said Juan, 'but I wonder why. It looks like there's a lot of rough customers out there.'

The laughing brown eyes looked into his. 'I'm Tormo, and Ricardo tells me I'm to be one of your boxing companions.'

They shook hands. 'My name's Avila – Juan Avila.'

'Yes, I know. Ricardo told me that, too.'

'Say, tell me,' said Juan, 'how is it that this Ricardo is so prominent around here? Does he own the place or something?'

The face assumed an air of superiority. 'Well, he has an interest in the place, but not the kind you might suspect. His interest is purely in manpower, and not in the mechanics of sport.'

'A most interesting character,' said Juan.

Tormo ran his fingers through his black hair. 'Indeed. I would say that such a description sums him up neatly. But for now, my friend, the trainer is signalling us from the ring. I see you're all set, so perhaps we will do a little sparring this day.'

The trainer leaned carelessly over the ropes in the far corner. 'Hey there,' he called. 'Hey there, Tormo! Bring the boy over here.'

He waited quietly until the duo had threaded their way through the bounding forms, then grinned down at Juan and said, 'Avila, you can hit as hard as you please. I doubt that you'll be able to reach him, anyway. Remember, he's not going to hurt you.'

Juan flashed the man a glance. He resented his attitude.

'Touch gloves,' came the curt command.

He lunged forward with the speed of a cat, and Tormo barely had time to elude the blow. A sudden jarring thud on the side of his head brought Juan up short.

'Well done,' cried the trainer. 'Remember, Juan, the other fellow has arms, too. If you don't cover yourself, no matter how fast your attacks might be, you'll never last a round.'

From then on Juan was in a daze. He was fighting a ghost that was never there. At the same time, it seemed as if twelve men were around him, hitting and tapping at him from everywhere and in every place at one and the same time. Panting and exhausted, he was driven into a corner.

'All right, break it up,' called the trainer. 'That's enough for today. Avila, your reactions are pretty good, and you're quick and have instinctive footwork. But you've no wind and are much too aggressive. Don't worry about the aches and throbs, that is until tomorrow. All the rest of this week you'll be one big pain.'

Together, the boxing companions left the gymnasium and turned their faces towards the Plaza de Quevedo. The little central garden there claimed priority over the broad and narrow streets that, star-like, met it. Throngs of humanity hurried by, disappearing into the hot and stuffy entrance of the Metro station, which had taken its name from Quevedo, that gay and cynical writer whose razor-edged wit had driven kings and courtiers insane with fury and rage.

The teeming multitude pushed them along. Like driftwood jostled and pushed about by the current, Juan felt himself sitting on the banks of this tideless river.

'I've a little money in my pocket,' he said. 'Let's go over to that bar across the square and have a glass of *clara con limon.*'

Tormo looked at him. 'I don't mind if I do.' They parted the beaded curtains, and the cool interior engulfed them.

Seated there, in the company of one whose intelligence and physical appeal he respected, Juan felt expansive and relaxed. This was living in the right way. This was good. But someone was missing. Hilda Krantz. Her face haunted his waking and sleeping hours.

'Hey, Juan,' said Tormo, 'wake up. The waiter wants your order.'

'Oh, *clara con limon,*' said Juan, struggling up from depths of remembrance.

Tormo leaned across the narrow table. 'I'll bet it's a girl.'

'True enough,' replied Juan. 'Love's a funny thing, Tormo. You feel when you're with the person that you're in heaven, and yet when you're away from her you feel like you're in hell.'

A laugh welled up from Tormo's trim figure. 'Frankly, I know little enough about love. Never had time for it myself. It's enough to keep body and soul together without worrying about such luxuries as love.'

Juan was interested. Here again was a story of ever-present need. 'Where do you work, Tormo?'

'Work? Well, if you can call it work. I'm employed by a local garage. Rather, I should say I was employed. They let me go last night.' He rubbed a finger around the rim of his glass reflectively.

'Hard luck,' said Juan. 'Any other prospects in mind?'

'Not at the moment. And I've a mother and sister to support. That's the hardest part of it.'

'Some day,' said Juan, 'things will be changed. The change

must come, and soon, else our nation cannot survive. Ricardo has opened my eyes to a great many things.'

'My eyes, too, have been opened, but perhaps it's too late.' Tormo leaned closer and whispered softly, anxiety written on his face. 'Juan, I'm in trouble. I knew I would be released from my job, so I helped myself to a little something to tide my family over the season without work.'

'No,' breathed Juan. 'And yet you're still coming to the gymnasium, where they're sure to look for you? Shouldn't you be hiding out somewhere until things cool off a bit?'

'Oh, I don't believe they'll ever find out who did it.' Tormo grimaced and leaned back in his chair. 'No one ever commits a crime with the intention of being caught, you know.'

'I think you're very foolish. I'd disappear for a time.'

'And where can you disappear these days? Our friends the Civil Guards could find a needle in a pile of hay. No, running would do no good.'

There was a commotion at the entrance to the bar and a voice thundered out over the buzzing drone of the customers. 'You there, Tormo! Stay exactly where you are, and don't move.'

Tormo dropped his glass with a loud crash. Faces turned towards their table. Juan wished he could disappear into the floor.

'Well, well, so we find you enjoying the fruits of your labours.' A great, hulking Civil Guard loomed above them. 'And who is your friend, if I may ask?'

'I met him just this morning in this bar,' returned Tormo, visibly shaken by the sudden turn of events. 'He doesn't know me at all.'

'Well, this is all very cosy,' said the man. 'Perhaps, Tormo, you would accompany us.' Without further ado, he pulled Tormo's hands behind him and clamped a tight pair of handcuffs on his wrists. Dragged to his feet, he was pushed angrily towards the door.

Juan felt shaken. Civil Guards and their sadistic brutality! He wished that Hilda were with him. She alone could calm the fevers that burned in his breast. Here was the story of passionate youth, for ever beguiled by an imaginary paradise, towards which practical purpose ever strives. Juan did not know then, as he would in later days, that they fail because they lack access to that never-ending, winding stair that begins in the dim recesses of the infinite, passes down into the light and range of eyesight, and dwindles away once again into the infinite. The faith of their childhood too often ended up being betrayed by the harsh, grim realities of daily existence.

And so, in Juan's being, conflict raged and he trembled on the edge of darkness. He walked with Hilda along the storied streets of old Madrid. He wandered with her down the country trails and they discovered together the secrets and mysteries of this strange and legendary land. And all the while, his ideas of life were slowly but surely evolving into a philosophy that could lead only to death.

Ricardo had given him a car for his personal use. Now, wheeling rapidly along the broad highway, Juan turned from his intense concentration upon the receding landscape to cast a quick sidelong glance at Hilda's seductive face, struck by the now feeble rays of the setting sun. She turned her finely chiselled features towards him and smiled into his eyes.

His usually pale features became suddenly flushed. He felt not unlike a playful puppy.

She reached for his hand, and held it tightly in hers. With a sigh she moved over and rested her cheek lightly against his shoulder. 'Juan,' she said, 'I feel as if I'd never really lived until I met you.'

He smiled, and shifted about on the seat. 'You embarrass me, my darling. I've never considered myself the great lover type.'

'Love? I never knew there could be such a thing,' she said, 'but fate has shown me that it's not just a dead word.'

Juan stopped the car on a hill and, without further words, put his arms about her, holding her as if she were a lost child. 'Tell me,' he said, 'how you managed to get mixed up with the Party?'

She sat erect and stared sombrely out of the car window. 'It's a long story, and not a really pleasant one, I suppose. There was a teacher at the school. His name was Schenk. About forty, I'd say, maybe more. They said he'd been a hero of the Great War. He was one who spoke of the wonderful world of the future. And I was anxious – oh Juan, I was so anxious to find that new world. A world where the cramped miner and the bent stevedore would find the satisfaction of equal remuneration for all.'

He reached over and patted her hand. 'Yes, I can well imagine. But please go on.'

Hilda turned her face from the window and looked full into his eyes. 'Well, the flattering presence of a lot of pimple-faced students served only to anger me, and the sticky innuendoes of all those older men sickened me.' She shivered and drew her coat closer about her shoulders. 'I used to talk with other girls about life, but in reply to my questions I received only giggles, or, more often, glances full of unspoken secrets.' She stopped and stared at her fingertips for an instant, then continued in the same vein. 'Juan, I had only one desire: to succeed. As a girl, what chance did I have, even if I did have as good a mind as the best of them? But my friend, Schenk, used to set the example for me, and I sought to emulate him. He never took a stand in a discussion, but rather he would lead his opponents out and finally would direct their thoughts towards his own point of view. You'd have liked him, Juan. He was a great man.'

'I'm sure I would have, my Hilda.'

'Yes, but then one day he introduced me to another man who had come from Berlin. Schmidt was his name, and he seemed to have a power that Schenk lacked. Though Schenk was a good man, his amiable socialism seemed at times to lack the fire and the force needed to conquer in our day. Schmidt had that force, and he had that fire. I'll never forget the way he looked at me that day, nor will I ever forget the words he said.'

Juan sat erect. 'And his words? What were they?'

'He said that he'd heard from his soft-hearted friend that I was interested in joining the Communist Party. Then he went on to say that I'd have to renounce my whims. I'd have to forget my family, for I'd be representing a creed that would gather me up as a spreading fire envelops a twig, to become at each burning greater and of more use. Yes, and he was right. I've learned to know achievement. I've learned to subjugate my fears. And I've learned to obey, even as I've been obeyed.'

Juan's eyes burned with a new light. 'How wonderful. This is what I seek from life. Some day this glory will be mine, my darling, and Spain will be ours.'

Hilda sighed. 'Yes, I've no doubt that you'll accomplish your purpose. But, Juan, you'll have to learn to live as an outcast in many ways. The police will pursue you, even as they've pursued me. You'll be forced to assume a different personality at times. You'll be watched, my Juan, and even hunted like a wild beast. But through it all you'll have a definite goal to attain, the smashing triumph of our cause. Just think,' she lay back and closed her eyes, 'together we'll erase the curse of our time: private property. A great new world will open up, and we'll help to lead the way.'

He looked down upon the winsome face, her long eyelashes brushing her cheeks. The next instant she was in his arms, her youthful body warm against his, and he felt as if the whole world were gone, and they were alone in time and space.

★

Madrid – city of gayness and noise, of lights, and people walking endlessly, smiling and greeting one another – was silent now. The drums of war had rolled forth their martial melodies. Where love and smiles had bloomed, now only fear and death patrolled. The silent nights were shattered by the rattle of musketry. In the Cuartel de la Montaña, a group of doomed young men and officers sought to further the rights of tradition, the ties of family and the prolongation of their faith. Automobiles crossed the deserted streets, mattresses tied to their roofs to protect them from snipers. Groups of *milicianos* invaded the houses, leaving behind them sorrow and tragedy. Civil War had come.

Juan Avila strode briskly towards his home. Arrayed now in the uniform of the Communist Party, black leather boots, black leather jacket, and a visor cap, his clothing formed a startling background for the red stars that gleamed dully from his chest and cap. The bars of his rank formed a horizon from which the star arose on its jet-black background. A heavy pistol swung on his hip, a symbol of his newly gained power.

The door of his house swung open, and he saw the face of his mother. In a flash it changed. Her eyes became as hard as agate and her back squared perceptibly. 'Juan,' she said, 'this is still my house, humble though it may be. In this place dwells the spirit of your dead father. You're my son, but with that uniform you've asserted yourself as an enemy of your family, of your creed, of your faith and of your friends. Where would you be if it weren't for the friends of your father? You criticise the Duque, but he saved you from prison. It's an insult to your sisters who are coming into womanhood. I suppose you want to see them despoiled by the free love that your creed suggests. You can stay here tonight, for you're still my son. Tomorrow, when you leave this house you will not return. I never thought I'd live to see the day when the fruit of my womb would be a leader of those who deem me an enemy.'

'Mother, I can do nothing except to bow to your will,' he said. 'But don't forget, it's for people like you and our friends, and for their betterment that this ideal has come to be. The Duque is not your friend, even as he isn't mine. It's because of the iniquities of capitalistic society, in which we've lived until now, that the policy of the will of the masses has sprung. With its unstoppable force, it shall erase and flatten those steps into a valley for everybody to walk, achieving their purpose.'

His mother's eyes flashed. 'Enough! You can save those high-sounding words for those who've need of human arguments to fill the void that's been produced by their own volition when they parted company with the only stream that can quench any man's thirst: the fountain of faith.'

So this was her gratitude for his attempts to better her way of life. Was this to be his answer from all those whose conditions he sought to improve? Inwardly he was seething, but he remained visibly calm. 'I'll leave this pistol and ammunition with you as a parting gift. I'll send you some food. You'll soon be in dire need. Pedro knows where I can be reached: at the headquarters of the Communist Party of Fuencarral.'

'I don't need your food,' she said. 'I don't need that any more than I need your presence. I'll take the pistol to defend our honour but to me, my son is dead.'

He bowed respectfully and strode away from the house. Little did he know of the direction towards which he set his face. Inside his mind a strange phenomenon was developing. Once he had been diametrically opposed to the rigid, unyielding world of his father. Of late he had begun to sense that perhaps the foreign organisations behind the mighty Communist Party were not to be trusted. Hilda filled him with a new, glowing warmth but he tired of the cold, calculating phrases of the Party intellectuals. He grew weary of the vicious brutality of their military men and the scheming plans of their politicians. And as he walked along the deserted street, oblivious to the danger about him, he remembered that he was to meet Rosenberg, the representative of the Communist Party, in a suite at the Hotel Savoy.

As he crossed the street to enter the hotel, he stopped to look towards the entrance of the Museum of the Prado and the botanical gardens of Charles III. It appeared, he thought, that long-dead human beings had sought to depict, through those who mastered the Arts, the beauty of a hallowed tradition inspired by the soul. Yet here it stood, in stark contrast to the ambassador of the soulless present. Juan struggled to cast these doubts from his mind. All had to be hated, for all had been corruption. Furthermore, the people had been neglected. Yet the unsolved problems remained. When the gaping doors of one of the world's most wondrous museums yawned open, its great treasures were given freely, for the most part, for the enjoyment of all mankind, rich or poor.

He turned, then, and entered the teeming, smoke-filled lobby, self-conscious under the candid appraisal of men and women. And then he saw her. Hilda Krantz, dressed as she had been the very first time they'd met. Now she wore, attached to her belt, the suicide pistol of the Russian women's political organisation. Her back was towards him and as he started through the throng to reach her side a soldier, garbed in the heavy uniform of the Russian army, spoke sharply to him. 'Follow me, comrade!'

Juan looked longingly at Hilda's retreating back, but turned dutifully to follow the guard. They walked along the well-lit corridor, where guards stood stiffly to attention, impressive pistols strapped to their trim sides. As he passed them by, he felt a chill almost as of a cold wind – the inimical stare of the International Communists of the inner circle.

A door opened silently, and he was presented to Rosenberg, a smallish man who peered at him owlishly through thick glasses with a piercing, intelligent gaze. There were a few desultory remarks, and then a discreet tap sounded.

With a cold smile, Rosenberg walked to the door and opened it wide. Hilda Krantz stepped composedly into the centre of that spider's web.

Escape to Freedom

It is moral cowardice to leave undone what one perceives to be right.

The Analects of Confucius

Pedro Avila skulked through the gloomy streets of Madrid. Not a light shone from the windows. Groups of men, many in their early teens, were shouting and calling to one another, keyed to a pitch of frenzy by the booming of the loudspeakers that had kept up a remorseless barrage of propaganda for days.

He had but one objective: to gain, through the university city of Madrid, the foothills of the Pardo. From that point he would follow the winding course of the Manzanares River, skirting the village of Colmenar Viejo and hiking towards the distant mountains. From that place, to Segovia.

His mother and sisters had disappeared into the darkness and confusion of Madrid, he knew not where, and yet he hoped against hope that somewhere, somehow they were safe. Perhaps they had reached the safety of the Nationalist side. In any case, to stay in Madrid was death. He knew he had no easy task before him, but he had hiked and ridden over the terrain many times. He was confident that he had a good chance of making it to the other side.

Now he was nearing the university city. The dark hulk of the state prison loomed on his left. Around it were tall buildings, filled with sharpshooters, he was sure. He did not know then that on the next day these sharpshooters would begin their fusillade into the courtyard of the gloomy place. Hundreds would die, ripped to pieces by the sudden onslaught of machine gunfire.

'Halt!' He was faced by a squad. Death stared him in the face. He realised suddenly that without a Popular Front identification card, nor badge of any youthful organisation, he had little chance of survival. He felt the bulk of the pistol and ammunition hidden inside his shirt.

To his right was a clump of trees; to his left, the broad street, while farther on wound the road belonging to the Parque del Oeste.

Running with all speed across the dark street, he plunged headlong into the lush foliage of the park. Bullets sang and danced about him. Yet, he reasoned, a fleeing figure was not of sufficient importance to make them organise a definite manhunt. Dodging from bush to bush and tree to tree, he plunged down the steep hill of the park towards the Manzanares River.

The moon on this sultry August night burned with its phosphorescent glare, illuminating everything starkly. In a flash he remembered conversations with the Duque, who had sought to explain to him the different planes in the composition of a modern painting. He saw those planes now: the trees around him, as if they had no perspective; the darkness behind them, filled with murderous patrols; the metaphysical presence of a town – thousands of minds thinking, some one way, some another. All were beings separated from normality by reaction to frenzied success or harrowing defeat. He wondered what had become of the Duque del Bosque; a prisoner of the Communists, no doubt. He shuddered involuntarily at the thought.

He crept over the turnpike road, around which the trees were thicker, and found himself in the corner of the old Bombilla. This was the place, he remembered, where the immortal Goya had painted scenes of revelry in bygone days. This had been the site of lovers' meetings, of crooning whispers, of children's playing. All gone. Death stalked its solitude.

Pedro crossed the river, but a trickle at that time of the year, on the side of the Casa del Campo. Climbing the *casa*'s wall, he walked softly through the wooded slopes and again crossed the road, northbound. The nearness of a patrol shocked him into hushed immobility, but he felt on surer footing now. Behind him was a wilderness of mountain ranges, where nature was his friend. Bushes took on human form. Stunted trees would protect his retreat. The spirit of the hunted animal that at last finds refuge surged through his veins, firing his every nerve. He gripped his pistol butt until it hurt. His grey eyes glinted along the barrel, seeking aim to vent his power. Pedro had passed from pursued to killer.

★

Juan had met once again with Rosenberg, and that owlish man had posed a question. 'Do you know anything of the White Aide?'

That great phantom, the White Aide! Whispers in the dimly lit streets of Madrid, clandestine broadcasts, pamphlets that appeared as if from nowhere. Directions from some mysterious source to enemy artillery units, and signs for aviation direction. All the teeming unrest that caused victims through sabotage. The helping, unknown and unseen, of prisoner's families. The White Aide had crept into the heart of even the most secret organisations in its stealthy, shadowy way. Nobody on the Republican side had been able to find out the source of their support, though it was rumoured that the Catholic Church was the primary supplier of both men and arms, through their militant Falangists.

'No, I know no more about it than anyone else,' Juan replied.

Rosenberg fixed his thick-lensed stare upon him. 'Probably true enough. None of us knows much about them. And yet it's essential that we learn of their activities. I have been watching you these past weeks, young man, and I see in you great possibilities of good for the Party. I'm going to propose something that I want you to consider seriously.'

'Naturally, comrade, I shall consider seriously any of your proposals.' Juan wondered what the man was getting at.

'You've become very friendly with Hilda Krantz of late. That's as it should be. She can be of great value to you, for she knows the workings of Communism. At the same time, together you can be of value to the Party. I propose that you and the girl conduct a campaign of propaganda throughout our concentration camps. In these camps I'm confident that you will learn a great deal about the White Aide. You will report directly to me. As you know, the biggest camp, Belles Artes, is operated by the Russians. Atadell, one of our most dependable assets is the supervisor. That is your first destination.'

'Is this an order, comrade?'

Rosenberg smiled thinly. 'I said it was only a suggestion. However, it's wise to listen to my suggestions just now, for you have a great future ahead of you, and I can be of immeasurable service to you in achieving that goal.'

The thought seemed sound, he could not deny that, and yet Juan shuddered inwardly at the idea. He had always had an extreme aversion to seeing captured things, whether animal or human. Once, he had even opened the door of his mother's canary's cage in order to give the creature its freedom. Yet now he was to walk among those human derelicts who were locked up behind bars like wild animals.

'One other thing. I have secured the release from prison of someone you will be interested in. His name's Tormo, and he will serve as chauffeur for you on this trip.'

'Tormo?' Juan was caught by surprise. 'I thought he was dead by now.'

'Hardly,' said Rosenberg. 'You can't kill such sturdy peasant stock. And that's what he is, you know. In any event, he will meet you this evening at eight, and Hilda will be ready to leave. I might add, you will not find Tormo as you last saw him. He has become embittered and somewhat brutalised, I fear, by his treatment at the hands of those delightful Civil Guards. But this bitterness will serve us one day. He knows the mountains like nobody else, and his strength and skill in handling the things of war will be invaluable to you.'

'Tormo,' said Juan. 'I can hardly believe it. He seemed to me to be just a harmless young boxer with a gift for stealing when it became necessary.'

'Don't fool yourself,' said Rosenberg. 'And don't cross the man, or you'll live to regret it, if you live at all. For now, goodbye, and don't forget your reports. I shall look forward to hearing from you.'

★

The sights of Pedro's gun were levelled on the back of a man who was searching through the trees. The moon played on the stalwart form. Fate had it that at that precise instant the man turned. Through some primordial instinct he sensed death. Was it possible that the man's eyes pierced the gloom to look and concentrate upon that death-dealing instrument? An expression of panic seized his face. Pedro's hand quivered. As the shot sounded, he knew that he had killed wantonly.

Then came hours of terror for him. Walking, looking, listening. Everywhere possible enemies lurked. Shots sounded far and near. The manhunt was on, yet not for him specifically. This he knew. Hundreds, like him, were like smaller grains of sand being sifted through a mesh.

A crash in a nearby thicket caused him a moment of acute panic. His heart had undoubtedly missed a beat. Action was impossible. He stood – rooted to the spot.

The glint of moonbeams picked out the form of a deer. Motionless, it looked at him with soft brown eyes. Like a thunderbolt, Pedro was struck by the idea that passion and hatred are fostered only in what is supposed to be the noblest creation of God's world. With sinuous grace the buck bounded forward, disappearing into the shadowed forest.

Dawn was beginning to colour the earth with the rosy hues of day. Pedro knew that with the rising of the sun his peril would grow. A sentry with field glasses, scanning the bald summits of the hills of the northern Pardo, could easily see any person moving between the scrubby oaks.

But he kept forging ahead for a time. At last, reaching the bare hillsides of Colmenar Viejo, from whose church spire anything could be spotted for miles around, he crouched beneath a thicket. He saw the towering mountains, kissed by the rising sun, striking the blue vault of heaven with their definite outline. The purple of shadow mantled the steepness of their sides. With dawn, there entered into Pedro's imagination the forgotten memories of his history. Now he peopled the slopes and jagged passes of the mountains with the Muslim hordes and the Christian knights, who, a thousand years ago, had surged back and forth in desperate battle. There too he could see, rising upon a knoll, the famous castle of Manzanares el Real, gate for many years of the disputes between Segovian gentlemen and the knights of Madrid. Wars had raged over feudal rights, over creeds and now, once again, Mars was inflicting its burning wound upon the already barren country.

Pedro looked from his hiding place, and saw, shimmering in the distance, the horizon that clutched tortured Madrid to its bosom. On the other side, relentless slopes glared back heat and drought.

At noon even life seemed to stand still. Only the *chicharras* kept up their rasping sound. Overhead, like Nemesis, a vulture leaned its mighty wings against the flawless air. Plumes of dust marked the trail of trucks coming from Madrid, full of beings with the zest and zeal of their creed, to which death was justice. The throb of the distant motors, even the sound of cries came drifting through the air like so many imaginary hammers. The pushing cordon of men crept behind him, like the sickle of the emblem that overshadowed his life's desire.

He remembered that he had many times spoken with friends in the comfort of a cafe, about the tragedy of death. Now, small in the vast cup of the earth, with nature around him, he found himself but a speck in the infinite. He had but one wish: to live.

Pedro saw the troops deploying upwards towards the still-distant summits. He would have to step warily to pass that line of frenzied idealism. His throat was dry, for he had not dared to venture out of hiding to seek the river, which like a silver mirror snaked downwards towards Madrid. He felt the pangs of hunger; but they were small compared to his thirst.

At last night fell, and he crept from his thicket. He remembered that a shepherd friend lived near one of the small villages. Perhaps there he could get some goat's milk or a bit of cheese. A shepherd's fare is scanty on the best of occasions, and this was not one of the best. Cautiously slinking from boulder to boulder, and bush to bush, he left the closely guarded dam of Santilana to his right and crept towards the deeper shadow where he knew the village nestled.

A dog barked – the worried tone of an animal that senses a stranger. Were they patrols, or was it the dog of his friend?

'Rey, Rey,' he called softly. And there, directly before him glinted the yellow eyes and the shaggy coat of Rey, the mastiff.

With an audible prayer of thankfulness, Pedro remembered the many times he had given the great beast food, scraps of his mother's tortillas. A lone man, in that dreary and desolate countryside, was no match for any mastiff.

Now a tiny flicker of light greeted him, and a subdued voice hailed him. '*Quien va?*'

'It is I,' replied Pedro in the same cautious tones.

The shepherd stepped forward. The moonlight picked out, with silvery gleam, the skinning knife held ready in his hand, for these were troubled times. 'Come in,' he growled. 'Make no fancy moves or, by all the saints, you shall not live to make another.'

★

Juan and Hilda were in the car, with Tormo behind the wheel. Clearly the car was not a good one, for it had begun to boil after the heavy gradient coming out of the valley of the Jarama.

'It lets out steam like a locomotive,' said Juan.

'Yes,' returned Tormo, 'we'll have to stop up ahead here at that fountain.' He gestured to the side of the road.

As is usual in Spain at that time of the year, on the high plateau of the Province of Cuenca, the sun comes out with strange force. On each side of the road were scrubby, rolling mountains and, between them, grasped by their lean shoulders, green little valleys trickled back down into the plain far below.

'I'm hot,' said Hilda. She pointed to an especially inviting strip of green below the road. 'I'm going down there to cool off.' Without further words she scrambled down the steep bank, and found to her surprise that it was farther than she had imagined. She must have walked a good mile when suddenly before her appeared a veritable oasis – from the arid to the bountiful; from rocks and scorching heat to trees and flowers.

She relaxed upon a moss-cloaked boulder, and, taking off her dust-covered shoes, dangled her feet in the cool water. Only the sounds of crickets, the mournful cooing of a lone dove, and now and then the warbling of a distant *jilguerlo* broke the stillness of the placid air.

And as she stared fixedly down at the glassy surface of the

pool, disturbed only by the rude ripples her feet had created, she saw herself reflected there. As she looked, the pool became a cone. In its whirling vortex was her mind. From it, definite shapes and forms manifested themselves, but, upon contact with the air, they disappeared. Her discipline of thought was escaping. All her life she had fettered her subconscious so that it had become a coldly-analytical quantity. Now it was becoming ascendant. About her was the mighty horizon. In the distance were the dimly seen mountains, their craggy hardness mellowed by time and space.

Juan stepped to the edge of the road. 'Hello,' he called, 'it's time to leave if we are to reach Motilla del Palancar by nightfall.'

Motilla del Palancar. Once a thriving centre for the growing of saffron. Square stone houses were built along a central way, a few sulking acacias giving an apology of shade in the blistering sun.

Here the Civil Guard, in the time of its founding, had erected a thick, sombre building of masonry, with the capacity for a platoon. Behind, there was a large courtyard for horses and equipment. This tragic building had known many a beating and many a brawl but it was to know still more, and worse. A concentration camp, run by the brutal prison guard, Atadell, for the Soviet secret police, had unfurled its bloody banner over the enterprise of the long-dead Marquis of Ahumada.

Juan's orders were clear enough. As the spokesman, coached by the perfectionist who was Hilda, he was to try to discover the secrets of the White Aide, while propagandising for the Communist cause.

The doors of the concentration camp yawned open to present the picture Juan had always dreaded to see. Lined up before him were faces that shot out of the mass like so many blows. These had been his friends in gentler days. Haggard eyes pierced him with darts of hatred and contempt. To them he was the embodiment of all their loathing for the foreign Communists.

Winter, with its extreme cold and the hunger that came with it, had left a damning mark. Hundreds had died from exposure and starvation. Juan involuntarily cringed at the sight of the wreckage that had once been human beings.

A pathetic figure, the fifth man to the right, attracted Juan's attention. It couldn't be, and yet it was: the Duque del Bosque. His hands were raw and bleeding, his roughened feet wrapped in sackcloth. About his shoulders was draped the sorry remnant of a military tunic. Once a dignified man, the contrast between his clothes and loose skin made him look like a clown, a tragic buffoon.

Juan passed before him in his spotless uniform and yet the Duque said not a word. Only his eyes held a world of suffering. Now, at last, Juan had realised his ambition. The Duque was a broken man, a dying man. And yet there was no joy of triumph in Juan's heart, no exulting in his soul. The eyes of the tormented prisoners burned into his brain until he thought he should go mad.

★

Pedro slid into the doorway of the hut in the uncomfortable position he was ordered to take. He felt the sharp prick of the knifepoint pressed against his kidneys. He knew that any move he made in that dim interior would spell death for him.

Suddenly, in breezy tones, the shepherd exclaimed, 'By the sainted Virgin, why didn't you say you were Pedro Avila! Sit down and be comfortable. This is your house.'

Pedro heaved a sigh of relief, and sat gingerly on the edge of a stool. He could scarcely mouth his thanks. 'This is a strange way to greet a friend.'

The swarthy features before him relaxed into an expansive grin. 'These are troubled times. Your own family can be your worst enemy. Hunger is everywhere, and distrust and betrayal go hand in hand with dislike. What do you want, my night-travelling friend? A little trip over the mountains, hey? You're not the first to come, oh no. There have been others, though they've not met with the same greeting. They could've been spies. You're my friend. How's your mother who cooks such savoury tortillas? May the saints praise her!'

'To be honest, I don't know where she is. I have reason to think that she escaped from Madrid to the Nationalist side, but that's a long story. Suffice it to say that I'm looking for her this minute. I suppose you remember my brother. His ways will end in death for him and in heartbreak for all of us. But, to get back to the purpose of this nocturnal visit: I'm as thirsty as those boulders up there in the sierras, and as hungry as a vulture.'

The shepherd arose, and filled a tumbler with goat's milk. A thick slice of bread, half an onion, and a piece of *Torcino* were handed to him. 'Now eat and be quiet. When you're able we'll talk. I'll go and have a look around. Some of those sons of Satan from the village are apt to be prowling tonight.'

His thirst and hunger satisfied, Pedro felt drowsy and tired. He relaxed on a pile of sheepskins in the corner of the hut, and was soon fast asleep.

Something wet and cold nudged Pedro's face. Awakening with a start, he rubbed his eyes, and found the shepherd smiling down at him, the dog by his side.

'Are you going to sleep all your life like the lazy señoritas of the city?' the man said. 'We must be halfway up those slopes before daylight, friend. Before the slightest streak of light comes, we have to cross the valley behind the castle of Manzanares el Real. You haven't said so in so many words, but it's clear enough that you want to cross those mountains.'

Together they climbed over one of the stone walls as they left the sleeping valley behind. The shepherd whispered, 'Be careful that you make no noise. This is wild bull country, and they're extremely nervous these days. There are a lot of dead bodies along the road, and the bulls sense things astir.'

Their course took them to the right of the castle. Slower and slower grew their progress. The shepherd's hand gripped Pedro's arm. 'We're in trouble,' he said. 'We've a *solitario* right in front of us and I think he's heard us.'

Pedro remembered that *solitarios* are the most dangerous of the wild bulls – outcasts, or sometimes a young bull that has not had sufficient prowess to fight for the supremacy of the herd. Pained by his wounds, and enraged by his solitary confinement, he is a dangerous animal. This was the beast that was sent to fight the tiger and the lion in the arenas of ancient Rome, nearly always winning in the process. These were the animals that had ripped the Christians to pieces in orgies of blood.

The shepherd, throwing caution to the winds, cried, 'Run for the wall on your left. Don't think about trees. They're too small anyway.'

Then, in a flash, Pedro was confronted by the horrible reality. A tremendous bull, horns glinting in the starlight, weighing at least fifteen hundred pounds, was pawing frantically at the grass, sending clods of earth arching over his broad back.

'Run, you fool!' roared the shepherd.

And so he did, as he had never run before in his life.

★

Juan and Hilda were in Alicante when the news came of a breakthrough of the Nationalists on the northern front. They sat in the car, stunned into silence by the enormity of the news.

'Have you heard the news?' Tormo stood outside the car, staring in through the open window.

'But of course,' said Juan. 'Get in, Tormo. We'll have to leave for Madrid at once. This turn of events will mean a new assignment for us all.'

Hilda reached over and took his hand in hers. 'It's been such a wonderful trip. I had hoped it would never end.'

'Wonderful?' Juan flashed her a look filled with amazement and jerked his hand away. 'It's been the most miserable experience of my life. How can you enjoy the misery of a lot of poor wretches who are locked behind bars?'

'Oh Juan, you mistake my meaning.' She turned her sweetest smile on him. 'What I meant was that I've enjoyed your company.'

He was not to be dissuaded by her charms. 'I'm not so sure, Hilda. I've watched you these past days. I've seen you almost gloating over men who were dying from starvation. And, what's even worse, I've never seen you flinch. I've begun to wonder what's happened to the sweet girl I once knew.'

'All right, Juan,' she said, 'I suppose I had that coming. You'll never understand me. Remember, I warned you once that I was first of all a Communist and only secondly a woman. This cause is too great to think about in your terms. Those men you feel so sorry for are fools. I knew that some day they would be swept away like leaves of autumn before the driving winds. Yes, and like the dead leaves they've become, they'll pass away.'

'Dead leaves? You can speak of human beings as dead leaves?'

She laughed mirthlessly. 'Nothing, my dear Juan, will stand in the way of the Party. Not you, and certainly not I. Remember, I told you that a man named Schmidt brought me into the Party. Well, there's a story about that man that should be brought to your attention, for I see that you're beginning to waver in your allegiance.'

'A story? All right, let's hear this story. Right now I'm hardly in the mood to listen, but perhaps you can justify your attitude.'

'Justification, my dear Juan, is not necessary for us. However, Schmidt came to me one day while I was in Paris. He looked surprised to see me so prosperous.' She smiled, and leaned back against the seat. 'Certainly I was no longer the shabby girl he had met in Düsseldorf. But he was looking different, too. Gone was the brilliance of his gaze; lines around his mouth bespoke bitterness and silver streaked his hair. Well, suffice to say that I was shocked by his appearance. I thought perhaps he was ill, but I learned, after a few glasses of wine, that he was the living embodiment of all those who fall somewhere along the line. A love affair had cost him more than he could afford. And I don't mean money. He'd failed to carry out his orders to eliminate the one he loved.' She laced her hands behind her head and crossed her legs. 'Yes, a love affair had cost him everything. He, my dear Juan, had fallen a victim to the weakness of feeling. And in this game we're playing there's no room for those who can't learn to subdue their every whim. The brain has to succeed. The will must conquer. Feelings have to be put aside. Needless to say, there was only one answer: Schmidt had to be eliminated. The uniform movement of the Party had been slowed down by this man who had failed to maintain his vigilance in time of need.'

Juan's tongue felt thick in his mouth. He swallowed, and was surprised to find how dry his throat had become. 'And I suppose I don't need to ask what happened?'

'No,' she shrugged her shoulders. 'I think you know.'

Juan lapsed into moody silence. What was this monstrous thing that took a warm and lovely creature and conquered her very will? In this girl beside him he sensed, as never before, the driving purposefulness for the final triumph of the Communist cause. He had always bitterly attacked tradition; how then was it that he rebelled deep within his being at the sight of these imprisoned men? They had lived for a losing cause, and now they had to pay the price. Was this the whole answer? Where had his restless seeking first begun? For humanity and the cause of the downtrodden? Yes, but if that were the case, why should he have turned from that creed that said from its very foundation, 'Love your neighbour as yourself'? Those shabby men of faith gave themselves to the ultimate sacrifice, which is the life of the individual dedicated to a creed. If that creed and faith existed, as surely it must, how had he missed finding it? He had delved so profoundly into their thought, never to discover its elusive meaning. And here was Hilda, as beautiful and desirable as ever, coldly spelling out the death of a man with amused indifference. Why did these doubts assail him in times of stress? Where was his flaw?

The Long Night

Long is the night to him who is awake;
long is the mile to him who is tired;
long is life to the foolish.

The 'Dhammapada' of Buddha

As Pedro bounded head foremost over the wall into a thick briar bush behind, he felt the swish of air, impelled by the great lunge, and the tremendous upheaval of earth as the furious beast slid to a stop.

Complete silence was required. He dared not move from the thorny embrace, for he knew full well the incredible resourcefulness of these animals, once that vesanic rage overpowers them.

The awesome head appeared over the wall, holding him fascinated. The bull could easily have jumped the barrier, but had never tried it, from its calf days to the present. Pedro's only thought was a hypnotic sensation of acute fear, a fear of being impaled on the huge horns above him.

A well-aimed stone from the shepherd's sling saved the day. With the thud of the stone upon the beast's flanks, it wheeled about and charged off in another direction.

Extricating himself, and with all his nerves jangling, a sorry-looking Pedro walked around the bend to where the imperturbable shepherd awaited him.

'Were you looking for some silly girl you left behind? Perhaps you want to be a bullfighter? You'd better wake up, or you'll be sleeping your last sleep on those summits. Man in hatred is far worse than any beast in rage.' His warning delivered, the shepherd whirled about and strode away.

It seemed, to Pedro, that the shepherd's plan was to escort him along the summit of the Pedriza, by the Pico del Pajaro, and from there on to Cabezas de Hierro. In this way they would circle the old volcano that formed the rocky Circo de la Pedriza, an amazing formation of rocks, all of basaltic granite, washed smooth by countless ages of water that streamed down to the valley. The winds and storms of time had acted as a polishing sandpaper, leaving weird shapes of birds and beasts, of unbelievable balancing tons of rocks on wedges, of deep and narrow crevices, through which the wind bellows and roars. Through the middle of all this rocky chaos a little stream bounded, curled, disappeared and appeared again, gushing forth to spread itself out in the valley far beneath. Home of eagles, and vultures, their eerie cries echoed from corner to corner, until the intruding men thought the ghouls themselves were practicing their witchcraft, apparent only in sound.

Onwards they crept along the weary miles of lung-bursting climb, ever more cautious. As the towering cliffs and boulders neared the summit, they were coming under the menace of ever-searching glasses.

At last the shepherd called a halt at the four fingers of Cabeza de Hierro. High above the world the air felt cool and fresh, free of the mire of cities and factories. Nature claimed its own.

'I'll accompany you but a short way farther,' said the shepherd, 'and then I have to leave you to your fate. If I'm missing for more than one night, my wife and children will pay the price.'

Pedro, breathing heavily from the unaccustomed exertion, gasped, 'You've already come far enough. I know these mountains well. Go back now. I don't want to be a hindrance to your family. I'll always remember this action on your part, and some day I'll repay you in due form. It's sufficient that one family should be broken up by this damned war.' He took the shepherd's hand and gripped it warmly.

'So be it,' said the shepherd. 'May God, Fate, Providence, or whomsoever watches over us be kind to you. I'm many years older than you, my friend, but up here in the mountains when the wind dies down and it's quiet in the valleys, I have thought in my uncouth way – for I can't read or write – that you'll one day do some great thing for Spain, and with all those youths who want to change. I wish I knew whether or not you'll succeed. These sierras have seen brilliant men come and go, and yet they still continue. That's life, I suppose. It's only a bridge between birth and death. Don't mention repayment. That which comes from the heart isn't repayable. *Vaya con Dios, amigo.*'

With these words he disappeared, bounding down the sheer slopes with the matchless poise and grace of one who has lived always between the crags.

Loneliness was a void into which Pedro toppled, as if he had been perched upon the highest pinnacle. There he waited, all the long day, until the darkness fell.

★

Juan reached for the tassel to draw back the curtains that hung in front of the window as if standing guard against the throbbing city outside. He saw, in the light of the dying afternoon, a grove of trees, interlacing their hungry branches. And beyond the wall he heard shouts and the sound of running feet, whistles and shots, and the cries of the mortally wounded.

The thick folds of the curtain resumed their motionless barrier against sound and light. Juan walked slowly across the great room and seated himself next to Hilda in a leather-bound *frailero*.

Across a large table of polished oak sat Ricardo, resting his back against the rich upholstery of his chair.

'Strange how fate plays its game,' said Juan.

'How's that?' Ricardo thoughtfully stretched forth a slender hand and took a cigar from the silver box that spoke so eloquently of Cellini's artistic influence.

'Well, I should think it'd be obvious,' said Juan. 'Here we are, sitting in the Duque's house, in the very room where I've found myself many times. Only in those days I'm afraid I didn't feel quite so much at ease.'

Smiling, Ricardo leaned forward for a moment, staring down at the cigar in his hand. 'Yes, like this unlighted cigar,' he said. 'It's an expensive brand, thanks to the Duque, but there are not many left now. Still, the cigar would be of no great value unless it were lit. The same with this place,' he gestured about the room. 'With the Duque living here, it was of little value to anyone. Now it belongs to the people.' Leaning back, he ignited a match with slow, precise movements. Round and round went the cigar, until an even glowing circle proclaimed its ignition. With a long sigh he expelled the blued smoke and settled his body into a more comfortable position in the great, velvet-lined chair.

Hilda spoke sharply. 'All right, Ricardo, I'm sure we're charmed by all this, but let's get down to business. I don't think we're particularly concerned with your attitude towards this place or the people at the moment.'

Ricardo fixed his cold eyes upon her. 'A woman of action, I see. Well, I should think you'd get weary of that after a while. Just think! The world spins round and round, attracting and being attracted. The moon around us, and we around the sun. Finally we all belong to the universe. Tragedy, glee, and action have been here for thousands of years. And then we're produced. A short sixty or seventy years of life. Who knows?' He waved his cigar as if at some elusive form. 'We're out, just like a candle, a tiny little flame in some tremendous cavern. Some people inherit and are pleased. Others mourn for a while, until time erases from their memories the things over which they mourned. Ah, yes, action. For that you need a goal, my dear. Something for which you can live, and fight, and die if need be.'

'Fine-sounding words,' said Hilda, 'but I must say I'm getting impatient to know what this is all about.'

He sat erect suddenly, threw the cigar to the floor and ground it out on the thick carpet with his foot. 'I'll tell you what this is about, my pretty,' he thundered. 'It's about you and your paramour here.'

'Now just a minute,' said Juan, starting to his feet.

'Oh sit down,' replied Ricardo. 'I grow impatient with noble people. In the first place, the Party isn't at all happy with the work you've done in the prison camps. Juan here,' and he pointed a ringed finger at him, 'did little in the camps except look sad and solemn. You'd think he was a missionary who was trying to spread the gospel, only we've begun to wonder what gospel he's spreading. And as for you, Hilda, it's really quite simple: you've become altogether too enamoured of this man of late. Think about it and you'll see that I'm right.'

Hilda leaned back in her chair and took a cigarette from a purse she wore by a strap around her shoulder. Her fingers were trembling somewhat, but she wore a cold, aloof expression. Now it was her turn to look at Ricardo as she had been looked at a moment before. 'And who are you to tell me these things? Our activities are under the direction of Rosenberg.'

Ricardo smiled expansively. 'Not any more, my dear. But I'm curious to know one thing. If you were required to give up your relationship with Juan by the Party, could you do it?'

A moment of silence. Juan grew pale and stared down at the ornate carpet underfoot. Somewhere in the distance a siren wailed.

Hilda appeared to be choosing her own words with care. She drew deeply upon her cigarette, expelling the smoke in a pencil-thin stream that curled about her face like the serpents of Medusa. 'If I had to choose, comrade? I think my record in the Party speaks for itself.'

Ricardo rose to his feet and strode briskly to the window. Whirling about, he levelled his hard stare at them. 'I'm glad to hear you say that, Hilda. Remember, my dear, the Party can offer us the world itself one day, but in order to accomplish that purpose we must learn to bear whatever personal discomforts may come our way.' He jerked upon the embroidered cord and the heavy drapes slid open. 'Out there,' and he waved his hand in an all-embracing gesture, 'is Madrid, and beyond that is all of Spain. This is the initial test for our cause. To lose this game would mean a realignment of the chessmen. The testament of Lenin is at stake. Through lack of organisation and purpose our side might, conceivably, lose. Such an eventuality must always be anticipated. But remember, comrades, the pincers are open, and this time Europe won't find the broad back of a Thessalian bull to save herself. There are many problems to solve. There are many interpretations of our doctrine, and such men as our Party ideologues, Marty and Thorez, are quibbling over them in a dangerous way. You, Hilda, with your far-seeing mind and objectivity, can be of great help to us. On the other hand, Juan Avila can be of assistance too, but only apart from you. We have no place for moonstruck love. Only grim reality is permissible now.'

'And what is planned for me, comrade?' Hilda was now all

Party member. Gone was the warmth and radiance that Juan had known; gone was the softness and the glowing light. Now only the cold, inscrutable face of the dedicated Communist met his glance.

He felt suddenly weak and tired. Bitterness threatened, for a time, to flood the room. Juan fought back the bitter words and the cries of anguish. This was no longer the woman he loved. This was a woman who could never love a tangible thing of flesh and blood. Hilda had become the calculating, bloodless machine that his subconscious mind had always told him she might be.

Ricardo left the window, then, and walked to her side. He dropped his hand upon her shoulder. 'Comrade, your mission will be to go to Valencia. There you will receive your instructions. As for you,' and he turned to Juan with a grim smile, 'you will remain in Madrid for a while until we see how best your talents may be used for the good of the common cause. Don't become impatient. You will receive your instructions in good time. And so for now, goodbye to both of you, and good luck.' He was already seated at the table, his head bowed over a great sheaf of papers and pamphlets.

★

Pedro laboriously ascended the crags from which sprouted the rocky Cabezas de Hierro. He saw, gently sloping downward from his perch, the saddle that united his rocky peak with the great bald mass of Cuerda Largo. Here the ground held but little earth. All was boulders and rubble, rutted and torn, cracked from their gnarled sides by the patient and ever-weakening forces of wind and rain. Little bushes could be seen here and there, gaining a precarious sustenance from the stony ground.

Far up the slope of the mountain summit, he detected the glint of a gun where a bored sentinel kept lonely vigil. If only the darkness would fall. In that flawless sky and brilliant light, anything that moved for miles around could be spotted. He seated himself as comfortably as possible, and rested his broad back against a smooth boulder. With half-closed eyes he considered what route should be taken. Those mountains seemed so near, yet he knew that they were a good five miles away over the arid, rounded slope that divided north from south.

The sun swooped majestically downwards, and space nestled it comfortably to its vast bosom. Such a tremendous movement; yet without a sound. With those last feeble rays, far overhead, a few milky clouds blushed their concern at coming night. Soon the stars would blink down at velvety earth.

Cautiously, Pedro stepped forward. He had dozed practically throughout the day. From boulder to boulder he stepped, trying to walk as the shepherd had done, and thanking Providence that he had remembered to put on thick-soled hiking shoes before leaving his home in Madrid. Madrid, the dark, dangerous, smouldering and passionate city that had been, only a short time back, so carefree and gay.

And the moon was rising, first cloaked in red, but as she climbed, shearing off her veils to emerge in all her silvery splendour. Shadows were like holes, and the lighted places were like columns that seemed to magnify size or diminish it. When those shafts of light crowned the ancient grey of mighty Pena Lara he veered slightly to the left. Crouching low, bounding, standing still and listening, he moved ever forwards.

Perhaps he relaxed his vigilance, and, since things had gone so well, optimism had smothered reality. The sharp crack of a rifle, not far away, and the whine of a bullet, brought him crashing back to fear and his plight. Sinking into a deep hole behind a sheltering boulder, he heard cries far and near.

He knew that the trenches began three miles to the right and two miles to the left. He had to get at that near sentinel, somehow, and silence him. Then he would have nothing further to fear. By the direction of the shouts it was clear that the line was sparsely held. The part he was crossing, being untimbered and flat, could be easily guarded.

Cautiously he made his way towards the direction of the shot. The rocks tore at his hands and clothes, but he was oblivious to pain. He stopped, for the sound of the sentinel's pacing was very near. How could he rid himself of the enemy without noise? Perhaps he could spring upon the man's back. But no, for the man would be alerted by this time and would be unusually quick to discharge his rifle at the first disturbance. Patrols must have been sent out from the platoon headquarters. He thought of stunning the man with a stone, for he was not wearing his helmet, the glint of which could be seen as it lay several feet away. Now his mind focused upon that helmet. He would don it, and, calling out to the guard, approach as a comrade-in-arms.

Slowly and painfully he inched towards his goal, until at last his reaching fingers captured it. Slithering back, he made a wide circle and, with firm steps, yet pounding heart, approached.

'Who goes there?'

'Stop your yelling, you human megaphone,' said Pedro in as firm a voice as he could muster. 'You already have all the sierras singing with your stupid shadow-shooting. Do you expect a man to come along bawling his name and occupation since his first birthday?' He kept walking forward deliberately.

'Give the password, or I'll shoot,' came the response.

With a flying leap from several feet away, Pedro crashed headlong into the man. Using all the strength that desperation and the will to live add to a human being, he pinned the sentinel down. Clutching the struggling man's throat with his left hand, his right closed convulsively around a stone. With a wrench he freed the heavy object, and crashed it down upon the head of his victim. A low grunt, followed by a rattling sigh. That was all.

Rising, he took the dead man's ammunition, rifle and hand grenades and fled up the slopes like a soundless wraith. Not a moment too soon. His alert ears caught the muffled tread of many feet: the patrol. As fast as his legs could carry him, he ran in a straight line towards the distant peak that guided him on as the polar star guides the lost sailor.

Crossing the dividing line he breathed deeply, gasping in relief, though he knew that before him lay many a dangerous mile.

His path sloped gently downwards, losing height as slowly as possible, heading due west towards the pass, Puerto de los Cotos. From that point he planned to go west once again, and, circling Pena Lara, leave that great mountain to his left. It would be safer to bypass the entrenched and practically surrounded town of La Granja.

Across the Puerto de los Cotos he went, darting from tree to tree. Here his friends, the pines, abounded. The dark hulk of what had once been a skier's clubhouse loomed ahead. He prayed that no dogs would be about. From defective human senses he could easily hide, but he could never hope to flee from the friend of man.

Leaving the line of trees, Pedro gathered his failing strength and ran with all speed across the road and upwards towards the slope ahead. Tall grass clutched at him, retarding his progress. At last, when his goal of trees was near, the feared dog barked, commencing an ungodly refrain.

A door was thrust open violently, and a raucous voice boomed forth. 'That dog would never bark unless someone were about. Up and about on your business. If another of those damned Fascists have passed us we'll never hear the end of it from the Comisari.'

★

The days passed slowly for Juan in Madrid. He sought to forget Hilda's face in the routine of Party duties, and yet, in the darkness of night the cold mask of her features would come plainly into view. How could a person change as quickly as a chameleon changed its colours? Perhaps he had been mistaken about her feelings for him. Surely she could not have loved him if she had rejected him with such finality.

And then he remembered that a girl Pedro had escorted to various social affairs was still living in the city. Perhaps there he would receive some information about his mother and sisters. They had disappeared into the maelstrom of war, and he feared that they were long since dead.

He approached the house with some trepidation. It was neither wise nor convenient these days for a known Communist leader to be seen frequenting familiar old places.

The door was opened a crack, and an old and tired face peered out at him. 'Who? Oh, Juan Avila.' The woman swung the door open, after fiddling for some time with the rusty latch chain. 'Come in, young man.'

'Is either of the children here?' he asked.

A trembling hand brushed her pale, drawn face. 'The children? No, I'm afraid you're too late for that, my dear. My son was ordered to the front, and my daughter, rest her soul, died last week of pneumonia.'

'Conchita dead?' He could hardly believe his own ears. 'But she was always so full of life, and so strong.'

'War, Juan, has a habit of changing all those things. But here, do sit down.' And she pulled forward an ancient chair. 'I'll light the candles.' She busied herself about the room, and soon the warm glow of the candles dispelled the gloom. 'And what of your brother, Pedro?'

'Oh, I don't know. I understand he's in a combat unit and has made quite a name for himself. Of course, he's on our side.'

'Oh, of course.' There was no sound of conviction in the woman's voice. 'I wish this war were over. I don't know what a good meal is any more, and not one of the family around. But I don't suppose you think much of that, since you're a Communist. I don't say that things were better before, but certainly they're in an awful state now. I had to stand in a queue for two long hours the other day for half a pound of beans. When I got them they were half sand. But you can't protest, for they immediately say you're a fifth columnist trying to cause trouble.'

He sighed but made no attempt to answer the woman. It felt good just to sit there in the comparative comfort of the place, the smell of old and familiar things about him.

Her voice droned on. 'Don't you remember, just five years ago it was, when Pedro came and took the children over to your house? Then all of you attended Christmas Eve Mass at midnight. It was held at the Duque's house, as I recall, and all of you got such wonderful gifts. Yes, yes. You can nod your head. You may think me a silly old woman, Juan, but I've lived much longer than you, and the demon knows more through age than because he's the Devil.' She smiled grimly, and closed her eyes. 'There's no question about it. All that we see about us has to change and will change. Do you think it's a normal thing for the population to go around flourishing great pistols before they're even twenty years old? Even if it is war, that's not right. If these people are so warlike, why don't they go to the front? Then perhaps my son could come home. That's where they're doing the fighting. Yes, and the dying. They seem to be marching all along the front, but that's neither here nor there. I'm not politically inclined, and only want to be left in peace. I want to live as well as I can without harming anyone else. I'll help all I can, but I don't want to be constantly pushed around like some dumb sheep.'

Juan had made a mistake in coming to this house before ascertaining if his friends were there. He knew it now, but it was too late. The woman's garrulousness was well known.

'By the way,' she continued, 'how are your mother and sisters? I don't believe you said.'

He rose to his feet, and gestured with his expressive hands. 'Oh, they're fine. A bit pinched with hunger these days like all of us. And now I must be going.' He strode to the door, and turned. 'Goodbye, and best wishes to you.'

The old woman gave him a strange smile. 'Well, have a good time, and don't think that people are so foolish.'

Juan walked down the crumbling stairs and out into the street. Had she known from the beginning where his family had gone? He had never thought that her son would go to the front. If he remembered rightly, the boy was not exactly of his way of thinking. But, since they had been classmates in school, they had sworn eternal friendship, no matter what their ideologies might be. Could he have joined up with the other side across those distant mountains? All his boyhood friends were disappearing, as if into thin air. No notes. No letters. No clues as to their whereabouts.

His footsteps took him to a bar in the centre of the city. As he entered the doorway, he looked about in horror. The place was jammed to overflowing. Men in uniform on furlough from the front, men carrying briefcases and looking serious, as if they bore the weight of the world in those bags. He felt like a stranger in their midst. There was only one thing to do. He shouldered his way to the bar and signalled the harassed bartender.

'Anis,' he said.

He swallowed it without much relish, and four more followed in quick succession. The doors of equilibrium and proportion were closed. The evening rolled by in a haze, as his steps took him from bar to bar. His brain was cloudy, but he felt light and cheerful all of a sudden.

Midnight passed, and he was alone in a bar behind the Plaza del Progreso. With loneliness, his bitter mood resumed. Lurching to his feet, he made his way with faltering steps towards the door.

The cooling wind of that August night came straight from the distant mountains. Not a light could be seen and there was only the noise of the whistling wind as it tore at the little heaps of garbage and dirt that lay in the unkempt streets. Acting on him as an antidote, the breeze cleared the fog of alcohol from his brain. Suddenly he felt very hungry. Since morning he had eaten nothing.

He walked towards the old Institute of San Isidro, and passed the entrance of the church that enshrined the patron saint of Madrid. How many times, as a child, had Juan entered that building to say his prayers before the annual examinations? He felt drawn, now, by curiosity, and turned into the vast building.

The place was a shambles. The beautiful fifteenth-century altar had been ripped to pieces. The tombs of the friars had been opened and their bones were strewn around. In the centre of the altar, a skull grinned nakedly at life, with a cap set on it at a rakish angle. Sacks in a distant corner denoted that it had been used as a storehouse but gloominess had forced its abandonment.

A voice echoed cavernously from a corner, where a light glimmered feebly. 'What do you want? Only the dead and myself live here.'

★

Dazed though he was through lack of breath, Pedro rose and staggered on, hoping to gain his second wind. He splashed into the brook and headed northward to avoid the sensitive nose of the dog. A half-hour of scrambling downstream found him in wild country. Pines and fir trees abounded. Between them, great granite boulders now and again showed their sloping sides. Pine needles carpeted his step. With dragging feet he climbed a hill that soared upward to his right. Would the hill never end? He felt as if he were on the verge of collapse. But at last the thinning trees proclaimed the summit, about which were similar hills, seeming, to his distorted senses, like bubbles in a cauldron.

The light of day was streaming into every nook and cranny. At last the summit. To the south lay the great range of mountains he had passed; to the south-east, the pear-shaped cone of Pena Lara and, from its mighty back like the fingers of a giant hand, the dwindling mountains crumbled into the great plain that stretched endlessly forward, in yellows and browns, towards the dimness of distance.

Drowsiness was creeping over him, like the unstoppable flow of water from a broken dike. And into a fissure between two great rocks he crept, brushing the ground, and digging with his hands a small cavity into which he lowered his exhausted body. Covering himself with sheepskins, Pedro closed his weary eyes on the light of day.

Light dispelled the grey veils of sleep. He opened his eyes and sat erect. The sun was on its way to its zenith. *Nine or ten o'clock*, he thought.

He could not adjust his mind to his actual position. The strain of the last few nights had been unbelievable. As the noises of the wooded slopes permeated his brain, things took shape. Glancing back into the cleft in the rock, he noted the sheepskins, the rifle and ammunition belt that he had taken from the dead sentry nearly fifteen miles away. There, too, lay the pistol of his brother. Upon seeing the arms, things of destruction made by that ingenuity through which human beings are distinguished from the brutes, he remembered death, persecution and fear.

Wasting no time, he bound the rucksack and ammunition belt tightly about him, and slid down the steep slope of the hill that had guarded him so well in his sleep. Reaching the foaming creek, he sank his hands and face deep in its icy clearness.

Down he went, here jumping a crag and there a rock. He passed one of the deep pools seen so frequently in granite mountains. Here the water, in its countless ages of passing, had created a cistern that could well have been the bathing place for legendary nymphs. Around him were the shiny slabs of granite, coloured as if the hands of some painter had followed a chance whim, trying desperately to focus the rainbow on their sides. Glittering black, rusty brown, black quartz, and farther on, the dark green of slate crept forward to add its presence to the colour scheme of the puzzle.

But he could not linger here. He would have to be careful when approaching the lines of his would-be comrades-in-arms. They would shoot at any target moving among the mountain jumble. He was fearful of the discharge of a machine gun upon the noise of his walking. To a lone rifleman he could shout his claims of friendship. In the case of the machine gunner there would be no hope. Something psychological grips the hand as the savage recoil grinds out its message of death, paralysing, for the time being, any other sense except that of extermination.

He had an acute feeling of discomfiture, as if he were being stared at and yet could not see. What was worse, nature had quieted around him. His keen eyes darted from left to right. The pines were sparser now and, before him, were beginning to succumb the mountain ranges, like waves of the sea spreading on to the beach.

Then a sudden start, a paralysing fear, as a perfunctory order sounded behind him: 'Halt and drop those arms. Don't move, or you're a dead man!'

The rifle fell from his grasp with a loud clatter. He dared not grip his pistol to cast it away, for fear his action would be misunderstood. What if this were the patrol from Madrid, reconnoitring enemy country? What explanation could he offer? And he had on his person the arms from a dead sentry. Through his imagination thoughts raced like shooting stars, seen, gone, appearing, disappearing, to leave no sound nor sign of their passing. The muscles in his back felt carved of wood.

A crunch of footsteps sounded behind him, and the point of a rifle was jammed into the small of his back. 'Walk slowly,' came the voice.

Three soldiers awaited them a hundred yards beyond. They were dressed in the uniform of a regiment of artillery. No red stars could be seen, but he knew that the Communist side also had regular soldiers. Then a fourth man appeared from behind a clump of bushes. He was wearing the stripes of a corporal, and Pedro, with a sensation of leaping relief, saw around his neck, hanging by a small, glittering chain – a *cross!*

Shadow of the Cross

The people that walked in darkness have seen a great light.
They that dwell in the land of the shadow of death,
upon them hath the light shined.

The Book of Isaiah

Juan walked towards the sound of the voice, his nailed boots ringing on the stone floor of the church. 'What are you doing here?' he asked.

'And what might you be doing here?' came the surly rejoinder.

He saw that the man was garbed in a soldier's uniform, a heavy *capote* around him, and a rifle between his legs. For all his seeming carelessness, he was holding the rifle with its muzzle pointed toward the intruder. 'I was chilled and hungry.' Juan said. 'When I saw your light I thought you might have some food. I've spent all my money.'

The man stared at him. 'There's a tin of sardines over yonder. Next to that pile of sacks. You can have some of them.'

A *brasero* next to the guard gave out a little heat, its glowing embers setting off a reddish glow, giving things a strange colouring. Overhead, the great pillars receded into blackness, and all about was the silence of the tomb. Here and there a gleaming bone was picked out by a small ray of light.

'This is not joyful guard duty you have, comrade,' said Juan, squatting beside him.

'It might be better, and it could be worse. After the first night in this place, life changes. With all these dead around, and their graves ripped open, one thinks a bit. As I say, life changes. I wish this experience could have occurred several years ago, I would have benefited by it a great deal.'

'In what way, comrade?' Juan paused with a sardine halfway to his mouth. 'How would such terrible duty have benefited anyone?'

A laugh welled up from the depths of the man. 'All those men yonder,' he pointed at the pale white of scattered bones, 'lived and thought and worked, even as you and I. And what are they now? Crumbling dust, some of them, and the rest, bones. Some of them must have thought they were right, and everybody else was wrong. Where are they now? They're all alike.' He lapsed into moody silence.

Juan suspected that the eeriness of his duty was turning the man's mind. He kept quiet, resolving to learn more about this strange apparition.

'I know what you're thinking,' said the man. 'You're not the first to come here, you know. Nor will you be the last before this war is over. Many's the night I have put out this light and waited in the gloom of yonder corner. You get accustomed to seeing in the dark after awhile. I've seen men and women, friend, thinking themselves alone, kneeling and praying, even as you and I when we were children. But we are told all that was foolish, and God does not exist. We've been assured that man is what he makes himself to be, and that there's no more to him than meat and bones.'

By his speech this was no ordinary workman, furthermore, he was an older man.

'Yes,' the man continued, 'things are changing. Even a short time ago nobody would have spoken as I do now. But men have gone to war, and they've seen people killed, and they've killed others, themselves. These men will come back on furlough and realise that those whom they so much feared before they left have been equalised by the use of arms. Often they'll find that the one they feared is not even equal in courage to themselves. It's a necessary awakening. Peace is what we search for, and yet in peace the mobster, the gangster and the criminal seek to reap their ill-earned crop. The law-abiding citizen works hard to carve a place for himself and raise a family. Those who have no moral precepts to stem their lusts move right ahead, plundering and breaking all that stands in their way. War comes on, and they're shown in their true colours. They'll never go to the front where all have equal chance for survival or death. No, the meek man stands behind his gun, alone and desperately fighting, while those who've pushed him around in the scavenging fight of life have flown and left him behind to die alone. You're younger than I, and will see more of life. I'm old and my time's drawing near. I've lost both sons in this war. My wife is ill and will not survive the winter. We have no money for medicine. That's why I volunteered for this job. But it has its rewards, you see. Since I've been here, a great calm has come over me. These things have always been and always will be, and yet we do not see them because we're too full of ourselves.'

A strange day, and a strange ending for it, alone in a ruined church with a guard who was an educated man and spoke of strange things. Yet were these things so strange? Juan felt a shiver go through him in the opaque silence that fell around him. It was not the cold. 'Thank you for the sardines,' he said to the man. 'What you've said is something most people probably know sooner or later, though it might be expressed differently. Age mellows the angles of youth.'

The moon shone through one of the arched windows, and the deeper mauve of a cross in its centre formed a dark shadow in the light shining on the floor. Juan stepped over that cross, remembering the shadows in the eyes that looked out from faces where privation and suffering had passed expression. And as he closed the door of the church behind him, the creaking of its hinges seemed to lift, in some strange and unknowable way, a weight from his being.

★

The corporal searched Pedro, and found the pistol. 'Where do you come from with all this ammunition and arms? You smell like a spy to me. In any event, you'll have an interview with the captain. Get a move on.' And he was shoved down a small pathway that wound between the boulders he had just left behind.

He felt disgruntled. Some welcome for one who braved all dangers to get there! Their greeting could hardly be called enthusiastic. *Such is life,* he soliloquised. He would not have lasted very long in Madrid in any case. *So be it. God's will be done.*

The querulous old captain had been recalled to the army after several years of retirement. He puffed angrily on an ancient pipe and poured a stream of whys and wherefores at Pedro's protesting ears.

Pedro could stand it no longer. 'What do you think I am,' he demanded, 'a damn fool? So, without the slightest regard for myself, I've walked over those mountains for days, spying out enemy terrain. And all alone. I plan to go back and tell the Reds all I know, carrying a dead Red sentinel's arms, and a stolen pistol from the Republicans' *Guardia deAsalto*. Nonsense! It's really very simple. I came here because I was against all that was over there. That's all. My father would have insisted I take this action. And certainly the Duque del Bosque would have been in full accord.'

At the mention of the illustrious name of the Duque the captain sat erect, and focused his watery eyes upon Pedro's face. 'My dear young man,' he smiled, 'why didn't you tell me you know the Duque? You must know that we're constantly being attacked in our rearguard, and those infernal *dinamiteros* from Madrid are continually harassing us with acts of sabotage. They creep over those mountains as if they were playing at toy soldiers. So you see, my friend, we must be cautious. Even now you will have to go through the regular procedure. We'll have to contact the Duque and find out about you.'

Pedro smiled grimly. 'Easier said than done. The Duque, or so they say, is behind bars in one of their happy little camps.'

'Most regrettable,' said the captain. 'Well, in any case, we have ways of finding out about your background. You'll have to remain in custody in a concentration camp near Segovia. Just a formality, you know.'

He was unceremoniously placed upon the floor of a truck that was going to Segovia for supplies. The sun came down with molten gold. Not a breath of wind stirred the air. Uniforms were everywhere, the khaki of the army; among them the spattered colours of the light green clothed legionnaires, wearing the tattooed arms and the cold faces of the professional soldier, and hiding behind that iron discipline the dark secrets of stirring passion. The yellow of colonial troops, with their red fezzes, and, now and then, a soberly clad civilian added a discordant note to the vibrant symphony of colour.

Trucks passed his own, crowded to overflowing with young men in blue shirts and khaki pants. On top of the vehicles was a great red-and-black flag, divided into diametrical halves. Pedro was startled. He had seen these colours in Madrid – the same colours as the anarchists. They must be Falangists.

And more trucks. Khaki and red berets, waving proudly a spotless white flag, the cross of St Andrew blazoned in red upon it. War rhythms and chants. Shouts and cheers. In all of them was the desire for ultimate sacrifice, the only surrender that can quench the thirst of a creed.

After a while, by the whirring sound of tyres, and the lack of street noises, he judged that they must be considerably removed from the city. The countryside rolled off to hazy distance on one side, and, as he turned, Pedro was confronted by rising slopes that ended in crags and the mighty range of grey, purple, and brown mountains that sat upon the plain of Spain, dividing it into two halves, north and south: the two halves of Spain, isolated from each other by a mighty wall; as different and remotely apart as the northern *jota*, that leaping, frolicsome dance, is to the passionate, tragic *cante hondo*; as different as the change from thick, red wine to golden sherry.

The concentration camp proved to be drab and uninteresting. He didn't really care. This was to be only a temporary stop.

Reassigned to a small group, he was led away post-haste to the gaping entrance of a wooden, barn-like building. As he entered the door, an impressive array of needles, cotton rolls, and boiling syringes bid him good day. A doctor and two medical aides in white stood guard over the display. 'Strip!' came the curt command.

★

'My dear Juan,' said Ricardo, 'we feel it's time you became of some use to the Party.'

'Nothing would suit me better.' Juan was growing impatient at the long-delayed promised action. 'The war's going on around me, and all I do is sit and think.'

Ricardo laughed shortly. 'Patience is a virtue, comrade. We'll need a great deal of it in the days ahead. But we do have an assignment for you, and I think you'll find it interesting. Of course it's not as exciting as being in the presence of Hilda Krantz, but,' and he blinked his pale eyes, 'that's a luxury few of us can afford in these times.'

Juan nodded in silent agreement. 'I suppose you're right, comrade. But get down to business. What do I do next?'

'Impatience again, my boy. Well, you're to go to the front at the River Cinca. There's been a bit of action up there, and the captain was shot and killed last week by a stray sniper. We think you have the ability to adjust yourself to such a task.'

'But I've no experience in commanding soldiers.'

'That, comrade, is another luxury we can ill afford these days. Suffice to say that you're needed, and we think you'll do the mission credit. There's really nothing further to discuss. You'll leave tomorrow. You'll receive a commission as captain in the Fifth International Brigade. You've had enough training these past few months in the art of war to be of use up there.'

Juan bid the man goodbye and walked briskly from the room. There was a great deal to be accomplished before he left for the front. Hilda must be informed. He would have to secure the necessary papers – a hundred and one details to attend to.

The plane left Madrid at noon. High above the city they soared, circling for a brief instant. In a moment they were swallowed up by a bank of clouds.

Juan must have fallen asleep. Now he woke with a start, as a voice behind him said loudly, 'We've arrived, comrade.'

Tarragona. The very sound suggests rises and hollows. Mountains and gullies follow each other in a constant, diminishing trend from the mighty Pyrenees, down to the slanting River Ebro. Greeks had considered them the feasting places of gods. Arabs had stopped in front of the Ebro in their northward surge, pondering deeply the wisdom of crossing that silent, powerfully moving flow, to meet that scarred and ribbed countryside.

And from the small window of the circling plane, Juan could see the winding course of the valley as it merged into the flats of the mother river. On the shoulders of the disappearing mountains was a cluster of white and pink houses. Across the river rose the tremendous castle of Miravet, once a fortress of the Knights Templar and later sold to the Knights of Saint John when that heroic order had been disbanded by the wilfulness of a French king. He could see the mighty pile silhouetted against the sky, its great watchtower soaring a hundred and fifty feet above the rest of the building. Tradition came from the rocks, echoed across the slopes, and with it came the muted whispers of Charlemagne.

He felt taut and anxious. Decisions would have to be made. Juan feared his lack of military knowledge. Difficulties and problems were construed by his imaginative brain. But he had a job to carry out. There could be no turning back.

Later he went to the front where he met his superiors. Everything was routine. The *Salud Camarada*, that had taken place of the normal *Duenas Dias*, was just as formal as before. The *Tu* in place of the *Usted* was just as distancing, and the disobeying of an order was just as severely dealt with as under the flag of the Foreign Legion a mile away. Maps! Plans! Radios! Orders! Counter orders! Munitions boxes! War – plain war!

Here were human beings with opposed ideals, facing each other across a narrow river, and both allegedly fighting for the rights of man. So it had always been from Hannibal to Caesar, from Alexander to Napoleon. And so it would always be. Now his mind was like a ship in a fog, floating upon the surface, yet strangely held by the lack of sight. Where was the flaw in this constant and unsolved problem of right and wrong? Where was the answer to this might or weakness?

His orders were clear. An advanced position called Latorreta had an excellent field of vision. Crossfire of machine guns could be most effective here against the enemy who encamped a bit lower. Between his position and the enemy was the River Cinca, practically dry now because of the dam several miles upstream. Patrols on both sides of the river haunted that dam on this sparsely settled front. Destruction of that barrier would end for ever the possibility of attack from either side. It was of utmost importance to both bands that this door be kept open.

He crouched down where a knoll jutted forward from the surrounding hills. Not a tree could be seen for miles around.

Only rolling, scrubby hills, now and again broken by great ridges of granite boulders. Where the water had cut its path, bare limestone presented its white face. Far away could be seen the jumbled mass of the Pyrenees, and to the south, the ridged slopes of the Alcubierre, where a hundred years before the Tigre del Maestrazo, with a handful of followers, had kept the wealthy provinces of Valencia and Castellon in constant fear of his inroads.

Looking through his field glasses Juan could see, across a mile-wide valley, another series of drought-dried gullies and crumbling slopes similar to the terrain on which he stood. A jumble of barbed wire zigzagged halfway up the slope.

Over there, men looked through sights, through field glasses, through periscopes. Telephones were at their command, waiting to crackle forth orders to artillery. The glinting, now and then, of a possible bayonet or a discarded tin, flashed back the reflection of the ever-present sun. Day was easy. But night would come, with its ghosts of attacking armies, of creeping volunteers filled with the lust to kill: easy ground for peasants who had fought their guerrilla warfare from the days of contests between Iberians and Celts, against Carthaginians who had set their bloody hands across the wasted lands, and against Roman legions, forced to use all the concentrated might of distant Rome and the genius of Scipio the African.

And in the immutable course of time, night followed day. A hush came with the mantle of darkness. Flares could not be used. They were bad for the morale of the men, for, after each brief flash, the darkness was even greater than before.

Juan rose from his cramped position and stalked around the dugout. Looking out at the weather-beaten landscape, Juan reflected that the hill, covered in barbed-wire, looked as if some inconsequential ant had weaved its path across it.

He did not want to seem a greenhorn in the eyes of the other men yet his activities in Madrid seemed suddenly very childish in the face of the awful fact that for every bullet he could unloose, for every bomb he might cast, another would come back, directed at him. And again he was struck by that mysterious phantom, fear, abject fear. His thoughts were paralysed; his actions were sluggish. Across the table, in his dugout, he could sense six pairs of eyes watching his every move; he knew the men were comparing their dead captain with the upstart before them. He knew what they were thinking, and he knew that his inner worry, no matter how carefully he strove to mask it, would be observed by those critical eyes. He would be blighted with the everlasting shame of the city Recomendado, the favoured one put in charge, with no credentials whatsoever.

★

Pedro had been ordered to strip, and now he cursed inwardly. He did not relish showing off his naked body before strangers. But he was the first in line, and was bombarded by questions. 'Name? Age? Place of birth? Occupation? Any venereal diseases? Last vaccination?' The corporal jabbed him with a needle and signalled him into a side room.

He stood there, undecided, shivering in the chill of the place. With a loud crash the door flew open and Pedro whirled about, to meet the gaze of another victim with blue eyes and chestnut hair. The newcomer had the broad cheekbones and ruddy complexion that whispered of Celtic origin. A broken nose and a humorous mouth conveyed to all the world an explosive and jaunty character. Short and stocky, he had the bunchy muscles of the typical Asturiano, those who claim for themselves the honour of being the first Spaniards.

'*Hola amigo*,' came a booming greeting from the naked intruder.

Pedro grinned sheepishly. 'Naked, man came to this earth, and we're naked too. Let's be friends. It looks like we're the first men of this new world.'

'My name's Pablo Maiquez, and I'm from Oviedo,' said the stranger. 'I was studying for medicine in Madrid when all this damned upheaval took place. Well, it was to be expected, I suppose. All my friends were here, and my family. My father is vacationing with my mother near San Sebastian. So I decided to walk over the mountains.' He clapped a jovial hand on Pedro's bare shoulder.

'Pedro Avila, at your service.' He punctuated it with a deep bow, flourishing his hand. 'Late of Madrid and more or less a student. I also walked over these mountains, by the way, and if they don't feed me pretty soon, I'm going to become a cannibal.'

Pablo grinned; white teeth flashing in his ruddy face. 'Well, don't take a bite out of bare me. Don't worry, friend. Our troubles will soon end. They've selected us from this motley crew because of the names we've given for guarantees. I hear you gave the Duque del Bosque. We'll get a plate of army beans soon, which means only beans, but plenty of them.'

A medical corpsman stuck his head in the door, and threw in a handful of clothing. 'Put this on. When you've finished come into the other room for some vaccinations.'

'Not again,' groaned Pedro.

They felt suddenly indecent in their nakedness, and slipped rapidly into the army pants and regulation *alpargatas*. A worn shirt completed the newly acquired wardrobe.

Pablo had preceded Pedro into the other room, and now he turned to him. 'I wish I had never studied medicine. I've delved too much into books where prophylaxis is the common denominator. Right now I feel like a bull when it comes into the arena wearing little flags that indicate its breeding ownership. By the love of God, look at the size of those needles. They look like the scimitars of Saladin.'

And off came their so recently donned shirts. A dab of alcohol, and the sensation of a direct stab from some strange Malayan kris rent Pedro's cringing skin. The plunger went forth like the piston of a locomotive. Out came the needle, and a medical aide slapped on some straight iodine with a brush.

He glared at his tormentor. 'What do you think you're doing, *burro*? Painting a door?' More explosive comments came from behind as Pablo experienced the same treatment.

The man looked up, disgust on his face. 'Big men and small hearts. Thin skins and little courage. Small men of Madrid, I presume.'

They were escorted from the room by a grinning, wizened guard. He led the way towards another drab, unpainted shack.

A barbershop opened its doors to them. Inside was one

barber's chair with a broken mirror in front of it. A basin and a jug of water were on a small stand, and flies buzzed merrily around. Tufts of hair, of all colours, formed an untidy ring around the base of the rickety chair.

To all appearances, the barber was trying to hold the walls upright. He leered at them, and lurched erect. 'Sit down, my children, and father will give you a nice trim. Which side do you like parted? Perhaps a nice curl on the forehead? Well, come on. One of you be first. It's hot and I want to finish my work.'

Pedro flopped down upon the chair, and the man wrapped a towel of dubious cleanliness around his neck. Placing the whirring machine low on his neck, he passed it rapidly up to his forehead. He stepped back and surveyed his work with studious concern. Then, he returned to his labour, clipping off hair to the minimum with incredible speed. Pedro's bare skull reflected the rays of the sun that slanted in the door. He felt annoyed and very foolish.

As he turned away from the chair, he saw his new-found friend, whom he thought would be angry, collapsed in a corner, the tears streaming from his eyes. Pointing his stubby finger at the bald head, Pablo gasped in a choked voice, 'By the prophet's beard, are you ever ugly.'

Pedro stalked away without a word. Thinking better of it, he turned and waited for his friend to suffer the same humiliation.

★

Juan had bidden his lieutenants to follow him on his first rounds and now he scrambled about among the rocks, unloosing, in his awkwardness, a shower of stones. The men growled about brigades of cavalry, and made it clear that no one had ever made so much noise in the history of the whole war. Why did they have to send some greenhorn from Madrid? The damned Fascists would be sending their singing babies over soon enough without all this ado.

And the next instant, as had been foretold, a string of hissing bees thudded nearby. Bullets sang as they glanced off stones.

Throwing himself prostrate upon the ground, Juan buried his

face in the pebbled earth. The amused chuckles of his companions burned in his ears. He felt as if he were engulfed in a mesh of black velvet. Without a word, he arose and strode away, feeling the amused stares of his companions upon his back.

A night bird shrilled out. Otherwise, all was silent. For the first time Juan understood the difference between the man from the fields and the man of the city streets. The first, where horizons help to broaden the objectiveness of life; the other, where doors and corners augment the mechanical necessity of movement.

And he remembered the faces of his companions. One, a student, full of fire and vehemence. A brilliant young man, but it was clear that he had become entangled with his everlasting friend, the bottle. The man oozed alcohol, although he kept himself remarkably under control. Another face came to mind, hard-lined and cold, in which many a tempest had come and gone, and all had left their damning stamp. The third, sullen and morose. War had engulfed him, and had embittered him. These were the faces of his men. These were the faces of war. But what were they fighting for? And his soldiers. Stocky, bold and hardy. Peasants from the mountains behind Castellon and Valencia. A tooth for a tooth and an eye for an eye had come down to them as an inheritance from migrations of Camit and Ammit races, blended with the Arabs and the Phoenicians. No respect here for the weakling. One suffered, and the other must suffer. Courage was their only hero. Their creed was only the direction and will of their leader whom they liked and followed, or whom they disliked and finally killed.

He knew, now, that this place would have eternal significance for him. Juan felt it in the winds that blew from the south, and he realised it in the beings that surrounded him. That riverbed worried him, for he had heard that the troops considered themselves strong enough to launch an offensive. The grapevine of the White Aide, mysterious and unknowable, was present here as everywhere.

The days passed in uneventful monotony. On the morning of the sixth day, he was warned that the troops were coming into the enemy trenches. He would have to go personally, with some of his men, to look over the terrain.

It was typical autumn weather, with the taint of frost in the air. They were wearing peasants' *alpargatas*, dyed black. Their faces were tinged with charcoal. As they moved forward, they came to the inevitable whitish spot that marked the passage of the old riverbed.

A Violent Land

For hatred does not cease by hatred at any time: hatred ceases by love.

The 'Dhammapada' of Buddha

Pedro and Pablo were at last free to go where they willed. Now they stood in the central square of Segovia, using one of the weathered sides of the little music kiosk as a leaning place. Once this place had rung to the sound of music and laughter.

They had eaten well, for Pablo's wealthy parents had sent ample funds, and he had insisted upon sharing with his destitute friend. Pedro was at peace with the world.

Before him rose the majestic cathedral, with its great ramparts of a rose-hued yellow, worn by the ages, still striking the sky with a theme of Gothic past. He felt himself dwarfed by the immensity of the great tower that had twice fallen, only to be reconstructed. On the farther side, the shouldered ramparts of the cathedral fell down to a narrow street. Across the street he could see more walls. Battlements of Segovia, the town that had never been conquered. Farther away, he could see the river turning at a sharp angle, and the spired castle of the Catholic kings climbing towards the sky like some legendary, enchanted palace, above a full four hundred feet of sheer crags.

The very noble and ancient city of Segovia was always feuding with Madrid. From her walls had gone the cavalcade, led by Alphonso VI. And he had conquered the castle of Magerit, once the pride of the Muslims, the impregnable fortress that closed its gates on the wealthy lands and kingdom of Toledo. Now again, eight centuries later, all the rancour and bitterness of the past flared up and was launched like a spearhead of revenge against those who were coming from Madrid to spoil her traditions and soil her culture.

Pedro yawned and stretched lazily. 'I'm content to sit here in the sun and bask for ever,' he said. 'I've walked enough these past days to last me a lifetime. I've forgotten that human beings can be in some other position than on their feet.'

Pablo agreed in emphatic tones. 'But nonetheless,' he said, 'we should be moving on. We could be here for a month and never see all the sights. I feel very uncomfortable in this dress suit. I'm bursting my shirt, and I could easily hide in my pants.'

'I suppose you're right,' said Pedro. 'But where will we go?'

'Any place but here,' returned Pablo, already strolling slowly away. 'We'll have to enrol in some army unit or something soon. I've seen men giving us suspicious stares already. We'll be drafted soon anyway, due to our age. The man who hits first always hits twice. At the moment we can choose where we'll serve.'

Pedro heaved a great sigh and stumbled away from the wall. 'Slow up, and don't walk so fast. You're just like my brother. Always wanting to be doing something. I don't know when you people ever think.' He caught up to his friend and matched his stride. 'Let's go to the *Comandancia* and ask for permission to see your family. They'll know a lot more about the general situation than we. In any event, we can go to some other town, mingle with the people, and hear what they've to say for themselves.'

'Sound words, brother philosopher. Let's go to the *Comandancia*.'

The usual red tape followed: the customary hulking sergeant; a pink slip for each of them, giving them a trip on the railway from Segovia to Salamanca; and then a trip to the telegraph office, and a wire to Pablo's father, informing him of the name of the hotel at which they would stay in Salamanca.

But they were not prepared for the sight that greeted their eyes as they approached the station. Hundreds of people were trying to crowd into the already packed train. Soldiers clambered through windows. Others sat on the roofs of carriages. Everything was jammed. Even the locomotive tender bore a weight of people on its roof. The train seemed fully cognisant of the terrible strain it must undergo on the long, slow journey. Now and again a wheezy gasp broke from the tender's whistle.

Without a word, Pedro clambered up on the last carriage,

followed dutifully by Pablo who cursed each step of the way. It seemed to be less full than the others but, even the passengers sat back to back and side to side, staring stolidly out of the windows. It was war, and these things had to be. There was no complaining, for it would do no good.

After what seemed to be an interminable amount of shoving and pushing, Pedro staggered on to a wooden box next to a window. Pablo almost fell on top of him, cursing bitterly as he stumbled over a soldier who sat sleeping in the aisle.

Do not talk. Do not breathe. Do not think. Just concentrate on blankness and the time will pass more quickly, thought Pedro grimly.

At last, far up the line came the clang of a bell, and a little trumpet blared forth. A wheezing whistle came from the tired engine. A jerk; a creaking of old hinges that sorely needed oil; the strain of overweight, and another desperate jerk. Then, immobility once again. The wheels ground away at the rails in a futile attempt to drag the load. Another jerk, and a square box full of heavy articles fell squarely on the head of the sleeping trooper. A stream of vitriolic language poured forth, yet at the obvious lack of sympathy and interest on the part of his fellow passengers, he subsided into fretful silence.

Now another engine was being coupled on. Distant shouts. More whistles. Louder bells. Greater jerks. And then – was it possible? – the train was actually moving.

Pedro glanced at his friend and saw that he was fast asleep. In the last glimpse of Segovia he saw, silhouetted against the rising ground that ends in the tiny village of Zamarramala, the crumbling chapel where the Knights Templar used to congregate, pledging fidelity to the cross and to their order, before setting out on their crusading treks.

Night began to fall, and with it came the soughing wind that sweeps across those sun-baked plains. Not a tree was in sight, not a house. Far away, a tiny spire heralded the presence of some small village nestling underneath a brink beside a small stream.

Pedro managed to extricate himself from the tangle of arms and legs and made his way to the window. The smell of autumn, the drying leaves and the myriad of late flowers, gave up to the oncoming dew the aroma of their secret vials. And he thought of his mother and sisters. If only people could realise that through bloodshed, burning and destruction nothing can be won, only the bitterness of the vanquished and the glee of the vanquisher. And from this, hate springs forth anew, to mushroom again.

But at last nature took its hold on his troubled mind. As his eyelids closed, the metamorphosis of conscience changed into the infinite land of dreams. Here were creatures that knew no weight to retard them, no shape to limit them, no pain to stop them.

*

The crescent of the moon was just beginning to appear over the far off hills as Juan, with his reconnaissance squad, approached the strip of sand in the riverbed. He crouched beside some bushes, and the men slid silently down behind him. What should he do? Rush it altogether? Try to reach the other side man by man?

At that precise instant a flare went up from his own trenches. He swore under his breath. Such an act could jeopardise the entire mission. The phantom of the White Aide flashed into his mind. But as the yellow flare hissed downward, he thanked Providence that it fell a hundred metres farther up the riverbed. Nearby bushes and tussocks leapt out in stark relief. Such stupidity must be dealt with. Voices around him muttered dire threats against the unknown somebody. Seconds after, the darkness seemed greater than before. Now was the moment to rush across the stream.

He dashed across, finding, to his surprise, that it was much wider and far rougher going than he had anticipated. His feet sank into yielding sand up to his ankles, which the stones twisted painfully. He could not avoid a loud clatter as he raced along, already losing ground to his companions. Juan cursed his unsporting youth.

The stutter of a machine gun preceded the whine of its murderous missiles. Machine guns from his own trenches returned the fire. Undoubtedly they had heard the commotion.

With painfully heaving lungs, Juan crawled over to where his men lay in a gully, perfectly concealed. Suddenly calm and composed, he threw himself prostrate and scanned the ragged cliffs where the enemy lay hidden. Should he try to wipe out some of the *Escuchas*, or should he restrict his actions to simple reconnaissance? The decision was his, alone, to make. He knew that there were Moors on this side of the river, and their reputation for hearing like foxes and seeing like cats in the dark was not to be ignored. In a flash he made up his mind. He would go all the way. It was essential that he regain his prestige that had sunk to a new low following his clumsy crossing of the riverbed.

Reaching up, he secured a firm hold on the stony ground and eased himself upward with utmost caution. He gasped at what he saw. Not thirty yards away lay the barbed wire of the enemy entanglements. Their line of lookouts must be very near.

As he rolled over the brink, a shower of small pebbles was dislodged, and things seemed to leap about him with added intensity. He held his breath, fearing the gusty draught of bullets that would end his life. But all was quiet.

Laboriously pulling himself along the dry earth, he slid forward. The words of the Party manual flashed into his mind. 'Elbows, toes, and then down. Elbows, toes, and then down.'

To his left was the mesh of barbed wire in which he felt he would inevitably be caught. Farther up was the dark line of the summit. Not a whisper. Not a stir.

And then before him was a figure, leaning nonchalantly on a rifle. With a sense of relief, Juan saw that the man's back was towards him. Fear, for an instant, threatened to crowd out the balance of his thoughts. In a daze, blindly and without conscious effort, he drew his knife from his belt and leapt through the air, driving the weapon deep into the sentry's back once, twice. The form crumpled and lay still.

★

Pedro awoke to find the train stopped in a barn-like place. Soldiers were everywhere, some herded like sheep into open carriages and others sprawled upon the station floor; some with the haggard expression of those who have seen the shrouded figure of death near them, others gay and laughing, for the spirit of adventure was in them. Only optimism prevails when achievement is a tangible goal.

Ever onward, in its timeless passage, climbed the sun. Pablo, crawling through a window and standing on shaking legs, looked up at Pedro and whistled through clenched teeth. 'One more of these nights, and by all the powers of hell I'm walking back to Madrid. A plague take that damn cavalry officer sleeping next to us. He's slept since yesterday without once changing position. He's made of wood, I tell you.'

Pedro stared down at the thickset soldier who was even now lying flat on his back, vastly contented. His hands hooked in his belt and his feet crossed, he was a picture of relaxation. What to him was this troubled world? Death would come for him when God willed it. If not, he would be back toiling in his fields, the sun blasting down in summer, and the winter winds cutting the buds from their stems. Toil and hardship had been this man's birthright; toil and hardship would be his end. If contentment would come sometime during the span of his living days, so much the better. If not, nothing could be done about it.

At last the switch was made, and the train laboriously resumed its way. Venta de Banos was left behind, squatting in the flat plains, wreathed in windswept dust.

The long, dreary day droned by. Thoughts slowly disappeared to form part of the grey mass, as it always happens when beings are pressed together without possibility of expansion. Physical discomfiture, after a few moments of peak acuteness, begins to subside, and a drowsy blankness falls on everyone.

Sometime during the interminable night, the train creaked to a halt. Packets were hurled all about. People jumped from windows, while others clambered in to take their places.

'Valladolid,' said Pablo, leaning interestedly out of the window, 'at least I think it must be. Let's get out and stretch our legs. They say this old wreck will be here for a couple of hours at least.'

Again a jammed station, and soldiers swarming everywhere: blue shirts, khaki shirts, Moroccan troops, and now and then the lighter green of the Foreign Legion – all milling about like a disturbed anthill. Dark-grey eyes and singsong accents told of Galicia, while ruddy complexions and startling blue eyes gleamed under the red beret of the *Requetes* of Navarre. Silent, aquiline-featured, sombre men proclaimed by their appearance their ancestry from the plains of Castile. And slim, dark men sang and clapped their hands with incredible rhythm, flashing white teeth in an ever-ready smile. Quick language and sibilant accents announced that they were from wealthy Andalusia. Here were youths and men in all their vigour, fired with enthusiasm and the all-embracing drive of a people who think of the past as of the present. Once again they were goaded to repel the intrusion of foreign influence that tended to break the chain that linked the future with the past. They would fall with a song on their lips. Men would die with curses on their tongues, defending the honour of their family names. An age would weep at the repetition of history.

Pedro shouldered his way through all this chaos, and the blackness of night engulfed them. 'It's too late to find anything to eat,' he said. 'We might as well go to the town proper, though, for you never know.'

And so they walked along the Calle de Santiago, leaving the massive Academy of Cavalry to their left. The looming cathedral was behind them now, and on the far corner a tavern blinked its smile at them through a crack in its curtained doorway.

Knocking on the door, they were greeted by a fiercely moustached old man who bade them enter. They seated themselves at a small table in the centre of the dimly lit room, and minutes later, two plates holding sizzling eggs and great pieces of ham welcomed their knives and forks.

'Oh brother,' sighed Pedro, 'I've been waiting for this all my life.' And, without more ado, down went the eggs, the ham and the half-bottle of wine. He leaned back and sighed happily.

The tavern keeper seated himself on a chair and, after the usual niceties, inquired as to their destination.

Pedro did not answer for a full minute. When he did, his eyes were dark and brooding, and a frown settled on his face. 'Alas, it's a long story, *patron*. Perhaps it would suffice to say that our destination is Salamanca. I don't suppose we'll get there before tomorrow at least.'

The man agreed, launching into a wild tirade against

Communists in general and fifth columnists in particular. He spat resentfully at the very words. So these were modern times. In his day they had paid attention to the political leader of the village, but now everybody wanted to know how and why and when and where. People had begun to sound like women who were constantly chattering, as if by all this asking and changing, things could be won. Rubbish. It is hot in the summer and cold in the winter, and the moon comes up by night and the sun by day. People are born and people die. Why, then, did people make all this fuss? He mourned for his son who had been killed on the distant mountains and wept softly in remembrance, his tears belying his fierce appearance.

'There, there,' said Pedro. 'I agree with you, and I'm sorry, but regrets will not change things. Regrets can only stultify. For now, my friend and I haven't bathed our faces in three days. Is there a fountain around?'

The old man, too overcome with emotion to answer, waved his arm in an idle curve towards a small door that opened at the back of the place. Then he blew his nose loudly into a far from clean handkerchief and stalked away, swearing loudly at all politicians.

Pedro sat motionless for a moment, remembering other faces and other regrets. He wondered, for the first time in several days, if his mother and sisters were still alive.

'Snap out of it,' said Pablo. 'That fountain awaits us, and I, for one, am looking forward to it with great glee.' Leading the way, he opened the door on to a small patio surrounded by a light stone wall.

The moonlight beamed in, and by its diffused light they could see the outlines of a typical Castilian well, its iron grate and pulley hooked on to a crossbeam. Removing the grating, Pedro lowered the bucket until a soft, sucking sound advised him that the water had been reached. Up came the bucket, clanking and squeaking.

All of a sudden he was thrown violently to the ground as the earth seemed to explode around him. A monstrous ram that, to him, looked more like the enraged bull Apis, glared at him with bulging eyes, daring him to rise again. Pablo, not far away, was wheezing and coughing, doubled up with laughter.

Pedro, who had little use for laughter at that moment, riveted his eyes upon the great beast that was walking, stiff-legged, backwards, preparing for a second attack. The bruised victim scrambled awkwardly to his feet and dashed madly for the door, Pablo close on his heels.

★

The white face stared up at Juan Avila. He was eighteen or nineteen at best. On his face he bore an expression of tragic surprise. Death had been meted out to youth. A mother would anguish. A father would sorrow. A broken-hearted sweetheart would weep in a darkened room. Goals of imagination had been thwarted in a single act, in one night, at one hour, at a given minute. What thoughts had crossed and interwoven in the brain of the dead boy before him? What needs had he experienced? What ideals had driven him forth from all he loved, to fight and die in this lonely land? And Juan remembered his brother, Pedro. A trembling possessed his limbs, and he felt as if he would fall. What would he have thought of the murderer at that moment, if his brother had been lying before him?

But duty, that stern figure, claimed its hour. For his comrades, after weeks and months of warfare, it was just another dead thing. Had the tables been turned, they might have been lying there. Like a bell through space throbbed his brother's words, 'What the hell's the use of it all?' Yes, what was the use?

This dead boy before him wore the uniform and the red beret of the *Requetes*, the wild fanatics of Navarre. He remembered tales of these tall, slim, blue-eyed people. Alone they had withstood, time and again, the concentrated attack of the queen's troops a century ago. Now, once again, grandfathers lifted their hoary heads, fathers followed the orders of age, and sons leapt to arms. With songs on their lips and a *jota* in the air, they had come down from their mountains to re-conquer Spain, as twelve centuries before their forefathers had marched forth against the Saracen hordes.

Time passed, and the only sound was the continual chirping of the crickets. Every noise seemed magnified now, and the very thump of Juan's heart sounded like a drumbeat. No wonder his ancestors had fled before the Islamic onslaught when, for the first time, they had heard the rumble of Almanzor's drums. But he had obtained the information he sought. Now he knew the type of troops and the exact positions and form of the enemy's defences.

As when he was a child, wakened in the dead of night, he felt that some unseen thing lurked in the darkness of the room. Was it possible that there was some force apart from the body? Ridiculous, of course. It was his overwrought imagination again, and the memory of his knife tearing through the young sentry's flesh. What would Hilda say of his ideas? He must brush these crazy notions from his head. There would be one last farewell for these enemies, one last remembrance of this night.

Pulling the pin from his Mills hand grenade, he signalled his men to do the same thing. One, two, three. He threw with all his strength. A moment later, there was a flash, and a deep explosion welled up from the darkness.

In the brilliant glare he glimpsed peering faces in what had been the impenetrable darkness. He saw the flash of gleaming bayonets. Raucous cries beat against his eardrums like so many files rubbed against iron.

Dashing wildly down the hill, he felt himself pursued by the whine of bullets. The man to his right gave a prodigious bound and fell, lying still. Another dim form faltered, staggered, and tumbled in a motionless heap. How many rabbits had he seen running before the hunter's gun? Doubling back and forth in an agony of fear, they had run until the shots had torn through their vitals, and then had screamed and sobbed in pain.

His legs felt numb. His mind was a blank. His whole body was exhausted. With the breath whistling through his clenched teeth, he flung himself down upon his face, safe on the opposite side of the river. Juan only knew that he had fled with animal fear.

But an inferno had been loosed by his raid. Death whizzed back and forth while trench mortars opened their thudding boom. Even a lonesome battery had opened fire, adding its mounting crescendo to the symphony of destruction.

With a louder roar, another battery began to fire. Eight guns thundered in a relatively narrow front. Dust and debris began to fall all about.

Juan sprang to his feet and rushed for the steep riverbank. As he scrambled up the sharp incline, a whistling approached nearer and nearer, slower and slower. Instinctively he dived forward. An ear-splitting crash sounded to his right, followed by the smell of burning and of cordite that stung in his assailed nostrils. He was hit as if by an invisible hand, feeling as though a vacuum had suddenly been thrust upon him.

The Waste Places

If the community is in trouble, a man must not say,
I will go to my house and eat and drink and peace shall be with you,
O my soul. But a man must share in the troubles of the community.
He who shares in its troubles, is worthy to see its consolation.

The Talmud

Pablo practically dragged Pedro into the lobby of the Hotel International. As his glance swept the room, crowded with people, Pedro compared them mentally with the soldiers he had seen in the station of Venta de Banos, sprawled on the hard ground, supported only by their convictions.

Here were civilians, dressed as though they had just stepped from London's Bond Street: military uniforms, jet-black trousers, the blue of shirts and the glittering of boots. There were young men, new ideals shining in their eyes, even their speech conforming to the groove of their creed. English, American, and French correspondents crowded the bar, living the good times of a hospitable nation caught up in the throes of war.

The picture vanished as Pablo turned to him and squeezed his arm. 'There's my father,' he said, pointing to a portly, well-dressed man who sat at a table with several people. With a wry smile, he added an afterthought. 'I feel as foolish as ever in my life in this stupid costume and sporting this sprouting head of cactus spines. I don't see why the devil they treated us like that.'

Pedro shrugged his shoulders, but did not reply, for Pablo's father was coming towards them, genuine affection reflected upon his florid face. As he embraced his son, Pedro realised that the man would never know how to express the feeling in his heart at that instant. His son had been given up for dead yet here he was, resurrected, as it were, from the tomb of Madrid.

Pablo again laid his heavy hand upon Pedro's arm and as the

introductions were made he stared, unblinking, into the blue eyes of Dr Maiquez.

In no time at all, the man had made it clear to Pedro that he was as welcome as a son. Clothes must be secured at once, of course. And then they could eat their fill at the grill of the hotel. He was a colonel, and Pedro noticed the insignia of the Medical Corps upon his arm.

As they wended their way through the throngs that crowded the street, Pedro absorbed the sounds, the sights of milling humanity about him. Salamanca: city of universities and of learning. He knew that for centuries their seats of philosophy and of law had been respected and known the world over. But this was the Nationalist capital now, and to it had come all the bureaucracy that accompanies a nation's managing team.

The voice of Dr Maiquez droned in his ear. They would go to Medical Headquarters that afternoon, he was saying. There was no reason on earth why they couldn't become soldiers in his medical unit. After all, there was a lot to be gained and nothing to lose. Most certainly there would be less danger than at the front.

Pedro finally could stand it no longer. 'I have no training in medicine,' he said. 'I was a student before the war began, and my father was the *apoderado* for the Duque del Bosque. When he died the Duque assumed the financial obligations of my education and my brother's. I have a mission to accomplish, Dr Maiquez, and I've not come this far to seek charity. Someway I must help to oust that organisation that has done so much harm, and has entrapped my brother in its tentacles. It's destroyed my family and my home. It's destroyed my friends and all that I loved. As soon as I can get my bearings I plan to enlist in the Foreign Legion.'

The old man was plainly angry. He spoke of idealists and the rocky road that such people must tread. Furthermore, he had seen many things come and go in life, and only those who travelled with power were in power. He thought it was wonderful that Pedro should want to fight for his country, but the young man was not to forget others were fighting too, in their own ways.

And when the meal was finished, Dr Maiquez insisted that he speak to some of his friends. The words that came from their lips jarred against Pedro's eardrums. He felt weary and ill at ease. The thought of rest was uppermost in his mind. The men spoke eloquently of suffering and heroism, and yet he could see little of either in their eyes. They spoke of the cause of civil strife, the clashing of ideals. But wars were no longer fought as they had been years before. No indeed. Now the wars were fought by masses on both sides, and only those who could place and replace the greatest quantity of men and machines on either side would win. Both of these fine young men had been well trained, and it was to their advantage to use that training for the betterment of all. Since Pablo had been trained for medical purposes, it was shameful to waste such talent. Words and more words, buffeting his ears, and the warm wine rendering him weaker by the minute.

'Gentlemen,' said Pedro, 'I appreciate your words. There's wisdom in your sayings, but I've always thought, with the folly of my youth, that right can be found where truth is followed. Tens of thousands are living and dying in distress this very moment. They, alone, made it possible for us to sit here in comfort. I'm an outsider and, frankly, I want to go to the front. My father would be there if he'd lived. I believe in God, honour, and the traditions of my country that my father held sacred before me. Please don't think me hasty or unduly ungrateful. But that's what I believe. With God's help I can act no other way.'

★

The telephone jangled into action. Juan picked up the receiver and queried in a tired voice, 'Yes?'

'Is this Captain Juan Avila?'

'That's correct,' came the reply.

'Well this is Ricardo. I thought you were wounded?'

'Ricardo? What makes you call here?' he said. 'No, I wasn't hurt very much. Just knocked dizzy for a spell.'

'Well, my impetuous friend, you're in a bit of trouble up there.'

Juan suppressed a yawn and seated himself on an ammunition box, empty now of its messengers of death. 'How's that?'

The voice on the other end of the line grew suddenly harsh

and cold. 'Report to your headquarters this afternoon and you'll find out. I'll be there to see you.' The receiver clicked, and a dull hum told him that Ricardo had hung up.

Now what had he done wrong? How could they expect him to carry out his mission with this constant interference? He felt suddenly as if a giant wind had blown the mists over a pleasant coastline. And to think that he had basked in the sun of a job well done. Obviously there were two solutions to everything. What was the use of worrying? Life wasn't worth a tinker's damn no matter how you looked at it.

The driver was curtly instructed to bring the automobile as quickly as possible, and Juan settled back for a long wait, for the vehicles were parked a long way from there in a canyon that ran parallel to the river, twisting its meandering way up to the deeper ravines.

It was always hazardous to attempt to leave the trenches. There was a distance of about a hundred paces in which one had to run the gauntlet of the enemy fire. Juan cursed his predecessor. It was preposterous that a man of his experience should have failed to ensure a method of securing relief in case of need.

As he ran rapidly across the intervening space, the whine of missiles was an accompaniment and goad to the rhythm of his legs. His knee struck a sharp stone as he dived for cover over the brink. Juan cursed freely.

Limping along, he crossed the half-mile that separated him from the canyon where the supply train was located in a rolling, scrubby, unprepossessing plateau.

But, the car was coming at last, bumping along wheezingly over the rough track. The road was bad enough in itself, but it would have been a much more comfortable ride had the driver not found diabolical glee in bounding and jumping over every obstacle in the way. The man made no attempt to avoid the numerous holes and ruts.

Then the crisis came. Juan saw the hood of the car disappear, as if they were diving in a hard-pressed submarine. There came a terrific jolt, and the sound of cracking. The car seemed to explode beneath them, followed by a desperate grinding of gears, then silence. Juan had been knocked forward against the seat and was gasping for breath.

Rescue came from a transport company. Juan instructed his driver to stay with the car while he sent back relief, and he felt the sweet taste of revenge as he did so. The village was four miles away, and over that rutted and explosion-pitted road it would take a long time before anyone could get through.

The driver of the truck volunteered the latest news. A jovial fellow, he had once worked for a fish market in Madrid. Juan was certain that he still smelled of fish, but his news was welcome, for only the official announcements had reached him at the front.

The time passed swiftly, and in what seemed a matter of only a few hours headquarters was reached. All around lay the messy, rolling plain, cut up here and there by small hills and gullies. Built around the ruins of some ancient castle, the village dominated, on one side, the deep ravine by which the road ascended. All was dry and dusty, with a constant wind moving across the barren landscape in a land that could breed nothing but dissatisfaction. Extremely cold in winter, it was terribly hot in summer, and there was little water, save when torrents washed away the scabrous ground between the rocks. Only sheep were herded there, and the houses were of stone. As Juan entered the sleeping village, an occasional mansion proclaimed this place the cradle of some long-vanished aristocracy. These great houses lay desolate, now, with their windows broken and doors hanging on rusted hinges. Through them had stormed the irate militia, bearing with them the hate of centuries that had seeded and grown since the days of the Hapsburgs and Bourbons. Now there was nothing left, save an old woman of incredible age sitting inside one of the doorways. Her gnarled hands folded in her lap, she wore a black woollen shawl that shaded the high-cheeked, hawk-nosed face. As they drove by, she gave no sign of recognition, save for blinking her hairless eyelids a bit faster over her watery eyes – eyes that had once flashed with the power of youth and the songs of spring. Now she looked upon the winter of her life, in the midst of the end of her surroundings.

Farther down the road, before one of the shabby houses, trucks were being laden and commands were shouted. All seemed to be in comparative order, and the work was being carried out with thoroughness and dispatch. Juan did not know then that he was at the headquarters of Marshall Tito, one of the most famous leaders of the International Brigade, a man who would count, in later days, in the forming of a nation in Eastern Europe, and in the final break with the powers of Russia. This was a man of incredible willpower and resourcefulness, trained in Russian political campaigning and sabotage. From the very beginning he had prophesied to his closest intimates what would happen if the Communist Party failed to achieve the total supremacy of Republican Spain. His prediction was to come true.

Juan cursed the war, his orders, and the world at large. Why could they not leave him alone to struggle with his own problems? He needed quiet. Even the front was better than all this sordid intrigue.

Ricardo greeted him with a cold smile and an indifferent handshake. 'Again you seem to have gotten yourself into a bit of trouble.'

'Trouble? I don't know what you mean.'

'Don't bother to make up any alibis,' said Ricardo. 'I have a full report on your whole operation the other night. Totally unnecessary amount of shooting going on up there. There are times, my dear Juan, when it's more expedient merely to sit tight and look over the scene.'

Juan was tired of the whole business, tired of Ricardo's ironic smile, tired of the critical tone of his voice. 'I simply did what I deemed right at the time.'

'Well,' said Ricardo, 'perhaps you did what you deemed right, but the fact remains that others did not think your decision was the wise one. For now, you are being relieved of your command and are to report at once to Barcelona's Party Headquarters.'

'And what,' said Juan, 'am I to do in that place?'

'In the Party we learn not to question our orders,' said Ricardo, 'but since you are possessed with boundless curiosity, I suppose it won't hurt to tell you that you're to serve in a training camp as an indoctrinator.'

★

Their quarters reached at last, Pedro walked to the window and drew back the curtains with one sweep of his arm. The rays of the setting sun streamed into the room in golden brilliance. Intense blue of the sky caused the yellow of aged limestone, the red of bricks, and the black slate of tile roofs to fill in the pattern of a picture without a frame: no soft blends, no pastel hues; only hard straight lines where a wall or an angle projected dark shadow. The cathedral lifted yellow lace towards the sky, hiding in a corner a theme of far-off Byzantium.

Pablo smiled broadly. 'And what do you see from the window, my friend, that can be of such great interest?'

'Many things,' said Pedro, turning from the window and dropping into a chair. 'First of all I see that the worldly change little, be they over here or over there. I suppose they won't be any different in the future. Enthusiasm, ideas, wrongs, rights – all these things are discussed for ever and anon. Some scientists try to prove that we've evolved from some lowly amoeba. Others worship the sun as the giver of life. Others? Well, other things. In any event, they're all in a quandary. We say we're right and they say we're wrong. Who knows?'

Pablo walked to the window and peered out at the gathering dusk. 'And you've discovered all that out this window? I must say, it's more than I can see.'

'The buffoon as ever,' said Pedro. 'Seriously, though, I didn't hear you say anything down there, when all those high-sounding words were flying around.'

Pablo sighed and threw up his hands. 'All right, you've got me there. Well, I suppose there wasn't much to say. I should accompany my father. Still, I'll be frightfully bored by it all. Life is nothing but a succession of working hours for him, and a trip to the theatre once in a fortnight is a magnificent concession for him. I've been living in Madrid these past three years, and have had a pretty fine time, if I do say so. I don't know. Anyhow, if one's to die, they say there's a bullet with a name carved on it. If the name corresponds to yours, too bad!'

'You'll have to do what your conscience dictates,' said Pedro. 'My conscience is pretty clear on the subject.'

'Easier said than done. The man who has a positive belief has only one way of thinking, but the other is cursed by endless possibilities. All sound reasonable enough, and all are worth trying. It's the problem of the cynic, I suppose,' said Pablo.

And so they talked, the daylight waned, and soon only the pale glow of the moon illuminated the place. Then, weary from their discourse, they decided, almost in unison, that a trip to the centre of town would be the only tonic to bring rest to their restless hearts.

What to them, at this moment, was the cold reality of war? Those on this side of the mountains had, obviously, never learned to understand the sacrifices, the planning and work, the physical and moral strain that is involved in being pursued like a hunted animal day after day and night after night. They had never known the sensation of being hunted down, where every shadow, movement, or noise spelled an infinitely more potent enemy. Compassion was hard to find.

They went down the stairs and out into the black night where five little stars made of electric bulbs indicated dens and dives. Bars, saloons and cheap cabarets cut the night with their pounding, insistent music. Lusty voices were raised in song. As they entered the door under the five illumined stars, the sign, 'LAS CINCO ESTRELLAS', glittered in Chinese-styled characters on the lintel.

Thick smoke enveloped everything in a bluish haze. A flight of wooden steps led upward to a small bandstand, where a varied assortment of instruments gave out a rhumba of sorts. There were uniforms of every description, hard-eyed women and youths on furlough, hoping to achieve legendary fame through heroism.

From wine to brandy they went and from brandy back to wine until the box-like shape of the place ceased to have dimensions. People around them no longer existed; they were just faces, a drifting mass of comings and goings. When or how they left the place, Pedro did not remember. Their bewildered steps carried them along the road of physical attraction, past snatches of conversation, to a cheaply scented room.

★

Juan began his journey that night, and it was a rough trip until he reached Reus. From that place he took the turnpike, but even here the going was slow and laboured, for vehicles jammed the way, and the dimmed lights made driving hazardous.

It was dawn when he finally entered Barcelona, the great cosmopolitan port of smoky factories and teeming millions. Here modern buildings of concrete touched the Gothic. Roman walls stood, tenaciously rooted to the spot, and, with their great arches, despised the crowded buses as they rattled their way down the Via Layetana.

A shattered city met his eyes. The throngs no longer swarmed from the Plaza de Espana towards the Palaces of Montjuich along the Paralelo. Only occasionally did he glimpse some lone passer-by.

As he turned towards the port, he found it heavily guarded. Some days previously, it had been bombarded by ships at sea. The city had become the focal point for long-range gunnery. Stretching northwards, all the way to Badalona, sprouted a great maze of factories, attracting the attention of any enemy ship that chanced to be passing by.

He would not have to report to his superior officer until the morrow, so he turned his footsteps towards a tavern that he had frequented on student outings in his university years. Jammed full of people, the low-raftered ceiling spoke of ages and the smell of wine seeped through every crack and cranny. Around him were voices raised in discourse: on the fortunes of war, on the winning side, on the undoubted end.

The fat bartender hustled about behind his display of bottles and potions, and in a distant corner sat a small group of men and women, the latter of bawdy aspect, yet pretty in a blatantly sexual way.

He commandeered a bottle of wine and a glass. Laden with this booty, he squeezed his way between the throng.

'Why, Comrade Avila,' came the greeting, 'we had heard you were gravely wounded after a tremendous attack against the enemy.'

A grim smile touched his lips. 'Exaggerations fly as quickly as the truth. It was a minor move in which only eight or so men took part.'

'Well, say what you like,' persisted the speaker, a fat, perspiring fellow with a sly look imprinted permanently upon his face. 'Still, it's well known around here that our Comrade Avila behaved himself in just the heroic manner we all thought he would.'

These were the men who made infamous the name of any creed, thought Juan. Clever, unscrupulous, and morally daring, they used physical pleasures to break down the altruism of youth, the faiths of maturity. He knew the type well. Soon he would be invited to lunch, to eat as nobody could at that time in starved Barcelona: English ham, caviar, French vegetables, champagne. Nothing would be missing, and the promise inherent in the bold-eyed women would be the ending for a physically perfect day. But on the morrow there would be the reckoning. A phone call would come, stating he had publicly made a series of criticisms against the government, and had used names too freely. From that point on would come the longer climb, until finally he would be turned into a creature of that organisation whose chief business was in selling to international dealers in France objects of art and jewels, stolen and looted from homes and churches. He knew the end results, and yet his whole being craved action. Anything to cut his train of thought.

'I don't know you,' said Juan to the speaker, 'but perhaps I've met you some place. In Madrid perhaps?'

The answer came too quickly. 'Why naturally. You met me at the prison of Bellas Artes.'

He knew the answer was a deliberate lie.

'Yes, I suppose it must have been somewhere,' he muttered.

The second man to his right was a typical ex-pugilist, the type always used as bodyguards. His flattened features and pig-like eyes were in themselves the solution of a miserable career in boxing, the art of which, although he had muscles, had been so sorely lacking that he was more beast than human. The third was a thin, tight-lipped little man, with steady, widely spaced eyes of unblinking stare, worn in an unchanging face. Juan could see that the man had developed an inferiority complex through a lifetime of misery due to his small size. He had been pushed by society into being what he was: a soulless killer, with neither dreams for the future nor repentance for the past. His only emotion was fear; the fear of one day being found without his gun at his side when weakness and horror of physical pain would again hover over him as they had done in his childhood and youth. As for the two women, one was pretty, in a dark, Mediterranean way: a classical nose, finely arched eyebrows, and two great, dark eyes that were wells of passion and lust. Small, even teeth under thick lips denoted, with the help of a strong chin, a mind bent only upon satisfaction of the ego. The second woman was more stereotyped. Trying desperately to imitate some actress of stage or screen, she faced him with prepared smiles, wrinkling nose, winks, and all the expressions perfected before a mirror. She reminded him of a cat that uses its tail when perched on a high limb over a pool to attract the attention of the fish.

Hilda, Hilda! thought Juan, *How different your face from the faces before me. Darkness is around me, and your light is far away.* But she had rejected him. She had turned her back upon him and spurned him for love of a creed. What was the use of all this? While some were dying at the front, others were scheming and plotting for personal power and prestige. If only Hilda were present. She would invest him anew with the burning desire to fulfil the Party creed. But that creed was his as well, though often it was pushed aside in his mind.

He presented himself at Party Headquarters at ten o'clock the next morning. As he waited for his interview, he pondered the strangeness of life. Only a few hours before, his every nerve had tingled. Now, tired and mentally slowed, his only longing was for open spaces, clean air and solitude. The action of wind had ceased, and quietude had brought only the emptiness of an empty dawn. Befuddled visions came to him in snatches: bare limbs and empty bottles; cigarettes strewn carelessly over furniture and carpets. Juan heard a familiar voice through the veils of reflection.

Ricardo stood before him once again, a frown settling down upon his face.

'You're rather late,' he said.

Juan smiled disarmingly, and threw up his hands in a gesture of defeat. 'Car trouble. I had trouble along the way.'

'You had trouble all right,' said Ricardo, 'but not with the car. However, that's neither here nor there. I hope you don't think I'm merely following you about. After you left, yesterday, I began to think that perhaps I should come to Barcelona and handle your case myself. There's one thing you must remember, comrade: the life of a leader is worth ten of his followers. The individual must bow to the will of the Party. There cannot be any stopping to face problems of reactions of any individual.'

As ever when rebuked, Juan felt a growing anger welling up inside. He had taken this censure in silence, but he could not bring himself to relinquish the idea that the individual should have something to say. Hilda had seemed to agree with him, for a while, and yet the Party had tamed her will in time. All his life he had tried to escape the system, but it held him like the coils of a giant snake, always ready with one loop to imprison the fighting arm or the kicking leg, until he found himself again engulfed. He had fought against his father's will since childhood; since then, all had been battle and unrest. He had aspired to liberty in order to overflow the great dam that channelled the swirling waters of humanity through the flume of custom and tradition. The wall had fallen, and the water had smashed down on all beneath, crushing in its inexorable passage all that had been. There was only one being who could get him out of this state of mental depression: Hilda Krantz.

'And what of Hilda Krantz?' he queried.

Ricardo smiled grimly and laced his hands behind his back. 'Comrade, I think you worry more about her than you do about yourself. She's quite well, and you'll meet her again one day, I don't doubt. For now, you have a job to carry out.'

The measured tramp of feet just outside the window drew Juan's attention. Another column of young men went into the street, heads held high. Creed upheld the weight of their packs, and conviction added strength to their limbs. On they marched towards some ephemeral goal, a challenge that would end, perhaps, with a mangled uniform as a shell blasted away their lives. And through his mind flashed the picture of scrubby figures, some in rags and others in discarded clothing. He saw again the swollen hands, the haggard features, the haunted eyes of distrust or hope.

'Are you listening to me?' said Ricardo.

'Yes, comrade,' Juan replied wearily. 'Please continue. I've been attending all the way.'

'I'm glad to hear you say that,' said Ricardo. 'It's time you came down out of that ivory tower of the mind and started putting your talents to work. This very day you will go to Bellas Artes. We have a man incarcerated there who will be of great interest to you.'

'To me? Why to me?' said Juan.

'His name,' smiled Ricardo, 'is the Duque del Bosque. Atadell thinks you should witness his confession.'

Death to Glory

When one subdues men by force, they do not submit to him in heart. They submit because their strength is not adequate to resist.

The Book of Mencius

Pedro crossed the bridge in the jolting, swaying truck, and Talavera met his eyes. Dusty. Filled with soldiers. A long sprawled-out town. Trucks seemed to be everywhere. Discarded automobiles, many riddled with holes, were capsized along the streets. Quartermaster depots. Milling, khaki-coloured humanity. Sunburned faces, wearing the carefree air of those who have forgotten, in the strife of battle, the subdued colours of everyday rainbows, meeting instead the devastating clearness of the brink betwixt life and death. Here were the wealthy and the poor, the proud and the humble, the courageous and the timid, the intelligent and the dull. All had come to the same strife, though Pedro did not realise it then. They had come under that unknown quantity that would, mayhap, cut their lives short.

The truck turned, then, from the principal thoroughfare and jolted over an open field studded with numerous barn-like wooden structures. In the centre of the space rested a flagpole on an emblem of the Foreign Legion, crossbow and musket.

Night came on, and with it came sleeplessness. It was hot. The bed of old straw, the raucous breathing and the snores added to his acute discomfort. He was plagued by bedbugs, and dreams – faces – mountain gorges – whispered voices. His father's face came into view as it had looked that day, so long ago now.

He had watched his father, then, fighting against a thing unseen, shaking his head, and the colour beginning to flow back into his face. And his mother, too, was there, bending low over the bed to stare intently into her husband's face. A curious insight

127

seemed to tell her that Don Juan Avila had but a short course left to run. Too late! Too late to break down the barriers of custom. How many times had she wanted to break down those barriers? How many times had she wanted to speak to this man as one who had loved him all her days? Yet that stern code that had been their legacy had forbidden it. A look of lost love had come into her eyes, and she had never seemed the same again.

The faces, the whispers, the voices appeared and disappeared as if all the world were pinpointed on this moment in time. And then it seemed as if a door opened before Pedro's eyes, and he saw his brother silhouetted against the bright light that flooded into the room. Juan's voice, as from some bottomless pit, moved upward in swelling sound. 'Father, they've killed you with too much work for too little reward.'

'No, no, my son,' came his father's reply. 'Don't say that. I've lived long, and as I desired to live. Now I'm going on the journey from which no man ever returns, but I've faith in my God. Juan, you must swear to me that you'll keep this family together. Remember, you're upheld only by the thin thread of life. Don't follow those who claim that all is centred upon this short span between birth and death. Don't follow them – don't ever follow them.'

And the voices faded away. Sleep fled away, and the time passed endlessly as Pedro stared unseeing at the corrugated ceiling overhead. Finally, a bugle brayed.

The days slipped by as if on the wings of the wind. Up at dawn; to bed at night. March, march, march. Left, right, march. Running, to sprawl in the sand. And always the blistering sun, going through him like water passing through a sponge.

Slowly those days became time units once again, filled with the good and the bad, with mirth and with sorrow. His iron constitution came to his aid. No longer was it painful drudgery to walk over the barren hills, to climb the grilling rocks, to jump down once again at a given signal and run like a fleeing deer, a heavy Hotchkiss machine gun on his unpadded shoulder.

At last came the day when the chorus rolled forth from the serried ranks of the unit, doing honours to Pedro and the legionnaires to be:

Soy un hombre a quien la suerte,
hirio con zarpa da fiera,
Soy el novio de la muerte,
y la estreche con brazo fuerte,
y su amor es mi mas fiel companera...

They wore speckless, white *alpargata* boots, white gloves, rolled-up sleeves. The deep drums rolled to the rapid beat of a hundred passing volunteers sworn to death and the principles of combat.

The unit marched past in geometrical pattern, the words of the full-throated chorus becoming, to him, some living, breathing thing. 'I am a man whom death has wounded with claws of a beast. I am the betrothed of death. I clasped her with a strong embrace, and her love is my most loyal companion.'

The thud of his footsteps mingled with the beat of the drums and the throbbing of his own pulse. No longer did he feel the physical effort of conquering the elements and distance.

At a raucous command the forward-moving rectangle froze. A file detached itself from the unit, and now each individual materialised into being. No longer was Pedro an existing entity. Instead, overpowered by the hypnotic spell of music, the clash of primitive rhythms and the tenseness of mental abstraction, he felt himself to be in a world apart.

Under the motionless flag they marched, reforming in another square on the opposite side. The passion had gone. Now only boredom remained, and the isolated fragments of a shouted chorus. *I am the betrothed of death – wounded with claws of a beast.* Then, endless filing lines: speeches, repeating the same phrases and words, and the spell was broken.

Pedro hoped to go to Dar Riffien when his six months of combat were through; to Morocco, and an old Legion base that had been recently converted into a training camp for officers. He would be a provisional officer. As the last drumbeats faded away and the setting sun cast its blue shadows across the stark surroundings, he thought he could hear the shriek of shells and the distant roar of artillery augmenting in intensity. The sudden, fateful sound of battle flooded in around him, and as he stood, alone, in the centre of the field that had, only a short time before, echoed to the cadence of a thousand feet and the roar of a thousand voices, he thought of the innumerable small items that had directed his life, pushing him ever onward towards some unknown goal. Within his being he felt a kindling of a new and strange flame, a mystic, unknowable dread, coupled with the ecstatic thrill of adventures yet to come.

★

Hilda walked down the stairs of the hotel. A phone call had come from Juan Avila. He would meet her in an hour, and his voice had sounded strangely different.

Juan Avila. She resented him in some ways. When she had criticised the actions of his companions, he had always only smiled and freely assented to her opinions, and yet she wondered if he really agreed. There had been that wall, building ever higher between them. Now, for the first time, she was unable to grasp the inner thoughts of this man. She felt frustrated and hampered at every turn. Even her friends used her for their own purposes; she knew that they secretly despised her for being an international agent who was trying to pry into their affairs. How she longed for the Parisian boulevards, the gay crowds, the intellectual surroundings. She wanted, more than anything else, to be a part of that bohemian atmosphere where speeches of revolution and death for the cause came easily around tables, with a bottle of cognac or champagne inspiring the mind to greater adventures. But here her utility seemed to have abandoned her. Everyone knew what she was. There were no secrets here. She felt that most of her effectiveness was wasted in the warring of one faction with another, the strife between one party and another. Everybody knew the only programme worth following was that of the Communists.

She recalled the face of a man. Once he had been youthful, strong and masterful, sure of all his acts. Shortly Schmidt had become a broken being, crawling like a wounded dog to the person he had created. Mists of the past were thrust aside by the spearhead of memory, and in a squalid room she saw that same man, once a friend, but now an enemy of the cause, starting up from the rumpled bed to find himself surrounded by hulking men; the crushing, violent blows continuing long after silence and death had fallen in the room.

As she walked up the stairs of the Party Headquarters, she caught a glimpse of Juan Avila, standing just inside the open door. He turned, and then their eyes met, and for an instant she felt the old heady sensation flooding her being. She stopped, and he rushed to meet her, grasping her hand with warm promise.

'Hilda, am I ever glad to see you.'

She couldn't seem to breathe for an instant. Her voice sounded faint and strange to her ears. 'And I'm glad to see you, comrade.'

'Comrade? Isn't that being a bit formal?'

'Formal? I don't know what you mean. The Party has instructed us on the proper use of names. But let's not talk here. We can go to my room at the hotel. They're not particular about those things any more. Now we're all equals.'

He placed her arm in his as they left the place and started down the street. For a moment he sensed a restraint, a tightening of muscles, but then she relaxed and smiled into his eyes.

'Well, how have you been, Juan?'

'Frankly, not so good. I've had the worst experience of my life these past weeks. But I'll tell you about it when we reach your quarters.'

'Yes,' she said, 'we must be careful. The walls have ears you know... But I'm sure that it's all for a good purpose. There are a lot of fools around who would injure our cause if they could.'

'Doubtless,' he returned dryly, 'but sometimes I think the fools who are doing the injuring are all *in* the Party.'

Spruced and clean, Juan looked attractive and very much his old self in the dimly lit room of the hotel.

'Well,' she said, 'what's all this news that you have to tell me? I'm dying to know why you're here in Valencia.'

'Just a few days' furlough,' he said, 'that's all. But there's more to the story than that.' His eyes grew dark and brooding, and he paced restlessly back and forth across the worn carpet. 'There's a world more than that.'

'Juan, do stop pacing about like a caged lion. Here,' and she patted the seat beside her, 'sit down beside me and relax. You make me nervous.'

'Nervous? Well, we might all be nervous at the things I've seen these past days. I saw priests, hung upon meat hooks while they were still alive, and the only cry from their lips was a plea for God's forgiveness upon their crucifiers. I saw men, goaded and tormented beyond human endurance, holding their peace and praying for those who tortured them to death. I saw the Duque del Bosque. Remember him? Yes, the same man, only battered and beaten beyond recognition. Do you know what they did to that man? They strapped him in a chair. Then they put a close-fitting box over that chair that corresponded to the shape of his body, enclosing him in it like a sardine in a can. And do you know what they did then? They had a small hole cut in that box, level with his eyes, and a door flapped up and down in steady rhythm. Every ten seconds or so a bright light would flash into his eyes. Then a bell would sound, and the process was repeated. Oh yes, but they didn't stop there. There was worse to come. So terrible that I won't even mention it, except to say that he died the most hideous death, one I could never imagine in my wildest dreams. And then you ask me why I'm restless.'

Hilda sat back in the seat and crossed her legs. 'You'd better pour yourself a drink, Juan.' She gestured with her expressive hands towards a decanter on a stand in the corner. 'You've had a terrible shock. Perhaps, though, it's not as bad as you'd imagine. Aren't these things necessary for the advancement of any worthy cause? Revolutions aren't won at tea parties, my dear Juan, and this cause is bigger than anything you've seen so far. There are confessions to be obtained, and sometimes the only way to get these confessions is through just such things as you've seen.'

He put the decanter down with an emphatic thump, and whirled about, his face pale and drawn. 'Necessary? Necessary, you say. Well, I'm beginning to think that a cause that has to be forwarded by such activity is no cause I want to align myself with.'

'Now, just a minute, comrade!' She was on her feet, her eyes cold and dark. 'I think you've already said too much. This cause, to which I've dedicated my life, will not stop for your petty grievances, nor for mine, for that matter. If you'll sit down and stop waving your arms around and declaiming, I'll tell you something that may be of more interest to you than all of this. Besides, I can't imagine you getting so stirred up about a man you've hated for as long as you can remember.'

Hated? Yes, he had hated the Duque, of that there was no question. But his hatred had been clean and pure, compared to the evil darkness that smote the man down. His hatred had been based upon personal injustice and not upon some intangible misalliance to some ephemeral cause and an even more ephemeral goal. He was disappointed, for he had expected a different reaction from Hilda Krantz. Would she turn him in to the authorities? But she loved him... or did she? A sudden chill seized him, and he fell blindly into a chair, covering his face with his hands. If he could only close out the faces – the screams – the prayers.

★

Pedro saw the Pillars of Hercules looming like a gateway, forbidding and dark. On one side, Gibraltar; on the other, Ceuta. The choppy sea lay between, and the vast ocean to the west. Here the wind bottlenecked, pushing and worrying the sighing, sand-laden, hot and angry winds of the Sahara.

Leaving Algeciras behind, the little ship ploughed its torturous way from the Bay of Gibraltar, pointing its bow towards the adjacent African coast. It was the month of mad February, and the sky was overcast with dark, leaden clouds. He feared the on-slaught of the levanter, of which he had heard much: a wind that would whip the cross-currents into a fury of foam in a matter of hours, driving them in every direction, curling and clutching at every ship or shape that ventured across the enraged surface.

The overloaded vessel creaked as the receding line of the Spanish coast appeared to pull the ever-growing skyline of Africa towards it. To his left reared the towering rock of Gibraltar, a means of concealment for enemy gunboats lying behind that sprawling fortress. But at last, with no untoward incidents, a narrow entrance opened its gates to the harbour of Ceuta.

Fitted snugly against the exterior pier, the light-grey cruiser unfurled its red-and-green flag from the stern. A hundred shouting voices raised their guttural accents, and a procession of ant-like figures, weighted down with crates and packages, formed a seemingly endless line from the bowels of the vessel to the waiting trucks.

He breathed deeply of the strange and mysterious smells. Africa. Dark legends and mysteries, and yet his first impressions were that he was in the heart of a European town. Uniforms were everywhere, the common denominator of every town he had entered since the war had begun.

A broad street edged with jewellery and clothing shops unwound before him and, as if spirited from a world of mystic legends, a towering figure wearing a white burnoose looked down at him with steel-grey eyes. Ancestry of the Mohammedan warriors was in every line of that powerful face. Only a flashing glimpse, a momentary glance, and he had passed with the springy stride of the Moroccan mountaineer. These people, Pedro remembered, had crushed in a single battle the might of the Visigoths and were still unchanged after the passing of the centuries.

A voice from a doorway hailed him and he turned to see a scrawny, sickly being, dressed half in European garb, and half in Moorish habit. A fez topped his head. Shrivelled and miserable, his pockmarked features inspired no trust. He flinched under Pedro's steady gaze, and retreated hastily, mumbling apologies as he went.

The culture of ages, the philosophies of great religions, the laws of habits, and the customs of environment faded into one dizzily revolving mass. Pedro compared the face of the shrivelled figure in the doorway with the forceful features of the striding warrior. Yes, he decided, life played strange tricks on people.

Then he stopped, enchanted by the view that spread before him. A wall of reddish hue surrounded what had once been the stronghold of the mighty Saracens. Within were waving palms, the hush and quiet of a people that knew how to rest under the vast vault of space. His eyes travelled upward, resting at last upon the lofty, climbing tower from which the muezzin chanted forth his ageless evening prayers. *La Illaha il Allah*; the proclamation that God is one God that begets not, had sounded over these selfsame walls in victory and defeat, in triumph and in sorrow. Pedro felt anew the shadowed groping of man's search for truth, the mystery of Africa falling like a mantle over his being.

Shifting Sands

He who is naturally in sympathy with men, to him all men come.

But he who forcedly adapts, has no room even for himself, still less for others.

And he who has no room for others, has no ties. It is all over with him.

The Writings of Chuang Tze

Juan lifted his face from his hands and lit a cigarette with shaking fingers. So this was what he had lived for all these days. He had always wanted to know how people lived in other countries, how people who strove were successful in their ambition. Now he felt tired, exhausted in mind and body. Yet his life would go on and on in its endless and aimless fashion. And Hilda Krantz. He had loved her once, and he supposed that he still did love the girl she once had been. She had changed before his very eyes, and yet he doubted that she had really changed. Perhaps, even now, he was in love with a dream, in love with a girl who had never really existed except in his imagination.

She lifted a glass of wine to her lips and smiled at him over its brim. 'Come, come, Juan. Lift all this gloom from your shoulders. Do you know where I received my true inspiration for this cause we find ourselves involved in?'

He had to admit that he didn't know. Juan was aware that she had lived for a long time in Paris, but he had heard other things about her that disturbed him of late. He had heard that she was much older than she appeared, that she used men only to discard them at the proper time. He had heard that her kiss was considered as deadly as a scorpion's sting. But all this was ridiculous gossip, of course. Wasn't she smiling at him even now over her glass of wine, as warm and friendly as she'd ever been? No, this could be no pose. Rather, the other attitude must be the pose, and this was Hilda at her truest. In all of Spain there could be no woman so beautiful as this enchanting being who sat before him.

'I'm glad to see you're feeling much better, darling.' She came to him, then, and ran her strong fingers through his dark hair. 'Such a bother about so small a thing, really. Of course it was a terrible shock for you, and why shouldn't it be? It would shock me, too, no doubt, and I know I'd die a thousand deaths myself.'

'Would you, Hilda? Would you?' He wanted desperately to believe her, to hold her once again in his arms and whisper of love.

'Well, of course, you silly thing.' She laughed lightly, and ruffled his hair with a playful gesture. 'There, now you look like a poodle dog I owned once. Seriously though, I promised to tell you something of interest, and perhaps it'll help to heal the wounds of this unfortunate day. I've been weighing the need to tell you something of myself, more than I've done already. I say, weighing the need, because often it's best for all concerned to keep one's secrets hidden. Well,' she turned and crossed the room, flinging herself down upon the low couch, 'come over here and join me, and I'll tell you all about it.'

Then came the story Juan had wondered about for so long. Hilda had left Paris, after the death of Schmidt, on orders from the Party, for she was a girl who could be entrusted with some of their inner secrets. She was to go to Russia, to see Communism at work in its native land. Her impressions of that place flooded out into the room, now, adding warmth and glow to the dim glimmer from the ancient lamps. She had seen Smolensk, and the tall grey of the Party building lifting its gaunt head above the spires and domes of times gone by. The brick chimneys of the little wooden houses sent forth their grey smoke again, and the black frost fell over the land, while the Veresina passed sluggishly underneath the bridge of the turnpike road that led to Moscow. Around Juan, now, were the rolling plains, with here and there a slight rise that rolled off like a turbulent river, while, farther away in the distance, he could envision a mighty forest that clutched between its sides the disappearing road. Napoleon had passed this place like the god of war, with faith in his victory and the urge of conquest in his soul. Later, bedraggled and weary, the remnants of that once mighty army had straggled by, leaning against the jeering scorn of winter. Juan did not know then, as he would later, that in his own time another army would pass that same place, and Smolensk would be no more. Only the smouldering ruins, the white faces, and the grey of the Party building would stand. He felt himself caught up into the spell of that mighty land, and as she talked he felt himself standing beside her as she gazed for the first time upon the pink walls of the battlements of Novgorod. He passed the gates with her, and felt himself in another world, with the glowing globe of the central tower of the Kremlin gleaming above the incredible minarets and dome of the cathedral. To his right he saw, as if he were there, the great bronzed globe, its sides covered with hundreds of sculptured figures that represented the battles of the czars. Hand in hand, he climbed with her to the top of the southern ramparts and saw, extending before him into the illimitable reaches of earth and sky, the flat lands of northern Russia. In the distance he could see the monastery of Yamok, surrounded by a few stunted trees. Farther on were the small islands of Malenki Morenya and Bolsey Morenya. The children skied, with shrill shrieks of joy, from the pink walls of the forbidding castle, downwards to the dip in the ground where the railway crossed to meet the bridge that would take it on to Moscow. Juan felt that he was standing there, staring into the shimmering distance, with the rolling forest of northern Europe sweeping onwards to the Peipus Lakes. Here the mighty bison had pursued his formidable desires from east to west. This was Russia – as vast as her plains, as cold as her snows, as temperamental as her music, as incredible as her legends.

And the glory, the mystic wonder, the strangeness of the scene faded away. His cigarette was cold and lifeless between his lips, and his throat felt dry and constricted. So this was the place that had taught Hilda her lessons of life. In that incredible land she had learned, first-hand, the gospel that would, by the power of the sword and the living word, be spread around the world. Juan felt foolish, and more than a little uneasy. He had said too much, and he had said it too soon. And as she looked at him, he felt a resurgence of the old love, flooding back into his frozen heart, melting the snows of hatred and kindling anew the fires of passion.

★

Pedro boarded the crowded bus and as it left Ceuta it seemed to be at the bursting point. But, through some strange power contrary to all physical laws, it was able to pack in another pushing, panting being at every stop. In the distance, nearly perpendicular, rock-ribbed mountains shut off from his view the hinterland of Morocco. This thin belt through which his bus made its protesting way was festooned with eucalyptus groves, striving to lessen the inroads of the hordes of predatory mosquitoes. The bus passed a small village, barely discernible from the window, then a long stretch of road, bounded on the left by the yellow sand of the coast.

With a series of laboured jerks, the bus pulled to a stop. Extricating himself from the crowd, Pedro stepped gingerly on to the sun-scorched earth. So this was Dar Riffien: a vast, red-brick building with white embellishments, and behind it a steep gradient that climbed to the jumble of mountains farther on. Clustered along the dry riverbed was a small village of square, whitewashed houses nestling against the eastern side of the central pavilion.

Pedro was assigned to the first company because of his height. Entering the barracks for the first time, he heard a raucous voice shouting out that a legionnaire with stripes had just come in.

Almost immediately an *alpargatas* came soaring through space and hit him squarely on the chest. Shrill cries, guttural laughs, and cries of, 'To the blanket with him,' smote his eardrums.

Before he knew what was happening, he found himself raised up bodily and thrown unceremoniously upon a large square military blanket. Up and down he went, losing all sense of direction or time. Head foremost or feet foremost he would come down. And each time he hit the blanket, his knapsack would land with a bruising blow on top of him. Then again, he went into the air.

With a breathtaking jar he fell prostrate upon the ground. A cry had announced the entrance of the company captain. He wondered, angrily, if this was the end or the beginning of the treatment. Dazed and sheepish, he decided they would not be so brave if caught alone. His eyes smouldered, the sparks fanning up from their smoky blackness. Then came the questions, the usual questions. There were mutual acquaintances to be exclaimed over, praise for his former company.

At last he sprawled in fatigue upon the topmost bunk. *Well, people are all alike,* he decided with a grimace. *We're just like flies upon a windowpane. You see a fly, and then it goes. Another comes along, and again you see a fly, and yet you never know whether it is the same one. Just be sure you don't make a nuisance of yourself. That's the way to keep from being swatted.* He was learning fast, he thought, damned fast.

And so Pedro found himself just another pawn on a vast chessboard of a country at war.

The next day dawned hot and murky. He loitered around the entrance of the camp in his free hour, gazing through the gate at the blue sea beyond. How fate played pranks with both men and nations! Spain was over there, just a day's journey away. For seven hundred years it had fought tooth and nail against the Saracen, finally bettering him in 1492. And yet, centuries afterward, those same Moroccan hills that bred strategy and tactics were preparing a spearhead of advance, an organised minority that sought to vanquish the monstrous disorder that had spread through Spain.

A taxi pulled up to the gate with a grinding of gears and a plume of acrid dust. Out jumped a soldier, elegantly dressed, his right hand holding an expensive suitcase. Nodding cheerily at the gaping sentries, the short figure and the jaunty air crashed in upon Pedro's mind like a sudden blow. Pablo Maiquez.

'Pedro,' came the words of recognition, 'such a coincidence!'

'Coincidence, hell,' said Pedro, slapping him upon the back. 'Let me direct your footsteps around here. You'll be lost the first day, even as I was, but you'll soon get used to it. First of all you'll have to give the usual information to our "hog face". Yes, there's one in every camp, and, unfortunately, we will not be in the same company, because they gave you such heavy food when you were young that it weighed you down and you never grew.'

Pablo gave him a look of knowing condescension. 'The same old Pedro I see. Always the cheerful one.'

'Well,' said Pedro, grinning broadly, 'you'll soon lose that tubby appearance. After your fifth day of ragout with carrots and turnips, and little else, except perhaps flies, you'll again be dreaming of steak and potatoes.'

'I've lived pretty well these past months, friend. I've enough meat stored away on my bones to keep me for a while.'

'Like a camel without water,' grunted Pedro. 'By the way, you can't be at the infirmary for more than five days without losing your promotion, so no matter what happens, keep on your feet. I had an inkling we'd meet again someplace, but not here, certainly.'

'And why not, I ask you?' said Pablo. 'I was frightfully bored over there, you know. Every night I had to tell my father all the medications, all the cures, every ugly muscle and bone I'd seen during the day. That'd go on until twelve at night. I'll explain all in greater detail later.'

Pedro laughed and kicked a stone out of the way with a well-aimed blow from his worn boot. 'Well, plenty of time for that. I'll leave you here, and you can go on in to see that piebald grass-eater. You'll be mauled around a bit when you get into your company, but keep your temper in check. Don't start a fight, whatever you do, for they're many and you're one.'

And so the incessant winds droned on, bringing with them the echoes of the Sahara.

★

His furlough was ended. Now, dressed as an ordinary *miliciano*, Juan Avila walked up the steps of the Palace of Montjuich. Ordinarily the place would have been teeming, but now it was deserted. He wound his way along the bridle paths, hidden by clustering trees. Every now and again he came upon some shaded nook where a couple were seated upon a bench. He scanned the faces with a quick glance, trying to discover what might be written upon them. Juan was beginning to feel not unlike a hopeless drifter. For some strange reason he was never allowed to become attached to any assignment, but was shifted around with alarming frequency. Now, he had taken over the political part of the Party work. It seemed that the Party did not trust a great many of its men, especially the Separatists of Cataluna. They fought like demons for their province, for their rights and traditions, but they could never seem to fight for the total proletariat revolution, even with the world at stake. He was to go to the Montjuich, for in that park strange things had been happening of late. Apart from the lovers' bowers, which held no interest save for the diseases that came from them, there were meetings being held that were hard to comprehend. He was to watch the people, mingle with them and try to learn their secrets.

As he neared the great stadium he paused to look around, and then walked unhurriedly to the low railing that delimited the flattened space. A vast view rolled out before him, with the low coast spreading its yellow ribbon of sand out to the south. Across it, from east to west, the River Prat intersected one of the richest black-soiled lands, squared into geometrical patterns, blessing its earth with harvests of every kind and species. Along the railway and the road that ran parallel to it towards Valencia, great factories encroached on either side. In the distance were the inevitable mountains, spurring out into the sea where the waves had cut them short.

He turned around and rested his back against the balustrade, looking upward at the fort of Montjuich. Once an impregnable stronghold, its might had been lowered by the guns of the British navy, helping to prolong the reign of the Hapsburgs over Spain. Now it was a prison, and through its square courtyards and gloomy dungeons white-faced prisoners kept their silent hope, hemmed in by gates that had been haughty in the reign of Charles III, and by lofty precipices that bounded on the sea. Filing in and out as the bugle blew or the bell sounded, these luckless men dreamt of the great city beneath and of the blue sea before them. Beyond that sea lay freedom – a lifetime away.

With a grimace, Juan turned away from the forbidding place and moved on towards a restaurant that offered a panoramic view of the city and port. There the foreigners and the pressmen gathered with frequency. Avoiding the road, he went by the footpath that led in the same general direction.

A glen with a small fountain met his eyes, surrounded by an Italian garden of great beauty. The usual neglect was apparent here. The box hedges were uncut and leaves spread a mantle of untidiness over the once geometrically perfect place. He walked through the garden slowly, musing on the centuries that had passed over this hillock, which had been transformed by the hand of man into a bower. Generations of gardeners had tended the flowers with loving care and children had romped there in carefree abandon. Now, hiding in the shadows, were fear, and hate, and death.

Rounding a corner, a shiver ran up his spine, for facing him were three men who gazed steadily upon him. His subconscious had already sounded a warning and he had sufficient willpower to keep walking straight ahead as if nothing were amiss. As he passed before them, he felt their icy stares boring into his back. With a sigh of relief, he turned down one of the side paths of the garden and increased his speed. When he considered that he had gone far enough, he stopped and turned around. No one was in sight. Had he blundered on to a secret meeting of the White Aide? If this were so, then it meant a chain of subversive activity all through the executive offices. He didn't like it. None of them had been wearing a specific uniform. One had a badge of the Communist Party pinned to his shirt; the other appeared to be a plain militiaman from the front.

Gradually climbing to a higher level, Juan worked his way through the dense undergrowth, reaching at long last the place where he had met the men. There, below him in the glen, they stood in an attitude of expectancy.

Time slipped by and, after what seemed an interminable wait, two more joined them. They were clothed in overalls, with no particular characteristics. Handed a paper by the newcomers, the taller of the group scanned it closely and then burned it with a match. The meeting was at an end.

They left singly, the last to leave being the obvious leader. There was but one path leading to the road, the one Juan himself had taken, so, allowing a short time to lapse, he followed cautiously. When he reached the road, he saw his quarry some distance away, walking towards the funicular station at a rapid gait.

Juan broke into a run as the man entered the station, arriving in time to buy a ticket and board the same funicular.

As Juan climbed the steps of the station at the end of the journey, he saw his man getting into a parked car. Quickly he wrote down the license number, and not a moment too soon. With a roar, the vehicle bounded forward down the Paralelo towards the port.

He reported immediately to his superior officer. No, he didn't know whether they would stage a reunion. Furthermore, the men had certainly taken a good look at him, and he might have been recognised, in which case the place would not be used again.

And then the words from his superior officer flashed into his brain like a searing iron. Someone had complained about him to the Party heads. He, himself, was under suspicion, but perhaps this latest report, if proved of value, would do much to clear the cloud from his name. He had been accused by some unknown party of favouritism towards a certain duque who had been known to be an enemy of all that the cause stood for. He had been accused of soft-heartedness towards captives. No, he could not be informed of the name of the betrayer. He must, rather, watch his every move so he could erase this blot upon his record.

Juan's eyes narrowed, and he clenched his hands until his nails bit into the flesh. Hilda Krantz! She had openly betrayed him to the Communist Party. She had accused him of treasonable policies. His better judgment had warned him, and yet he had thought, even in Valencia, that she still loved him, that she was really the girl he had known in Madrid. Ricardo had known all along what sort of person she was. Why hadn't he told him? But no, he despised Juan too and would be only too glad to see him out of the way. Juan groaned inwardly at this trick of fate. He would have given her everything he possessed to have fulfilled her every whim. Why had she repaid him in such fashion? And to think that he had heard once that good was repaid a thousandfold. The man's voice broke through his thoughts, warning, imploring, urging him to take great care. He would have to remember that only with complete submission to the Party's rules and decrees could the war be won.

Pedro waited on the corner where he and Pablo were wont to meet, unless his friend got into trouble. This had been their place of reunion from the very first. He had formed a friendship with old Mahome, a strange and interesting Moor, who seemed to be rooted permanently to that particular spot. He had erected a small table and sat cross-legged behind it now, surrounded by a teapot and a varied assortment of thick glasses, no two alike.

Pedro found solace and comfort in his conversations with this old man. This was the wisdom of age, of life and of the man who cares nothing for time and can ponder endlessly over things that seem of small import.

Now he waited impatiently in the shadow of the building. The mournful wind trying to find its way into the sheltering pocket behind the wall supported the pessimism of his thoughts.

The old Moor took one look at him and grunted, 'Ah, you are exceedingly sad, my friend. What's the trouble? No money? That's what you Christians seem to like most of all. Perhaps it's the war. Yes,' he nodded his grey head, 'I know what wars are. I fought on both sides of those Atlas Mountains until I grew weary of it all. That was long ago. I journeyed to Mecca after that, a trip of many months' duration, and all the way there and back I had nothing to do but think. I thought of the past, of the present, and dreamt of the future. Already I was old, and that was long ago. Winter was settling in my bones. I've been to Casablanca, and I've had many wives in my time. I've been to Marseilles, too, and other places that you call civilised. There were times when my hand would clutch eagerly for gold, and a dancer's lissom form would make my blood run hot, but that has all been washed away. I've thought of the shifting sands of the desert, of how the wind blows on and on for ever. I've thought of my sons who have died in the wars, and of my daughters who are married. Finally, I've come to the conclusion that only by seeing life in its constant change, and not being an actor in it, can peace and tranquillity come to the human being. Your ways are far different from mine, my son, for you belong to those people who have conquered Africa – or, at least, it is your flag that flies. Our flag once flew from Cordoba, though dissension and division brought it down again. Things will happen to you whether you worry about them or not. Think about these things, before it's too late. And now, the best medicine of all – a glass of tea?' He handed Pedro a long glass, filled to the brim with the green-hued Moorish brew.

Accepting the glass lengthwise between his thumb and forefinger, so he would not burn himself, Pedro sipped the fragrant liquid.

At his smile of approval, Mahome nodded assent. 'Truly, it's good, and your face now reflects that goodness. Those who follow Muhammad's rule are wise. I've seen drunken men – how foolish they look! The coward becomes a lion, the sage becomes a fool, the knave becomes dangerous and the felon becomes a leader. And yet your world says that we are the ones who need civilising.'

Pedro sighed and put the glass back down upon the table. 'It's not our purpose to try to civilise those that don't need it, friend. We only want to better the condition of those who live in poverty and squalor. You know that many do. Look at that poor old woman over there.' He pointed a forefinger in the direction of a shrivelled crone who was weighed down by a load of sticks she seemed scarcely able to bear. Behind her trailed a much younger woman, carrying a far lighter load. 'Is that justice?' he asked.

Mahome smiled. 'Those are customs, and those two would have it no other way. Remember, when they arrive at their house the younger must obey the older.'

'Oh, I suppose you're right.'

'And where are you and your tardy friend heading for this day?' asked Mahome.

'We're leaving for Tetuan. That is, we'll be going if Pablo hasn't fallen into trouble again.'

Between Two Worlds

The human heart is deceitful above all things, and desperately wicked. Who can know it?

The Book of Jeremiah

Juan wanted desperately to return to the front. There beings lived and died who were, after all, human. This was to be a revolution of the people, and not a revolution of tools. Obviously there were two kinds of people in the world. There were those you could look to with ease, like open houses into which you could stray and be at home. Others kept themselves locked against all intruders. Nothing could be known of what went on inside. He knew now, perhaps too late, that Hilda Krantz fell into the latter category.

They had located one of the men Juan had followed in the park, and Juan had witnessed his confession. Bruised lips and swollen eyes; a bloody, battered shape that had once been a human being, broken physically and spiritually, agreeing or disagreeing with whatever he was expected to affirm or deny. But there was still a slight spark of defiance glinting from under the battered eyelids. Juan had not identified the man, for he could not be sure that the shapeless form before him was the same. Too, he felt little sympathy for the man who had requested that he make the identification, the same man who had guided the Duque through his nightmarish death. He would say nothing. Let him find out for himself. He was nothing but a damn foreigner anyway, interfering in Spain's business.

Juan had returned then to headquarters and requested permission to go to the front. There, from the Pyrenees to the Mediterranean, was a line of men who were protecting him at this very moment, and striving desperately to win. Now the front was pushing ever forward towards the Mediterranean, and the northern provinces had already fallen. Asturias no longer flew the red banner, and many had fled to the mountains to fight out, singly or in groups, the battle that the army had lost. Those bands were dwindling, with only the rocks as their friends, dying for the mountains to remember and mortals to forget.

And soon his wish came true.

High up on the mountain slope a bush stirred. Only a circling vulture saw the motion. It knew there was no wind to move the scrubby plant. The great wings cambered slightly, the spiral became a trace smaller, and the bird dropped several hundred feet. Matchless eyes soon found the cause of the disturbance. Under that sheltering bush Juan lay, sprawled upon his stomach.

He stared through his field glasses for a long time without blinking. Far beneath wound the road of the Puerto del Pico, over which poured the supplies and replacements from the hinterlands of Avila and Salamanca towards the harassed Madrid and Toledo fronts. There was to be a great offensive. Somehow this means of revitalisation had to be blocked.

Juan was told to pick a group of men who knew the mountains and cut off the road where he deemed it wisest. Tormo had been a natural choice and Juan was delighted when he discovered him in Barcelona. For him, the discomfort of sleeping on bare rocks, with no blanket to keep out the night air, was as nothing.

It was a beautiful morning. Day was dawning and larks in the fields were singing their gay melodies. The fragrance that came from the little wild flowers that dotted, here and there, the few shady nooks in which they grew, was borne to Juan's nostrils like the kiss with which a mother awakens her child from its slumber. This was the song of nature, with thankfulness for the morning, giving to mortals the smile of hope for the future. Yet he was, at that moment, occupied in the tremendous surge that can only be stopped when the fulfilment of unleashed passions has lost its power. Only then would the pendulum of thought swing back, recovering in its passage the objectiveness that is like the constant direction of the compass, which, no matter how it may turn, to the right or to the left, always swings back to the north. So age counsels youth, and even so youth forgets that counsel, to become in turn aged and repentant, striving, itself, to counsel.

The mountains roundabout were silent with the stillness that only nature can give and space confine. To the unaccustomed it boomed with the absence of sound.

Juan seated himself on a rock. Turning to his men, he said, 'Comrades, you must obey my orders implicitly, for in them rests the safety of the entire group. We have a most important mission. I know that each of you has vengeance to mete out, and not for yourselves alone. You will avenge your mothers and your grandmothers before them. You will avenge all those who for centuries have been dying bone weary. Tormo, I know what you have to avenge, and I know you can be trusted to carry out your end of the bargain without fail. See those mountains yonder?' He swept his arm in a wide arc. 'That's how you have to be. Unmovable – unquenchable – indestructible. If one of you should fall, there he must lie, and there will be the bones of one more patriot, bleaching, withering and turning to dust, so the winds can pick him up again and rest him upon the soil of this great land which belongs to us, and one day will be for us.'

The three men looked at him. Here was the leader they had hoped to find. But Juan did not feel as sure of himself as he sounded. If only he could stay up there in the mountains, then he could be himself. Perhaps, as dusk was falling and the breeze from the valleys whispered the legends of Spain, he would feel some rejuvenation of his spirit. A new dedication might possess his being with all the fire and fury of his youth. Maybe then this misty dream would come true, and the world he hoped to find would become a reality. But he could not afford, in this hour, to reveal his inner turmoil to the faces around him. He could not tell them the truth; the truth that only Hilda had guessed. Somewhere, somehow the road had turned, and he had missed the crossing. He felt lost in some dark and aimless wilderness, the barren shadows of his life beginning to flicker across the screen of his mind by day and by night.

★

Pedro and Pablo left the Plaza, which was surrounded on three sides by modern buildings, and their boots clattered noisily against the concrete pavement as they hurried past the two Mejaznias, Colonial Civil Guards, reclining their stalwart forms against the brick of the arched entrance. A prostitute lurked in the shadows of a building, fearfully scanning the forms of the guards.

This was Tetuan, old and new. Here the monumental pile of the Alcazaba surmounted, on its knoll, the town. Below it, and half encircling it, sprawled the intricate, narrow-alleyed, criss-crossed city, full of whispers and secrets, a throbbing, pulsating attraction for youth.

'What'll we do?' asked Pablo, looking expectantly at his friend.

'Well, our term's nearly finished,' said Pedro. 'I recall your barely escaping from two predicaments around here. We've been lucky not to have been picked up by the military police. As things stand right now, I still think my collarbone was broken in that last fracas – it's bothered me a lot of late. In the light of all that, I suggest we go to some downtown theatre or something. We might hire a taxi and see the sights. I mean *see* the sights,' he emphasised, as he noticed the humorous glint in Pablo's eyes. 'Have you any idea, my friend, what would happen to you if you were found in that uniform, in any of those places we've been frequenting? Besides, we're lucky not to be fattening fish this minute.'

Pablo chuckled noisily. 'Yes, brother philosopher. You ought to shave your head, put on monk's robes, and preach to us lowly sinners. Tonight's our last one before God only knows what. In fifteen days we may be dead. Who knows? Let's have one fling, anyway, and away with all these damn doldrums.'

'True,' sighed Pedro, 'we may be dead in fifteen days, or in one week or a day. Does that mean we have to squander away the rest of the time that remains? Some idea! And as for the monk's cassock, better men than I have worn it, and not for that have they been criticised.'

'All right, my testy friend. No offence meant. Why are you always so solemn? I'll never figure that out if I live to be a hundred years old.'

No, their lives were not the same, thought Pedro. Plant a vine inside of a greenhouse, water it every day and fertilise it when needful, and a great vine will grow, rich with green leaves. The grapes will be luscious and fat. Plant that same shoot outside where thousands of others are growing, competing for life, battling against wind and sun and drought, and it will be small, the leaves not so green, the grapes not so large, the skins thicker. Yet the flavour and aroma will be stronger. Why was it, Pedro wondered, that man, as well as plants, became tougher and more durable only through suffering and trial? Water is pure only when it runs. So with the mind of man.

'Pablo,' he said, 'you'd be a lot better off right now if your father hadn't pampered you so much as a child. He tried to shield you from those very things that made him the man he is.'

Pablo shrugged his massive shoulders. 'Casting all sentiment aside, my friend, perhaps you have a point. In any case I haven't denied it as yet, and that's a point in your favour. I do what I can, but why always harp on the tragedies of life? You never seem to see the gayness. I, for one, prefer to be gay and happy while I have a chance. I can be happy today, and tomorrow perhaps not.' He stopped abruptly and stared about with interest. 'Well, see where we've walked to. We're in front of the selfsame place where you pulled me out of that mess the other night. I would never have thought that miserable little cur could put up such a fight.'

'So we're in front of the tavern. So what?'

'So what? Haven't you any adventure in your bones?'

Pedro chuckled, but his eyes were mirthless. 'Pablo, if you don't go in there because of me, you will be twitting me about my cowardice for the next fortnight. If we go in together, trouble will occur. I don't want to run like a scared rabbit for two miles, provided I'm still in any condition to do so.'

'Then don't come along,' said Pablo. 'But I'll wager a small bet that some interesting things are going on in that back room. If you must go, goodbye for now, and we'll meet at the post, I presume.'

'I presume,' said Pedro, walking away, mixing with the milling crowd of pedestrians, the burnoosed figures striding noiselessly along, their heavy *babuchas* lacking the familiar tap of heels on pavement. The women wore voluminous garments that draped their figures. Henna enhanced eyes gleamed interestedly over the gauze veils, their small feet and expressive hands conveying the promise of uncontrolled passions.

★

Gredos, that mighty pile that looks as if it were flung from heaven, lies athwart the centre of Spain. From its dizzy heights, Juan could see the Tajos River, winding far away. On the opposite side, rambling mountains crisscrossed and merged into each other, until they finally flowed into the northern plain. Over this mass toiled the road that he must somehow block. It wound and dipped, to come up at last farther on, then climbing once again until Puerto del Pico was reached. There the road stopped, as if enthralled by the picture below. Heavy mountain boulders swooped down, and from a hundred canyons the rocks had bounded forth, until the valley below looked like the playground of some long-vanished god. In one mass of hairpin bends the road lost height. Romans had stared aghast at this place, and moved on to Fuenfria. Yet man had succeeded here as elsewhere, toiling, sweating, labouring, dying to conquer nature, to further human progress, to come into contact with peoples of another place.

Juan led his small band along the westward side of the Alberche, climbing slowly. It was well past midnight before he called a halt. He had walked long and fast to try the mettle of his companions, for in the future there would be days when they would have to flee like terror-stricken mountain goats from the circle of the wolves.

He had picked out an angle formed by two boulders. This would be a good spot to sleep, for it covered all approaches. Fine sand seeped through the place where the two rocks met, making excellent bedding for tired bodies.

'Well, Tormo,' said Juan, 'you've stood up very well today.'

The man grinned broadly. 'I've observed you, comrade, from the very beginning. This has been our trying-out day. I'll tell you one thing, though, I can still walk all night and feel hungry when we stop.'

Yes, just as Ricardo had told him so long ago in Madrid, this was a dangerous man. How he wished he could smoke. But that would be wonderful for the Civil Guards – a nice little whiff of smoke on a lonely mountainside. They would probably think the mountain goats were having a party, and he grinned at the thought. Between the patrols of cavalry and the long noses of the Civil Guards, this country must be humming. The guns would need cleaning, for the winds of evening had carried much dust.

A sharp-eared fox rounded the northern boulder and stood motionless. Juan nearly discharged his gun at sight of the animal, but remembered himself in time. Now the moon swept over in its graceful trek across the sea of blackness, while the white sand sent back its beaming smile, the rocks turning silver to greet the newcomer. Nature's child slunk away, for, with the smell of grease, powder and man, death was near.

Juan was well on his way by morning, heading for the Tres Sorores. From that point he would command a view of all the mountain ranges, for there was only one peak that was higher, the Muela de Almanzor. From that place, he remembered, the mighty Muslim warrior, Almanzor, had scanned the luckless plains of Spain, soon to suffer his unstoppable inroads. From that peak the warrior had stormed ever northwards, until, with thousands of prisoners and laden with booty, he had returned to Cordoba, there to pour down the throats of his hapless victims the molten bronze from the bells of the cathedral of distant Santiago.

Juan cursed the slopes of lava clinker and loose stones that dragged at his feet. Every two steps he would slide back a foot, amidst a shower of pebbles.

Soon the sun was setting again, but he had achieved his first goal. A wall of granite sheared away from him, downwards, crumbling on to a little lake formed of some long-dead volcano. It was cold at that altitude and dirty patches of snow lay around. Just behind the glassy sheet of water he could see the gaunt fingers of stone, vast monolithic monsters that looked, from a distance, like three old women with bowed heads. And so this startling appearance had given them the name, Las Tres Sorores, the three sisters.

'We have to talk only in whispers,' said Juan, 'and travel in a group only by night. One must be our lookout always, and, since we all know how to imitate a partridge, I think, its song, thrice repeated, will be the alarm. If you hear shots fired, find your way back alone. If you're caught, I think you know what to do. If you fall into the hands of those Civil Guards over there, those dear ones will find a way to make you tell everything you know. Tormo, you'll climb up one of those fingers, and from that perch you'll see a hundred miles. It can be scaled easily on the northern side, or so I've been told. Only let your head show. We'll sleep here tonight, and tomorrow you'll climb up there.'

Tormo's flawless light brown eyes stared at him. Not a discolouring speck could be seen. His were the eyes of the mountaineer, accustomed from birth to dreaming while looking over vast spaces.

Juan lay back and stared up at the illimitable space. Ideals come and go, of this there was no question. Philosophies seemed to be like boulders that were pushed along by the current of life and were smothered or cast aside while others passed over and anon. Progress, success and competition, these three were the awful trinity to whose mighty speed and in whose wake he had chained himself. Now he wondered why he had chosen this particular road. And yet the other road seemed as dark and incomprehensible. Would he have made a different choice if he had to choose over again? He wondered. Tranquillity and peace – that was all he sought. Was it too much to ask of life? Like serried armies rolled the mists of sleep, blotting and erasing the definite forms of thought.

★

Pedro wound his way ever deeper into the Moorish quarter. Every now and again, in a crooked corner or before some dark recess, glowing embers would attract his attention. There, over the ever-present coals simmered the kettle of tea. The figures sat motionless behind their small tables, draped in a burnoose bearing the colours of the *cabila*, or clan, to which the wearer belonged. Beggars in rags, pockmarked, blind or feeble, pleaded for alms, their piteous cries echoing around the crowded streets. He instinctively feared them, their unclean appearance arousing in him a feeling akin to revulsion. And yet the Muslims brushed past these creatures, sometimes dropping money into their outstretched hands without, apparently, being inopportuned by their possible states of disease. He observed the saintly and dignified old men, looking like long-forgotten biblical patriarchs, addressing the wretched beings with their rolling and sonorous, 'Salaam Alai Kum', to be answered in return, 'Alai Kum Salaam', by the crouching figures. And he remembered stories of another figure of another land and another day, his arms around the lepers, his hands raised in blessing.

A long time had passed since Pedro had left Pablo at the doorway of the tavern. He felt uneasy for his friend's fate. Stopping in mid-stride, he turned about and set his face toward their place of parting.

He became more and more fearful as he approached the familiar corner. An excited group of loiterers peered interestedly in through the open doorway of the tavern. Hesitating for a moment on the threshold, Pedro steeled himself and stepped resolutely into the room, shouldering his way through the noisy throng.

The setting for a comic opera greeted his eyes. In one corner crouched Pablo, an overturned table before him. A figure sprawled incongruously upon the floor. Broken bottles were strewn about, the chairs and tables overturned in fantastic disarray. At a respectable distance, three beings, renegades of their religion, outcasts of all societies, dressed in half Moorish and half-European garb, scowled angrily from bearded faces. The sullen bitterness of those who have turned criminal through hatred of humanity burned in their fevered eyes. The bartender lurked in the shadows, weighing the possible outcome, for to the victor would he lend his aid.

And Pablo, undaunted by his predicament, blue eyes flashing in his tanned face, was crying forth his rage and defiance. They were three, and he was but one. Why didn't they come out and fight like men instead of hiding like miserable worms? They must be women to fear one lone man.

Then, seeing Pedro's form silhouetted in the doorway, he leapt over the table, hurling a bottle with great strength as his feet touched the floor. Pedro joined the fray, landing a stunning kick on the side of the man nearest him, his victim crumpling to the floor with a startled oath. The other two darted through the doorway in a flash, elbowing their way frenziedly through the mass of gaping onlookers.

With still no words spoken between them, Pedro grabbed Pablo's arm and yanked him bodily through the door. Pablo grunted in pain and clutched his side. As he brought his hand away, Pedro saw that it was covered with blood.

Death, the Proud Champion

The sage says: Who receives unto himself the calumny of the world is the preserver of the state. Who bears himself the sins of the world is the King of the world.

The Tao Teh King

Morning dawned as ever, and Juan awoke to a cool breeze that fanned up from nowhere. A lark trilled, while farther away a canary tilted its fluted voice to coming light.

He smiled with satisfaction, for he had caught two partridges in the traps that he had arranged the night before. To skin them, feathers and all, he slipped each of the birds through the slit he had made in the skin, running from the breastbone to the tail. Necks and lower legs had been hacked off first. Peeled, the birds were cut into two halves.

With the aid of the practically smokeless dry roots of the tomillo plant, Juan built a small fire in the crevice of a great rock, concealed from view. As he watched the birds, broiling over the tiny flame, he saw himself, as it were, straddled over the fires of destiny, helpless in the grip of the heat and furore of war. Tormo would soon be climbing the great monolith, and they could be on their way about their separate tasks. He felt impatient to be up and about, pitting his wits against the skill and the cunning of the other side. There was something immensely stimulating about the situation. Tonight he would pass over this terrain, and he must know it perfectly. His men would have to search the valley well, for any slips would mean their end. And things to remember – the thousand and one items: remember that glasses flash in the sun, and the sound of a rolling rock can be heard a mile away in this clear air; remember too that the principal interests are the paths used by the patrols to see if they are afoot or mounted and what kind of troops they are. Mules will doubtless spell trench mortars, and the presence of shepherds can be the greatest danger of all, for they are the most implacable foe.

The underbrush began to thicken as Juan descended the hill, so he sought clearer ground among the rocks along the steep sides of the canyon. He bounded from boulder to boulder, pausing every now and again to listen, waiting for the sudden hush of crickets and buzzing insects, accompanied by the rise of birds. Such activity could spell only one thing: the common enemy, man.

He had worked his way down a good mile when some primeval instinct caused him to flatten himself against a boulder. A small pebble jumped into the air, bounding down into the floor of the canyon. He waited in tense silence, cursing inwardly. The primary rules of caution, which to violate in the mountains spelled death, had eluded him over all the months of war. Had the man or men seen him? Were they waiting for him to move out from his place of hiding? No doubt about it, there was at least one man lurking somewhere about, for a wild creature would not have dislodged any gravel.

A soft noise, above and beyond his head, drew his attention. The hand that gripped the rifle was sticky with sweat. It was no place to use a rifle in any case. With agonising care he placed the gun upon the ground before him. Buckling his pistol firmly about his waist, he stealthily drew his knife. Glancing upwards, then, he saw, on a projecting boulder, a young man, seventeen or thereabouts, dressed in shepherd's garb. Even from that distance he could make out the lithe, firm form beneath the shapeless garments. He carried no arms, but a sling hung from his right hand, and to his practiced eye it could be as lethal as any gun. Juan thought of the timeless ruse of throwing a stone to distract the shepherd's attention, but he knew, too, that the keen eyes of the boy would detect the object in an instant. Sheathing his knife, he picked up the rifle and eased himself backwards.

He climbed upwards with laboured breath until he was above the young shepherd. When he calculated that he was more or less on top of the intruder, he edged forward. Slowly the brink came towards his face, and he breathed deeply, seeking to regain his composure. Another inch, and he looked down upon the statuesque form of the young man. His hand was shaking as he drew the knife from its scabbard. He thanked his dead father for teaching him the art of knife throwing when he was still young. Back the instrument went in a slow arc. Then – like a striking snake, the hand snapped forward as a boy throws a stone, the palm upwards and the knife blade flat upon the hand, point up. In the final split second, the wrist flicked forward. A flash, and the missile of death had crossed the intervening space and buried itself up to the hilt in the broad back. A sigh, as a sob, trembled from the suddenly rigid form, and with a shuddering gasp it toppled over the brink. Soon there would be that inexorable speck circling downwards. After it another, and yet another, all advised by their mysterious telepathy of the presence of death for miles around.

*

At last Pedro's long-dreamed-of day arrived. That morning the entire band of buglers, fifty strong, and as many drums, thundered out his last *reveille* in Dar Riffien.

Both he and Pablo were being sent to the northern front, for the situation there was turning in favour of their side. Pedro was happy. He had received the third in line of promotions, while Pablo had lost many points, due to his injury sustained in Tetuan. He had continued to drag himself, by sheer power of will, across the interminable reaches of sandy beach and mountainous background where the deployments had taken place. The word had spread around all right, but no one recognised his condition by any outward sign.

Now Pedro stood on the bow of the ship, filled with mixed emotions. He could hear the distant bark of a dog, the howling of a jackal, reminding him anew of wild and throbbing Africa that lay just behind the thin coastal strip with which men had sought to encase that legendary continent. For thousands of years its winds had strewn over the earth the legends of bygone civilisations, of disappearing peoples, of mythical treasures. Beyond loomed the Atlas Mountains, snowbound and aloof from the teeming shoreline, forest cloaking one side of its slopes, while granite boulders flanked the other, disappearing at last into the endless waves of the Sahara.

The Bay of Gibraltar and its looming fortresses reminded him that Nelson, with calmness and valour, had won his battle with doubling odds. Pedro leaned over the side, suddenly interested in a row of dolphins that had taken up the course of the ship, playing about the bow in their inimitable, boyish fashion. How free and easy were those movements, appearing to accelerate their downward plunge, as their pointed snouts touched the water following a soaring leap into the air. Carefree and gay. For them there was no heart that sorrowed for loved ones and home, no soul that yearned for peace and rest. He wished he were a dolphin, skimming lightly over the waves of the sea; anything but the thing he was at that minute, a machine, practised and tooled and prepared for war and death.

As he stared intently at the waves below, the scudding foam assumed a thousand familiar forms and shapes. He saw again the face of his sleeping brother as he had raised the candle aloft in that long-forgotten room in Madrid. Peacefully he had slept, with the rhythmical breathing of untainted youth, his black curls nestling on the pillow, a frame for the incredibly long lashes that cast blue shadows across his illumined face. He had loved his brother in that moment, loved him as he had never loved before or since. For that face had become a symbol, a symbol of serene peace. And then those great, dark eyes had opened, and the spell had been broken. The lines of ever-deepening cynicism had crept over that face, and the eyes had lost their warm glow. Soon the hard, uncompromising face of a brother that had lost his way had met his eyes. And he remembered that he had prayed late that night – beseeching – imploring – praying that his brother would not be lost for ever. Shapes and forms, flowing out behind the ship like some dark and fathomless spectre. Where had his brother and he gone their separate ways? In the school? Yes, but that had been only the outward evidence of the deeper division. Who cared for that lot of fools with their tangled beards and waving hair who spoke constantly of the day when everyone would be equal? But Juan had cared, had followed them down that labyrinthine path. He had wanted always to be a leader of men and he had never learned how to be led. Juan had sought happiness in his own selfish way but had he been so selfish after all? His father had fulfilled something in life at least. If the sons were fortunate, the family name would be carried on. Juan had taken a stand, and he, Pedro, had taken a stand. Pedro wondered how, in the final analysis, history would deal with their choices.

★

Rolling ground beneath the canyon greeted Juan, and, glancing back, he saw the great peak he had left behind. He had walked for five hours, and yet there was still a long way to go. There were shepherds prowling about. Then he would become a shepherd. Hiding his rifle in a crevice, he secured his pistol beneath his thick, corduroy jacket and walked boldly forward.

A mile away, to his left, he saw the fluffy bodies of sheep. His heart skipped a beat, for he recognised the red fez and the yellowish grey of a colonial *candora*, the half-coat, half-jacket that a Moorish soldier wears.

He was greeted with a long searching glance. 'Where do you come from?' said the Moor.

Juan calmed his inner quaking long enough to smile engagingly. 'Don't you know me? I'm the shepherd that grazes the sheep on yonder mountain.'

The Moor stared at him suspiciously, his hawk-like nose and glittering eyes giving him the appearance of a falcon about to strike. 'No, you don't look like a shepherd to me, nor sound like one.'

Juan's brain was functioning at feverish speed. If the Moor attacked him or took him prisoner it was the end of his mission. If he did, by chance, succeed in killing the Moor, which wasn't likely anyway, there would be a hundred men after him like bloodhounds after the scent. More than likely, someone was already looking their way.

'I've come to buy that big ram yonder,' said Juan, pointing in the direction of the flock. 'Whether you think I'm a shepherd or not is of no consequence. I need just such an animal, *paisa*.' He used the term all Moors have employed since the days of Moroccan warfare, a friendly gesture.

The man answered slowly and deliberately in the clipped, pidgin Spanish that employs only infinitives. 'You've come all this way to buy a ram, and you don't know if the animal's even for sale?'

'Most assuredly. I bring good money.'

'I don't want your money,' said the Moor. 'Walk towards the village along that white path yonder, and go slowly. I'll stand here, and if you turn about I'll shoot you. I don't like you! Go!'

He felt sticky all over. There was neither tree nor shrub behind which he might hide. That Moor would drop him at the first sign of a provocative move, and with a single shot. If he neared the village he would find the questions embarrassing. He cursed his folly for having wandered so far from his companions in his reconnoitring.

He managed a weak smile, though he could feel his knees trembling. 'You lose money, friend. I have to buy a ram someplace. Mine is lying over there where you see those vultures circling.'

The man did not reply, only the lock of his rifle broke the stillness as he snapped it into the ready position. Taking the middle of the path, Juan ambled slowly downwards, desperately seeking for some solution to his plight.

He counted his steps. One, two, three. About a quarter of a mile beyond he spotted a slight dip. Perhaps if he reached that cleft he would be safe, at least for a time. He steeled himself against the urge to run. Pace by slow pace he neared his goal, his practically noiseless footsteps sounding, to him, like the tolling of the cathedral bell in distant Caceres. Ten more steps to go. Now was the time. The muscles in his lean thighs and calves tautened, and he crouched ever so slightly without losing a stride. The right foot went forward. Doubling and leaping in frantic desperation, he crouched again, and jumped head foremost, as the red-hot sear of a bullet tore across his shoulder, followed by the sound of the sharp crack of the rifle. The second bullet whined harmlessly overhead, striking the ground just above him.

This was a serious predicament indeed. The blood flowing from his shoulder wound ran in rivulets down his arm. He was suddenly nauseous, vomiting wildly, even as he edged backwards and tried to look around. His pulse raced even faster as he saw that the declivity into which he had half-fallen merged into a dried-up winter water course that passed under the road. The local citizens would be dashing towards the Moor now. Doubled up in agony and fear, he rushed across the intervening space and dived headforemost into the lip of the road drain. Squirming through in a frenzy of action, he emerged at last on the opposite side, noting with satisfaction that the blood had ceased to flow. He brushed off his clothes with a hurried hand and ran as fast as his legs would carry him in the direction from which he had originally come.

At last, his lungs seemingly at the bursting point, he veered away from the road and set his face for the mountains on the far side. From that point he would have to risk his life in order to signal his men to wait for him.

Without pausing for breath, he ran, leapt and bounded up a narrow ravine, placing his feet with the sure agility of a hunted animal. Pain knotted his shins. His breath came in noisy wheezes. His back ached from running in the crouched position, but he would not give up the flight for even a moment's rest.

Rays of light were appearing over the crest of the disappearing ravine. Juan was nearing the summit with a final great effort. He plunged into the shadowed recesses and lay there panting, gasping for the breath that refused to enter his tortured lungs. His clothes dripped sweat. He was bathed in fire. For two hours and more he had dashed blindly up those jagged slopes.

His time of agony fled past, and his breathing was regular once again. Crawling cautiously from his sheltering nook he saw the road, like a thin ribbon, stretching across the saddle that united the two great mountain ranges. He could see the mighty peak of Las Tres Sorores where Tormo and his companions awaited him.

No doubt they had heard the shots. And then he remembered, with a shock of fear, that he had counselled them to flee upon hearing the sound of gunfire.

He was on a weather-beaten, flattened mountain, its summit formed of one immense granite boulder, dotted with pockets where rain water rested until the wind and sun evaporated it. The water had dug from the sides of that peak, in its constant passage, first a line, then a crevice, and then a fissure. A bush had at last gained a precarious foothold, and, with the attack of ice and nature's elements, quartz had finally given up the battle, and another ravine was begun.

Throwing himself down upon the flat top, he took out his signalling mirror, an item with which they were all equipped. Peering through the pinhole in its centre, he aimed at the three great fingers of rock, six miles away. Catching the reflection of the sun, he flashed once, and then again. His eyes pierced the distance in a vain endeavour to see the crevice where Tormo was supposedly hidden. And then it came – flashing back, one, two, three. He replied with one long, lingering glimmer of light. The prearranged signal. Now the men would leave their posts of observation and go towards the village, nearing the road.

As he skirted the rounded dome of the mountain and plunged downwards into the gathering dusk, he leapt from crag to crag, sliding over the smooth granite surfaces. If it was difficult for his enemies to catch him by day, it would be practically impossible for them to catch him by night unless they used dogs. The dim mass of Las Tres Sorores was still faintly discernible, when with the suddenness of a changing scene, day was projected into night – from bright blue to cobalt, from cobalt to navy blue. The silver stars could not be seen, for his eyes had not yet accustomed themselves to the dark.

Three hours later he was topping the brink that gave on to the lowest part of the valley. Pausing to rest, for he ached desperately in every muscle, he looked around, impressed with the silent stretches of space, bulwarked by the towering mountains that were barely distinguishable against the faint sheen of the stars. Far to the right, on the almost indiscernible distant horizon, a yellow mushroom was slowly appearing. Soon it would become drenching light, revaluing the mimetism of nature.

And as he wended his way towards the middle of the valley, he could barely see the white ribbon of the path that disappeared in the direction of the mighty peaks above. Lookouts of the enemy would most surely be found along this valley floor. He crossed the path and followed it on the farther side. They would not expect him to appear from this direction.

As he feared, the blurred sound of whispers caught Juan's keyed-up hearing.

★

'Wake up,' said Pedro, shaking Pablo's shoulder roughly. 'Our train has reached Sevilla. You've been asleep since we left the port of Algeciras.'

Pablo grunted and rubbed his sleep-laden eyes with closed fists. 'I could sleep for ever, I think. I must've really been fixed up properly in that damn tavern.'

'Yes,' Pedro agreed, 'you've had one rough time of it these past days. But don't say I didn't warn you. Maybe you've learned your lesson.'

'I doubt it,' said Pablo.

The station door opened before them, and with it, the smoke from burning coal and the throngs of humanity disappeared. Wondrous fragrance of azahar, the orange blossom flower, prevailed through the narrow streets of Sevilla. Here, for count-less ages, men had walked, impressed by the awesome splendour of fabulous art. The Greek, the Roman, the Goth and the cultured Arab had left the trail of their passing; the poet, the shadows of his legends; the sculptor, the substance of his statues. Rose-hued towers were surmounted by climbing wild roses, the purest tradition of Sevilla. An old culture of thought and being absorbed in its artistic embrace the driving power of countless warlike invaders.

'Isn't it a shame?' observed Pedro, leaning back against the worn cushions of the taxi that was wheeling them about the timeless streets.

'Isn't what a shame?' queried Pablo, turning his face from the view of the busy city to cast a curious glance at his companion.

'Oh, just thinking out loud, I suppose. I was about to say that it's tragic that all these things we see about us, this city that looks as if it were conjured up from the pages of some legend, could be destroyed in one short hour by bombs. It's taken ages to create this place, and yet two hands on a typewriter could set the forces in motion that would devastate all this glory.'

'Here we go again,' chuckled Pablo dryly.

Pedro sat upright and stared fixedly through the window, the strong lines of his face etched clear and sharp against the glare from without. 'I can't say why, but ever since Dar Riffien I've had the curious presentiment that I'll never live to really feel and know all this beauty that surrounds me, which I've only so recently begun to awaken to.' With a short laugh he settled back again upon the sagging cushions. 'I know what's going through that head of yours, my friend. You're about to say I'm morbid and overly melodramatic. Maybe that's the simple answer. I tell myself that I'm imagining things, it's all sheer nonsense; yet the thing becomes more real to me with each passing day. Just now I saw a figure there in the street, alone in the shadows of a building. I thought of my mother, but then I saw her face. Just another stranger.'

Pablo slid his arm firmly across Pedro's broad shoulders. 'You've been working too hard, much too hard. You've never heard a word from any of your family in all this time. It's certainly not unnatural that you should feel the shrouded figure near you these days. We all feel close to the edge, and all our worlds have been broken to bits by this damn war.'

'I suppose I've no right to feel gloomy,' said Pedro. 'A lot of people are worse off than we are.' He shook Pablo's arm from his shoulders and sat erect. 'Here we're in a fascinating city, with nothing but time on our hands at the moment. I'll keep my doleful reveries to myself, provided you keep your well-meant remarks to yourself. Let's enjoy our stay here. We'll have to see the cathedral. It's supposed to be the second largest in all the world.'

'Now that's like your old self,' returned Pablo, his eyes sparkling in the shafts of sunlight that streamed in through the open window. 'You'd never know there was a war on by the looks of things here, though I suppose there are plenty of empty stomachs here as elsewhere. But before I cease my admonitions, I'll say one other small thing. Wherever you go, friend, you'll always leave behind a wake of loyal followers. They'll remember you as a pretty fine fellow. There,' he pointed out the window, 'I've said it all, and there's your cathedral.'

As they crossed the great square, its surface dotted with orange trees, they were awed by the immensity of proportion and size. In silence they crossed the threshold, the cool dark interior fanning out into breathtaking reaches of space.

All the world, the noise and the tears, the struggle and the grind of life seemed to fade away into silence, with now and then a distant, echoing step, a murmur of a voice, a whispered prayer. Buildings made by man and creeds inherited by man were pondered in the hush of the Christian church, the silence of the Muslim mosque, the quiet of the Jewish synagogue, the stillness of the Hindu temple. Meditation and equilibrium. Here too, Pedro felt the power of thought was present, and yet the chains of imperious necessity demanded the attention of the mind. Floating off into space of higher levels had been rendered impossible; more so, now, with the menacing presence of death in the near future, the blood-red life in the present.

★

Juan held his breath and peered over the brink. Eight men huddled together immediately below him. Orders were being whispered. Their spokesman had decided that the flashes of light he had seen that afternoon proved that their quarry lay in hiding somewhere near the Three Sisters. Patrols of cavalry would keep them from escaping by the road, and it seemed to him that they would most likely attempt to dynamite that potential bottleneck in the road just after the second curve to the incline began. The Reds were angry at failing to break Brunete, and they would do everything in their power to break this supply line. He dispatched his men without further words, and Juan saw two men slip quietly away to the left. Two scaled the steep right bank, and one each crouched in the brush beside the path. The speaker and the last remaining man began patrolling from side to side.

Like a formless ghost, he backed away from them and followed the men who were to guard the farthest brink of the already steepening ravine. They were not of this part of the country, that much was certain, and so they would have no better knowledge of the terrain than he. He allowed them to get a short way ahead, following them by the heavy thud of their footsteps, the occasional thump of a rifle butt against the many boulders. A typical group of soldiers, he decided. Probably thinking to themselves that the enemy had a hundred ways of escaping, so why would he choose this particular spot? After all, this path was one of the very few that led directly into the village where sentries were placed at all times. Surely they would have chosen a more roundabout course, or changed their object of attack. Counting on these things, Juan edged ever nearer.

Now the light of the moon was beginning to give form and substance to that which had been shadow. He dared not attack the two men, that much was clear. And then he found it: his only avenue of escape.

There was still a good half-mile to the end of the slope, and as it tilted upward the way was ever more difficult. The sides began to be great shelving slabs of granite. Juan inched along toward a crevice that had appeared magically under the light of the moon. Steeper and ever steeper grew the great slab, until he found himself spreadeagled upon it. He moved his foot forward with great care, and then his hands, furthering the motion with the other leg.

He dared not increase his speed for fear of slipping, and he was feeling so weak and tired that he knew one false move would send him crashing down among the thickets below. Then he felt himself slipping and sliding, forever gaining speed. The ground rushed up to him. Bracing himself for the inevitable shock, he gripped the hard surface of the granite, the long red ribbons telling the story of his physical endeavours, the slashing and tearing from the corrugated stone. He was stunned for an instant by the shock of the fall.

Strangely enough, no voices hailed his rapid descent – not a stir nor a sound. Slowly he came to his feet, a burning rawness where his knees and hands had scraped along the granite ledge.

And then, as he picked his way cautiously along a chain of brilliantly lit boulders, the chirp of a partridge, repeated three times, rooted him to the spot. As if from nowhere appeared a shadow. 'That was close for you, comrade,' came Tormo's quiet voice. 'I've been watching you for the past half hour.'

Juan fell piqued that Tormo should have seen his approach. He had hoped he wasn't quite so obvious. 'I was only trying to see if you would recognise me,' he said. 'I see, though, that you're as blind as a newborn kitten and have to speak to someone before you recognise him. As soon as you provide me with a drink and whatever you have to eat, we'll have to be off and away from here. We have to blow the road up by tomorrow night, or never. Curse that damned Moor.'

'Yes, we know,' said Tormo. 'We saw everything that happened. Although I lost you when you climbed that mountain on the other side of the road.'

'I'll sleep for a few hours over there between those boulders. Awaken me before dawn. Those stupid soldiers down there have unwittingly told me that the curve in the road is the weakest spot.'

Shadows and light, and in between them darker shadows. The immense clock of the vaulted heavens signalled the passing of time with the changing of its moving pattern. Darkness was around them, touched here and there with the molten silver from the moon. He ached in every muscle and his nerves shrieked for relief. Tiny specks of light could be seen from the direction of the village where a door carelessly left open, or a window un-shuttered, let out the subdued light within. Otherwise all was darkness, and the moon slid slowly behind the looming mountains. Shadows among shadows.

Way of Destruction

Purity is for man, next to life, the greatest good. That purity is for him who cleanses his own self with good thoughts, words, and deeds.

The Venidad of Zoroaster

Juan squatted behind one of the stone walls he had met as they neared the village. This would be his most difficult moment. They would have to move across the road, still more than a mile away, and meet on top of the rising ground that merged with the peak on the far side. The sound of a barking dog would be the signal for his band to group together.

Cautiously he descended the slope that was still in shadow, though the lofty peaks behind glowed with morning colour. Far to the west, the last stars were putting out their lights, as if shamed by the oncoming power of the sun. The plan had been decided upon. Hairpinning down in two great curves, the road, like a ribbon, cut across a steep, rubbled slope that towered above, shearing off for hundreds of feet to the boulder-strewn canyon below. This was the place he would dynamite, starting a landslide that would project thousands of tons of rock across the road, blocking it for days. And his place was well chosen, for the water in its constant quest for easy passage had merged and rutted around a tremendous boulder that held up a large section of the towering mountain.

A great truck came lumbering down the steep slope of the road. The scraping of its brakes could be heard clearly in the still mountain air. Juan smiled grimly. Fate was strange indeed, a hard mistress to follow. If that truck had chosen to pass a few minutes later, driver and passengers would have been crushed to pulp under hundreds of tons of rock. Those men would never know how close they had been riding beside the white clothed figure of death.

Through his musings, he heard the bark of a dog from the direction of the bush where Tormo and the other men were in hiding. He stared down at them, and his thoughts were a jumble of conflicting emotions. The fuse was very short. In order to flee from the action of the explosion and the resulting landslide, they would have to get up and run. Their fleeing figures were bound to attract the attention of guards posted higher up. The small bundles of dynamite had been placed, and now he needed only to ignite the fuse for the explosion to occur seconds later. If he did not answer the signal, the men near the boulder would not move. What were their lives against the bigger picture of war? And yet he had been taught from childhood the sanctity of human life. But clearly there was no choice.

With trembling fingers he lighted a match, shielding the flame behind his jacket. A tiny spark formed in the centre of the seemingly harmless brown cord he held in his hand. With a hiss the light disappeared within.

The earth shook around him, and the boulder was no more. Far up the mountainside, where before grey and brown had been, white appeared. Boulders began to fall, and with a great grinding and jarring the landslide began to the accompaniment of a blinding cloud of dust.

Tormo, with burnt clothes and singed features, stood upright now, shaking his fist in the air. His frantic yells were drowned by the ear-splitting crescendo, and then a huge boulder, as if thrown from a sling, hit him squarely in the chest. His arms flailed outward, and he was launched down into the swirling, yellow dust beneath.

Where before there had been a road, now there was only an ill-formed mass of rubble, a great cloud of dust hanging over the scene. Nature, through the craft of man, had forestalled man's handiwork.

★

Pedro awakened with a rude jolt as the truck lurched to a sudden stop. A pale, rose-hued light mellowed the harsh countryside, and as he peered sleepily around the corner of the truck, rolling, scrubby, treeless hills, now and then broken by great ridges of granite boulders, met his view. Where water had cut its path, bare limestone presented its white face. Far away the jumbled mass of the Pyrenees, and to the south the ridged slopes of the Alcubierre. A tangle of barbed wire bracketed his position, and across a mile-wide valley he could see another series of drought-dried gullies and crumbling slopes.

The River Cinca.

Not a bad location, he decided, though the other side could doubtless say the same thing. If those monkeys over there took it into their heads to attack, they would be picked off like so many partridges running across the floor of that riverbed. But, and the thought paralysed his motions for an instant, he would look equally vulnerable in case of an offensive from his side.

Now everything lay quiet, and only the jumble of wire, the presence of armed men in that usually desolate region, and the occasional crack of a rifle spelled the fact of war.

He climbed down from the truck and walked to the parapet that looked out over the cloud-banked reaches of earth and sky, his eyes coming to rest at last upon the stark whiteness of the riverbed.

So this was war. A jumbled mass of barbed wire and a lot of half-starved men stared at each other across a valley. Somewhere over there, on the other side, was his brother. He flinched unconsciously at the thought. How did he know that Juan was even alive? There was good reason to think he was dead. Warfare; the inevitable clash between two ideals. Juan was bitter, and bitterness was a bad counsellor. He knew that now, but his brother had never learned the age-old lesson that it is better to work with known evil than with unknown good. The whole thing was absurd from the beginning. Everyone knew that things needed to be improved, but it wasn't through a division of wealth that people would become richer. Only the state would become richer, and who cared for that? What did the state care for his childish memories and dreams? It sought only maximum output and would exact it cold-bloodedly. No, he was sure now that he had found the answer on this side. Time alone would be the final judge.

Juan was back in Valencia with the 'well done' of Ricardo still ringing in his ears. Now he was in a sombre mood, sitting at one of the tables of the Cafe Commercial in the old Plaza Real, renamed Lenin's Plaza.

Three o'clock in the afternoon, and Valencia's damp, sticky heat fell on him. Besides, he had come to hate crowds of late, the constant jostling and pushing about.

He clapped his hands for a waiter, and, after a short time, receiving no response, he arose violently, upsetting his chair. A waiter rushed over, thinking his patron would not pay. 'What's all the hurry, *amigo*?'

'No hurry at all,' responded Juan. 'Service seems to be something you people know nothing about, so I've chosen to go elsewhere. How much do I owe you for this miserable drink you call coffee?'

Always he was bothered by people. And that Ricardo person. Juan was certain that Ricardo's interests in Hilda were something more than platonic interest in the Party's welfare. Every time he had tried to contact her since arriving in Valencia he had received the same answer. She was busy and would be unable to see him. He had some questions to ask that woman. It was clear now that she was avoiding him for that very reason.

The waiter looked annoyed but kept his peace. A man in the uniform of the Communist Party, with a tremendous nine-millimetre Astra pistol strapped to his thigh, was no one to fool with. 'Five pesetas,' he replied.

Juan slapped the desired bill down upon the table. All these cafe people were the same, not one whit better than the damned enemy they were fighting.

His steps directed him toward the lower part of the town. Had he but known, he was retracing the steps of that long-dead and practically mythical hero, the Cid Campeador who, mounted on Babieca, his white horse, had taken the teeming castle of Valencia when already a corpse. His reputation as a fighter had been so great that tied on the back of his faithful charger, his body had preceded the array of Christian knights as they had neared the ports of the castle. One look at that form in the saddle, and the old Moorish king had capitulated. He was past his seventieth year, anyway, and life was sweet. All the king wanted from life at that instant was a shaded nook where a pool with a fountain would create the music of coolness behind him, the scent of orange blossoms around him, and the calmness of space for his mind. And so with Juan Avila, as he walked these same streets. Peace for his troubled mind. An illusion and a snare. Peace was a word that had no substance, no tangible form. All of life had become a mad battleground, and the warfare in his mind continually raged.

A tavern appeared before his wandering eyes.

The place held few customers, and the characteristic zinc bar top and gaudy pictures of past bullfights decorated the room. Behind the bar were great barrels in the lower tier, and smaller ones on top, while little signs on the spigots denoted the kinds of wine. From the ceiling hung flypapers, around which buzzed merrily all those that had thus far escaped a sticky death.

'*Salute*, comrade,' smiled the bartender. 'The street is very warm today. What will be your pleasure?'

'A glass of *Priorato*,' returned Juan, 'the heavy wine of Tarragona. Don't bring it cool either, for it cuts the flavour.'

'One needs wine these days,' said the bartender, filling a glass to the brim with the thick, ruby-coloured liquid. 'Our memories play pranks with us at night. For some strange reason, it's only when we are in bed and the darkness around us that we see most clearly what we did, and what we should have done. Isn't that so, comrade?'

More words. A bartender-philosopher. Up in the mountains more was done and a lot less said. The day would come when all these fat *patronos* would be swinging from treetops.

He gave the man a bleak glance, paid for the wine and left. Silence fell heavily on the tavern, only the swish of the beaded curtain at the doorway breaking the stillness.

Tavern after tavern opened their doors to his wandering footsteps and at six o'clock he found himself before the door of Hilda's hotel. With an aimless shrug, he stepped into the lobby, to be confronted by people in city clothes overflowing the couches, the plush armchairs and the soft rugs. Foreigners again, he thought. Two or three Americans were having themselves a gay time in a distant corner with some girls, and the rest were a mixture of French, English, Russian and German. Were these people of the same creed, fighting for the same ideals as he? Never! They were enemies and always would be.

Going straight to the reception desk, he asked for Hilda Krantz, only to be informed that she had left sometime before with a man named Ricardo. Ricardo again! That name was beginning to rankle. No, she had left no messages. He turned away and left as silently as he had come.

The hot sultry night was unbearable. Women, men, and children were at the doors of their houses, leaving the darkness to care for their small, stuffy rooms. The old houses had been taken away from the former tenants and were filled with *milicianos* now. Brilliantly lit, they also exuded humanity. Everywhere was a spirit of unrest, for news had come that German and Italian aviation had taken its toll on cities far behind the lines, and more was to come. What would a bomb do to these densely packed quarters? Though there was a ring of Russian anti-aircraft guns around Valencia, and in the town were various units of Russian Ratas, the latest word in aviation to protect them, they were still uneasy.

His wandering steps took him toward the Lonja, the first stock exchange of the known world, while the moon languorously dripped her light through the unmoving palm fronds. A heavy sky blanketed the earth. But the beauty of art and the poetry of ages were not required. Juan was wrapped in the darkness of his thoughts.

Soft strumming of guitars, singing and the rhythmical beat of palm on palm announced that he was nearing one of the downtown cabarets that was doing a booming business this night, with drunken sailors and drunken officials, and, in a corner, a few people of the Party looking solemn and reserved.

In the centre of the room, garishly lighted, a girl with undoubted gypsy blood was dancing with cat-like grace. Red shoes and brown legs could be seen, now and then, twinkling through the heavy skirt, arms twisting in the lithe movements of ancient Egyptian murals. Her hands expressed the passions that swirled through the mind, her head keeping cadence with the rhythm of the age-old music, coming back with a snap at the end of each musical theme. Her body was sinuous and graceful, like flames that unite smoke and the burning tier. *Flamenco*. Strange music that uses the individual instead of the chorus to express its feeling.

He sat down at one of the few unoccupied tables and a scantily clad waitress took his order. Depositing a bottle and two glasses upon the table, she seated herself across from him. 'Well, moody man,' she said, 'what's on your mind?'

'I asked for one glass,' said Juan. 'I think there are enough clients here to keep you busy.' He spoke without an upward glance, for his eyes were still turned inward upon himself.

Accustomed as the woman was to the rebuffs that society gives to those who flaunt its customs, she inadvertently blushed. 'You people are all alike,' she said, springing to her feet and moving away through the thick pall of smoke.

All alike? Yes, he supposed that he wasn't really much different from the other Party people in the room. Yet he had sought to somehow remain apart from the sordid intrigues that went on about him by day and by night. Perhaps he had failed in this in the worst way any man could fail. He had turned into just the sort of machine the Party sought, and yet he knew that in his heart he would always rebel against the stifling, stultifying force that threatened always to mould him into a final pattern, a yielding and pliable bit of clay for the potter's wheel.

And then, *bolero*, and a second dancer joined the first. They came together, stopped, slithered around one another, with one hand on the waist and the other held high, their bodies arching suggestively and a smile parting their lips. *Bolero*. All in the room could feel the proximity of man and woman. And Juan thought of the scorpion dancing before its mate, the kingbird wheeling high and low. Music, with its rhythm, had opened the doors of imagination to fulfil the promise of the mind.

Hilda Krantz. Out with Ricardo this night. Probably warming his bed this very instant. He felt suddenly ill at the thought. She had betrayed him, the only man who had ever loved her honestly.

And then – was it his overly stimulated imagination? – through the door she walked, Ricardo by her side. Tall and supple; her blonde hair sparkled in the bright shafts of light; her features were as flawless as in the face he had known. A dream? Without a doubt, a dream. And yet she was still there, smiling, and laughing up at Ricardo as he helped her into a chair in a distant corner. Hilda Krantz. How could she do this thing? The girl he had once sworn to love for ever now lost to him through some evil magic. A monstrous organisation had cost him the girl, the only girl he had ever loved.

He was standing beside her then, staring down blindly at her hair, a thousand conflicting thoughts whirling through his brain. And Ricardo's voice acknowledged his presence. She laughed nervously, and he saw a look of fear as she whirled about. From that instant, all was darkness. He did not know that his hand had raised a bottle aloft, bringing it down upon Ricardo's head with a report that shocked the room into strained silence.

All he knew was that he was running like one possessed, while the sweat trickling down his arms and back calmed his interior fever. The billows of alcohol receded under the strenuous action. He slowed to a walk and then to a crawl, his chest heaving mightily under the exertion. He was dripping wet.

He did not remember then, as he would later, that Hilda had cried aloud her love for him in that packed and sweltering place. Not until many a trial had come and gone was he to learn the truth.

Betrayal

Others have taught this maxim, which I shall also teach. The violent man shall die a violent death.

The Tao Teh King

Juan was to learn, too late, that Hilda had betrayed him through sheer boredom. Once, long ago, she had experienced a dream on a train, and that dream had been returning all too often of late to haunt her. There had been the usual blast of the train whistle, the hissing of steam, the cries of station master and conductor, last goodbyes, the hurried steps, the fluttering of hands and kerchiefs. Ridiculous people had run a short way beside the train windows, smiling bravely at those who were departing into a strange and new world. At last came the final movements, a teeming passageway, the organising of packets, suitcases, and bodies. And she had shortly fallen fast asleep.

She had seen herself as if she were a point – far up and above a molten stream of seething lava that streamed past her with the force of life. Along this stream sped lights, with ever-increasing speed, disappearing and vanishing for ever. With the lights had come the music, the music of marches and the beat of drums. And then the shapes. Not limited, yet undoubtedly individualistic, the procession had kept moving on. All had been grey, save for the red under-flow and the yellow gleaming sparks. After it all had come a face, with brilliant eyes of diamond blue. Without a sound the face had shifted past, then, all of a sudden, it turned and pointed a finger at her, coming towards her with fixed eyes, without uttering a word. Bigger and bigger had grown the vision, until her whole sight had been filled with it. There it had stopped! Those lips had opened, and a wordless command had come from them.

What she had dreamed on the train as a young, inexperienced

girl came back again and again, with the same shapes walking on the molten stream, the sparks of light like life flitting away. The thousand memories, the thousand faces, the crawling, pleading forms, and the crushing, violent blows were returning to plague her waking and sleeping hours.

She had felt that she was growing soft. No, she would not let herself come under the influence of Saturn, dark and brooding, who had confided his desperation to mortals as Greece sought to advise humans of the erring propensities of pessimism. She would have to get away. Away from Valencia, with its interviewing of young and old on furlough who answered all her queries with the usual veiled replies that she was unable to fathom. Somehow she would have to break loose from this place, before her mind became as stagnant as the fetid air.

Juan Avila. He had unwittingly given her the passport to greater adventures. All too often such a stratagem had failed, but this was different. Somebody had to do the thinking and the planning, and treason was always a hook that would be snatched up in a country where the enemy had spies everywhere. Juan Avila would be that traitor. He would unwittingly make it possible for her to soar into wider fields of activity.

Once she had felt that she understood the mind of the Spanish people, at least in so far as her specialty, propaganda, was concerned. But why were men of Juan Avila's mettle constantly on two sides of the fence at once, and violent in both extremes? Lack of proper coaching as to Communist fundamentals, she decided, was obviously the cause.

And so she had betrayed him; had opened the way to his eventual death, if so the Fates willed it. Love? Her love for him seemed to have lost itself in the twisting, turning maze of war. The Party had given her the power, the material comforts, the success that she had always sought. The Party, alone, was worthy of her dedication.

Now, as her car raced toward Madrid, she recalled with something akin to terror the evening not so long ago when Juan had finally caught up with her in the cafe. Whose fault had it been? Surely Ricardo had not said enough to warrant his brutal beating in such a fashion, and yet Juan had escaped into the black night, unknown, and, as far as she knew, unapprehended to this day. She supposed it would be her duty to tell the Party the name of the guilty man, but she found it hard to bring herself to do so; love again, that elusive word that became more than a word only when it was least desired. In that hour she had felt a quick flash of the old feeling, the rending, tearing sensation in the pit of her stomach. No, she could not bring herself to report him a second time. Perhaps even now it was too late to heal the breach between them, but somehow, someday, she would try.

The winds of the plains forewarned her that summer was spent and winter was nigh. Soon, those far-distant mountains that seemed to ring every horizon would be capped with snow. People would huddle around their charcoal fires while children, naked and barefoot, would run out with blued hands to seek any pittance the traveller might give them. Animals would vainly search for food that had always been provided for them in the stables. As the wolves come down from the mountains when the thick snow pushes the grazers ever downward, so would man, in the throes of famine, seek whatever he could find to overcome the dire necessities for keeping body and soul together. Ragged figures would lurk in the shadows of government warehouses and supply depots. Children would be sent by their parents to squeeze their emaciated forms through windows and ventilation holes to steal, here a potato and there a few beans. Dogs and cats would disappear, slowly but inexorably, with the oncoming cold as the heat that keeps the body alive would crave more calories to feed the dwindling human flame. Women would forget the troth of tradition and give up their bodies to feed their families. Famine would be known near and far, as if the worst of earth's evils had to be topped. From the Pyrenees would come great, scudding masses of clouds, their yellow rims filled with snow. From the Monegros, the wind would whistle over those bleak and barren lands. As a scythe it would fall upon the untenanted fields further down, shrivelling and burning that which promised to grow. From the mountains, bursting floods would strew havoc along the canyons, uprooting trees and killing the animals that thrifty peasantry had tried to hide. Black would be the cities, and every now and again bloated bodies would glare in lifeless wonder or hate at the winter of tragedy, of man-made chaos.

As she neared Madrid, the ugly and hungry hideousness of the squalid suburb of Vallecas opened its doors. The thud of distant guns announced the presence of the enemy in the still-distant Ciudad Universidad, harassing Madrid night and day. She sensed the appalling change in the town, and she asked the control how things were going. The answer was characteristic enough. They would never pass this line. Madrid would be their tomb, but with their damned guns and aviation they were pounding the city to total destruction. They had already gotten the range of the telephone building, and the Gran Via was no longer safe. Even the Barrio de Salamanca was being bombed, for they seemed to be trying to localise, from the Casa del Campo, a battery or groups of batteries that were in the Retiro. Besides that, there was no food in the city and ugly lines formed every day before the bakeries and the food markets.

Arriving at the Plaza de Atocha, she saw the beautiful Paseo del Prado, its left side practically in ruins. Where once the great Hotel Savoy had stood, there loomed a mass of twisted rubble. People wandered around with dazed expressions, far different than the faces of 1936. Fear and death were everywhere in the grip of chaos.

She found the thoroughfare practically deserted as she drove to the Ministry of War on the broad Calle de Alcala. A soldier ran out, crying to her to get into the Metro station, waiting with its packed humanity for the rain of death from the sky. A nearing whine came overhead as she was pushed inside. It seemed, as it neared, to lose speed and the whine lowered its treble cry. A fraction after there sounded an ear-splitting crash followed by the pungent, oppressive smell of sulphur and ozone.

Voices were croaking out all around her now. There was still another to come, they were saying. Around this time there were always four, and they spread over the cobbled stones like water. Complaints about not fighting back again, and answers about those who talk but live on the fat of the land, rose around her.

A woman next to Hilda glared at her in hate, whispering loudly about the damnable foreigners who live at the Hotel Gaylord and think that they are the great organisers.

Glances, filled with distrust, ringed her round like so many barbed spears. There might be some more bombs, but she was getting out of that place at once. Each day she felt more alien to these people she had once thought she knew so well.

But a rough hand pushed her backwards as she was leaving the entrance of the building and a harsh voice growled, 'Orders are orders, comrade! If you're so brave, go to work in a hospital or go to the front and help out. They need all the help they can get out there.'

The next shell fell far away, only the double report of its explosion and echo filling the silent street. People came from their hiding places, then, like ants after a storm, here pushing aside a hanging door and there pulling on something that had been alive only seconds before.

Badly shaken, she climbed into the car. Paris became an obsession. If she could only get there for one week. It would be different then. She had to think out a plan, so her activities would be conducted in the most feasible manner and so she could acquire some liberty of action that now was practically non-existent. Her political activities had changed of late and for some reason she had been unable to do any effective work at all. Juan Avila had been little help with his attitude on the concentration camps at the beginning of the war. She had never overcome the distrust of men like Ricardo.

She was glad to hear that Rosenberg was still in Madrid. Perhaps he would be of help to her. But as she faced him she saw that the strain was beginning to tell. He looked tired and old. Little did she know that his span of influence was fast nearing its end. Things were not going as he had planned. The Basques were being pushed back and his big campaign at Asturias had fallen through. In the south the front seemed to be holding, but casualties were desperately heavy. Troops of the enemy were pouring through Aragon towards distant Valencia in the east. There was only one solution to the dilemma. The Communist Party would have to take full charge. If he could only win time, then this ultimate success would be achieved. Yet it seemed at times a hopeless struggle. Anarchism seemed to be more to the liking of the people than the sterner disciplines of the Communist Party.

'Where do you want to live, Comrade Hilda?' he asked.

'Anywhere.'

'Now that anywhere you speak of is not easy to find. If you want to be of any use to us, you will have to begin all over again. You're too well known around Madrid, and you haven't accomplished anything in Valencia. By the way, what of that young man? What was his name?'

'You mean Juan Avila?'

'Yes, that's the one. He showed great promise once, and yet I've heard little about him since, and what I have heard hasn't been too complimentary to us or the Party.'

She flushed, averting her eyes for an instant, yet he had caught the expression on her face. He smiled wanly, and continued in the same vein. 'Yes, life plays funny tricks on us, Hilda. I presume you know more about this Juan Avila than you care to discuss.'

'It's not that,' she lied. 'It's just that I know nothing at all about him. The last I saw of him was over a year ago in Valencia, and I suppose he's back at the front.'

'I suppose so,' he agreed, 'if he's still alive. Now, for your lodging place. You'll have to stay around here for ten or twelve days and make yourself as visible as possible. That shouldn't be hard. The war seems to have been gentler with you than it has with most of us. Let everyone know that you're planning to go to Belgium and France to recruit members for the International Columns. Imply that you're going to bring supplies and ammunition, and all the help that the proletariat of the world can offer. This campaign has turned against the people of Spain this year. You'll have to go to the front and talk to the men. Get their impressions. Sacrifice yourself a bit, for it's very necessary just now. We have to get rid of a lot of vacillating characters who are well liked by a considerable minority. Wherever you go, you'll have the support of the Party. And don't try to fool me, comrade. I know all about your activities in Valencia, and especially your little report concerning our mutual acquaintance. He'll be dealt with in due time, but this other work will have to take up your time for now.'

New horizons had opened for her, activity to plan and scheme, and to vanquish again.

Her quarters were in a private house in the once wealthy family abode of the Guindalera, well furnished and luxurious. With a sigh she slipped into bed, drawing the covers tightly about her. Night fell and sleep came on as though pushed forward by the crackle of machine guns, the deeper boom of trench mortars, and, now and then, the crash of an exploding shell. All blurred in her brain as physical weariness overcame the senses. Tomorrow would be another day.

★

The treeless plain that rolled out to the south was nippled by a hill. Hungry eyes looked at that hill from both sides of its smoke-covered cone. Shells had been bursting for the last three days and the moment of attack was drawing nigh. From this prominence the road to Aranjuez was completely dominated, and with it the surrounding dreary fields.

Juan could barely see the hill from his place of observation in one of the ruined buildings of the shunting terminal of the Estación de Atocha. A narrow slit between the sandbags made it possible for him to observe the battleground.

As his vision became accustomed to the gloom within and the light without, Juan saw, all about him, the ruin and chaos that war can produce. It was a bitterly cold day, and in the nearly roofless building the wind moaned through the cracks and crevices. Broken bricks and splinters of decayed woodwork were littered all about. On blackened walls, posters and letterings, bound together with hearts and arrows, reminded the human being that love can bloom, no matter how adverse the surroundings.

Another change of assignment. The whole business would be laughable, were it not such a serious thing. Incredible how much waiting around there was in war; for that moment of violence, that instant of action, there was always an hour, a day, a week of preparation, of suspense. He hadn't imagined that war could be like this. How he longed for those days before the revolution when he had known the thrill, more than once, of addressing, in closely packed quarters, beings whose goad was resentment and whose spur had been envy. Flushed faces and sweaty brows had confronted him, and eyes had been like voids that he, alone, would fill with his ideas. Youths, devoid of havens, had been looking for pilots to guide them across the tempest-tossed sea, and as the crash of applause rang out, it had been to him as the thunder is to the sailor, for when the thunder rolls the sailor knows that danger from lightning has passed. But had it really passed? Was this haven to be found in a war that had already cost a million lives and more, and was the ideal worthy of the sacrifice? He wondered.

And yet here he was, at the front again, before the enemy guns, with death hovering ever near. Life and death: paradoxical enigma that could never seem to resolve itself. To live is to die for the creed of the Church, he had been taught. Yet was this the final answer? Was this the sum of life? Those same followers of the Church, those peasants from their farms, had saved enough money on occasion to go into the city. The theatre, the films, and even the newspapers for those who could read, had told them another story. A society had prevailed through corruption and influence, while they slaved and worked. They, too, began to see themselves, in their dreams, in houses, going to bullfights, attending the best schools, well clothed and no longer barefoot. And then they had awakened to grim reality, plodding forth like a castrated bull with neither fun, nor spark, nor life. Was this all that the Holy Church had to offer? Was this the good life of the brotherhood of man?

A blue-eyed young man, clad in leather, came up to him. Speaking in the rolling French accent of Marseilles, he said, 'We have a couple of companies of tanks in those buildings to your right. Once those buildings were part of the Villaverde. The tanks are the latest Russian models, and they say they'll do wonders. They've already been tried out in the battle of Brunete, where, had it not been for the incredible stupidity of certain leaders, we could have marched straight on to Navalcarnero. We could have cut off all the supplies for this entire front from there. The tanks will be coming out in half an hour or so, and the brigades will attack immediately after. They'll cross more or less diagonally in front of us.'

The pall of smoke around the knoll grew in density, and, as

Juan peered out from the rude shelter, he felt himself curiously abstracted from this play of tragedy, victory and, perhaps, defeat. He could see the helmets of the men, moving restlessly among the masses of twisted rubble a few hundred yards away, extending in a great half moon before the shelter. Full of the desires and passions of the young, those men had harnessed those forces to the cloth of uniform, the yoke of arms. Fanatical in creed, they sought to defeat those who were opposed to them. And what of that great balance? The balance in which losing and winning hung was read only through that telltale pendulum that swung slowly at first, and then ever faster to the winning side. Before that motion, what aspiration? What wishes and thoughts crossed through each and all of these competitors for success?

A rat scurried across the rails where ice had formed in the drying puddles. Here and there, little clusters of snow tried to hide in their soft whiteness the hard grey of the silent ground, as cold and meaningless as his life at that moment; as desolate as his future. And where would he go from here? What bleak goal awaited his searching heart? He wished, of a sudden, that things had somehow been different. Perhaps if he had worked a little harder to follow the doctrine of the Party, had spoken more often of the importance of the world revolution, he might even now be in the arms of Hilda Krantz, instead of courting death in this hellish place. Was it true that a man, having once set his hand to the plough, dare not look back again? That seemed to be the case, and yet that was too simple, too much of a pat answer. No, life was a series of complications, growing more complicated each day. First there had been his youthful wish to struggle against all that he had known in his childhood, the frantic desire to throw off the chains of custom. Hilda Krantz had captured his heart for a time, that heart that reacted like a wild thing, fickle and untrustworthy in moments of greatest need for positive reactions. And yet her own heart had rejected him at a time when he needed her most. Forced to choose, she had not hesitated to cast him aside. From then on, all had been darkness and madness: his constant shifting from assignment to assignment and, even though he had been commended by the Party for his mission in blowing up the road, a coldness, an aloofness, and a suspicion about the 'accidental' deaths of his comrades. So even then, in his sacrifice of human lives for the Party's cause, they had found occasion to question his sincerity. Now he was cooped up in this observation post, readying information to be relayed to those agents who would recruit French and Belgian volunteers for the international columns.

With a visible start, he peered through the narrow slit in the wall. Like little beetles, first one and then two tanks came from the tangle of ruins. Time to put on his helmet. The aviation would surely be over soon, for a distant murmur was growing in intensity. He saw arms of the scattered soldiers pointing upward from their huddled positions. Then, far up, like a flight of ducks winging from the east, he saw the dots grow into a recognisable form. Three... six... nine. And to the left the same formation. About him were the usual reactions of the human being towards death, violent and unpredictable death. How many times had he heard Hilda Krantz talk about the ways the body could be mastered and subdued through sacrifice for the creed, how discipline could command the weakness of instinct? Yet here he was, fumbling with icy fingers at the chinstrap of his helmet. What was wrong with it all? Hadn't she spoken to the youth of nations in packed halls and stadiums? With the inspiration of her words the thousands had risen to their feet as one, the rhythm and words of the *Internationale* making whole cities shake with their power. But those words had failed to convince him, had left him untouched. What brand of creature was he that, of all men, he alone remained aloof from her ideas? He had loved her with all the power of his being, and yet his inner mind had rebelled against that force that upheld her, that had made her the woman she had become.

'Here they come,' said the blue-eyed soldier. '*Salud*. If those damn German planes hadn't come along, it would have been so easy. Now I'm not so sure of anything any more.'

A rising wail came from the sky, ever increasing in its pitch.

'On your face!'

The very world seemed to burst about him; hot and heavy explosions like the thump of a giant fist upon a great pillow. Dust and rubble were falling all around, and one of the buildings next to his shelter seemed to disappear, as if some gigantic child had become tired of his little constructions. Then, after an eternity, silence, and the receding drone of motors.

No Hiding Place

> And the kings of the earth, and the great men, and the rich men, and the chief captains, and the mighty men, and every bondman, and every free man, hid themselves in the dens and the rocks of the mountains; And said to the mountains and rocks, Fall on us, and hide us from the face of him that sitteth on the throne and from the wrath of the Lamb: For the great day of his wrath is come; and who shall be able to stand?
>
> The Book of Revelation

Hurrying forms scuttled from place to place, and Juan saw others carrying stretchers, appearing as if from nowhere, forming later the procession of those whose lives had changed, never again to be as before. In this procession would be those who had touched the world, and would touch it again, finding interested listeners so long as their conversations remained optimistic. These listeners might be of the same creed, but they would always want to know that victory had been won through the toll of their sacrifice. Time would pass, and their conversations would be repeated; while others would come along with the same tale of sacrifice, and without success as their companion. Bitterness of disbelief and the sadism of jeers would become their final comrades. Who cared one whit about a man who could no longer work, simply because he had gone to another country to fight for an ideal? After all, the healthy and the strong were competing for that maimed one's occupation. Life would have to continue, and success would have to be achieved. One more derelict would be formed, with only bitterness and defeat for himself, and repudiation from his fickle and fleeting followers, only a dead weight to the churning machine that had to move ahead.

He felt cold and numb. All the squalor and filth that battle leaves behind were around him. Here, an old sock; there, a burnt piece of wood; while farther on a discarded tin glinted feebly through a layer of dust. All were bound together, now, by the biting winter winds that seemed to laugh, mocking the tragedy of mankind enacted by a day, a year, a lifetime. These same winds had, with their soft fingers and jeering cries, moulded the granite on which man counted to protect his fear-torn body. A strange being, man: in moments of triumph, that being knew himself to be all in all, the sum of all creation; yet, in times of distress, man turned always to that infinitely greater being who, alone, can bring triumph to a soul steeped in tragedy. Triumph and tragedy; the sum of life. And this was his life: tears and laughter, sorrow and warmth, triumph and tragedy; the tears of unrequited love, and the laughter of childhood innocence; the sorrow for a family that would for ever be doomed, and the warmth of passionate desires fulfilled. Triumph and tragedy, the culminating forces of life and death! But what of this longing, this eternal gnawing yearning in a heart that would not, that could not find rest? He had loved, and he had lost that love, and now only the thick pall of smoke around a knoll, the inferno of diving planes, the shrilling of whistles, were the tangible forms of reality.

Like small wisps whipped away from a cloud bank by a relentless wind, here and there a lone man, and then a small group, climbed over trenches and ran, doubled forward, sprawling out to lie inert and still. And always, there was another to take the place of the fallen, while the clock stopped and life faded away. Cries of agony mingled with the shriek of falling shells. There was the bright red of blood upon the grey, cold ground.

Wretched refuse of war teemed and rolled about him like some endless sea, a sea of faces and an ocean of death. They rolled in masses upon the hard ground.

And night came on, a night filled with his bedraggled companions clustering in dejected groups, seeking to console each other with the thought of the thousands of shells that had landed on the enemy trenches. The sky was lit with the glow of a hundred burning buildings, the symbols of a pyrrhic victory.

Juan met the captains of the companies that had taken part in the unfruitful attack that day in an old barn that had once served as a storage place for hay. Men of different nationalities confronted him: Germans, Spaniards, French and Belgians, but not one Russian. As usual their great allies were absent when needed most. He flushed at the thought. Words and more words, and yet action was something that seemed to be alien to their natures.

He spoke to them, as persuasive and powerful in his speech as ever, but with no conviction in his heart. He had seen this day of battle, and it was only through the help and arms of other nations that the will of the people had been thwarted. But this had been the case only for today. Tomorrow and in the days ahead the world's peoples would raise their heads and see what was happening to the valiant race of men and women that had suffered so much for so long. It behoved the International Communist Party, the only group that thought in terms of the entire world and not of a single nation, to save these people from that nucleus of society that had ruled them, and was desperately trying to win back the authority that they knew they were losing. They must all measure up in the days ahead, for he who failed would be condemned as an obstruction in the path of progress of the Party, and as a weakling who had allowed his instincts to win over the directing force of will power. He sought to impress upon them the difficulties under which the Party laboured. The will of the people was behind this movement, but the governments of the capitalist nations were standing in the way. They would have to expect hard times, for even with the success of their cause in Spain, the work would be far from finished. There were a lot more countries that needed subduing under the creed of the proletariat.

Words, words. He was mouthing words now, and he knew it: words that had lost all meaning to him, that had ceased to have depth or perspective. How easy it was to talk; how difficult to believe.

He made his way to his car, leaving behind him the black earth with its patches of dirty snow and grey, crumbling walls. Another day would dawn, and the knoll would still be there. There would still be a few buildings left standing, and the wind would continue to moan and sough its way through leafless branches and broken windows, carrying with it one more history, one more page of the book of life.

★

Hilda found herself the centre of attraction. She was relaxed and gay again, flowing with that warmth Juan Avila had once found so irresistible. Overwrought and nervous in the midst of war-torn Spain, she was again that creature of charm and seduction she had been in those few fleeting, golden months before the war. The multicoloured picture of that most fashionable of cities, Paris, had fashioned a blanket on which she could lie down, logically disposing of her troubled feelings. No longer was she surrounded by faces torn with distrust, revenge or fear. No longer was she oppressed by hard, granite boulders, by great crest lines of mountains that surged on like waves of the sea, flattening and crushing all that opposed their wedlock to time.

She had been returned to Paris after days and weeks of effort on the Spanish front. Those days of darkness were behind her now, and the easy and imaginative speech of mankind's problems came easily in the aura of comfortable surroundings as did the quoting of books of bygone ages. Poets and musicians could interpret the passions of mankind in words and rhapsodies; yet how different was the picture that now and again crept through her thoughts in the stillness of night, of bloated bodies, of shattered ruins, of a torn and burnt earth where only the faith of creeds could sustain waning life.

A young artist, clearly of Polish extraction, toasted her silently across the room. She returned a gay smile, raising her glass, sipping, blowing a kiss from its sparkling rim. He wended his way towards her through the clusters of men and women, his pale green eyes giving him a look of eternal impudence.

'Well, Andre Dubrowsky,' she said. 'I haven't seen you in years. When was it, anyway?'

'Too long ago to be comfortable,' he replied. 'Besides, I'm afraid I was a frightful boy in those days, hardly old enough to even smile at you with hope in my eyes.'

'Such words,' she said, 'are calculated to get a girl off-centre, I'm afraid, but you should know that I'm not exactly a peasant on her first visit to the wicked, wild city.'

'As to that, how can the stars afford to look up at the moon?

You've always been so surrounded by courtiers that a nobody like me would never stand much chance.'

'And how are things going with you?' She had led him to a small divan, strangely unoccupied and apparently unnoticed in the midst of the throng. 'I hear you've been doing pretty well in your work.'

'Well? Perhaps you're joking. They seem to think I'm much too conventional, and conventions are not exactly the pearl of highest price these days.'

She smiled and gestured to a passing waiter. 'Another cocktail please. Andre,' and she turned to him, 'you've never been very conventional with me. Besides all of that, they tell me you've become one of the most popular young men in all of Paris, and most desirable as a companion.'

He shrugged his shoulders, and placed a cigarette between his lips with slender fingers. 'Enough of all that. How're things with you? The papers tell us that the Republican government is winning all along the line and that those rebels will be pushed back, right out of Spain as a matter of record.'

Hilda hesitated for an instant, as if framing her words. 'Yes,' she said calmly, 'it just so happens that I accidentally got myself involved in that war when I went to Spain the last time. I was interested in the colour schemes of Sorolla and the country that's been depicted by Ybanez. All of a sudden I was in Valencia in the middle of a revolution.'

Her companion looked at her with a strange smile on his face. Taking his smile for approval, she continued to relate her story, her view of the progress of the war until then. The war could have been stopped, she was saying, if only the people would have helped. Unfortunately the countries of Italy and Germany had been testing their war equipment upon the poor, helpless people of Spain who were only trying to uphold their national liberties. But, and her words had taken on new colour, all that would change, and soon. The government troops were doing exactly what Andre had indicated, pushing them back irresistibly. Some day the youth of the world would realise what was at stake. Then the story would have a happy ending. How she wished she could believe her own words. Things had not been going well, not at all.

The Republicans were on the verge of general rout, and yet the game was not lost, provided she could secure enough funds and volunteers from France to ensure the continuation of the war until the Communist Party had sufficient time to consolidate its positions.

Each day she knew more and more the need for an outlet for her pent-up emotions. Those emotions had lain dormant for thirty years, locked up in the dark recesses she had built around her character. Juan Avila had tapped those passions for a time, had almost succeeded in tearing down that wall of defence, but Ricardo had decreed that they must separate for the good of the Party. The good of the Party – everything seemed to be for the good of the Party! And Ricardo, no doubt, still was suffering from his cracked skull. Fortunately, the man had been too embarrassed by his relationship with her to press charges against Juan, choosing instead to secrete himself in his quarters until he should recover from the violent blow done both to his body and his pride. All that control she had once sworn was her major asset, was being broken down, shattered bastion by bastion, even as some besieging army of old had relentlessly crumbled the defences of long-thought impregnable fortresses. And again she remembered the half ironic, half tragic expression on the face of Schmidt on that day so long ago, the day she had felt his nervous hand on her arm. She had known then the only answer to his plight, and his eyes of diamond blue had pleaded silently with her, longing to be understood. But she had thought only of the tragedy of the organisation being stopped in its tracks through the blunderings of one man in a position of responsibility.

What was happening to her of late? She realised, with horror, that her individuality was coming to the fore once again in all its basic form. She must somehow subdue that driving force, if only for a night, a day, a week. And yet it seemed to her that it was a losing battle, for how could she for ever fetter the longings of her heart? Yet how could she rebel against that very thing that she, herself, had taught and advocated, the thing that had made her what she was? Oh fickle and perverse heart! She wished she could tear the thoughts from her mind.

Action, alone, was the way to escape these damning ideas. She was growing weary, again, of her assignment; the usual contacts, the dull conversations, the tedious flattery of words and deeds. Her real work in recruiting had not yet begun, of this she was certain, for she would have to reorganise from the top to the bottom. She must somehow find a way to persuade a group of young men, through their natural credulity and enthusiasm for adventure, into a single unit. Somehow, someway she had to enlarge the International Brigade. Someway she must prove to herself as well as the Party that her role was not altogether one of uselessness.

'Hilda, come back to earth.' The voice of Andre Dubrowsky buzzed in her ears. 'You've been a million miles away on some distant planet.'

'What?' She took a deep breath, lifting another long-stemmed glass from a passing tray. 'Let's drink a toast, Andre. To Paris – the city of love and colour,' and she smiled deep into his impish green eyes.

★

As he sipped his glass of wine in the fetid atmosphere of the unventilated cafe, Juan considered the fortunes of war. How simple it was in life to commit a grievous error, and how quickly one's enemies grasped that mistake and waved it aloft; yet, how difficult to maintain the line demanded by the Party, and how seldom was due praise accorded him. Anyone could make a mistake, yet the Party had no place for the seemingly natural weaknesses of mortal men. Rather, those weaknesses were to be preyed upon, exploited for the greater cause. Again he had reported to headquarters, only to receive the usual cold reception, and the usual icy stares of disapproval. Discouraging.

He had thought to be gay that evening, but his increasingly bitter mood had taken hold of his spirit. All about, the city was held in the thraldom of terror and death. The black-faced houses and the darkened streets, armed *milicianos* on the corners, revealed only by the flickering gleam from glowing cigarettes, and in the distance the booming of exploding shells, the rattling of machine gunfire.

Tomorrow he would return to the front.

Tomorrow death would stare him in the face again, and suddenly he was afraid. Afraid of the darkness and the cold, afraid of the rain of terror from the sky. Death. Death and life and all the myriad facets that composed them. Working and striving and labouring. And for what? What rhyme or reason could there be to this jungle, this oppressive jungle of life that crowded in around him on every side? Birth and life and death, and all a part of the meaningless pattern of existence. And always in his breast the gnawing hunger for something more than he knew. There must be more to life than this insane comic opera existence, this mad rushing through a world filled with all the horror and terror of the great unknown beyond the veil. The great unknown was always there, waking or sleeping, for ever mingling with his thoughts and desires, for ever trailing him down the labyrinth of his days. Damn the great unknown! Damn the Church! Damn all those who had taught him from earliest childhood that there was a judgment to be faced one day! Damn all those who had filled his mind with fear for an unknown, blind future! The Party had told him that he was the master of his own destiny, a destiny cradled and nourished by the supreme power of the earth, the Communist Party. Only the Party would be his judge, only the cold faces of the Party leaders could pronounce his doom: the cold faces, and the hard, unblinking eyes.

Madrid. The city that he had known and loved. He had known every nook and corner of her, had known the history and whispered legends of every building, of every fabulous personality. Madrid. No longer the city of smiles and song, the city of gaiety and laughter. Death, and darkness and chaos, and its inevitable surrender to that power he had once sought so valiantly to overthrow.

The crackling of exploding shells was growing in intensity now and the hush of doom had fallen upon the city of death. No hiding place. No place to flee from the desolation that confronted him.

And tomorrow the front again, and the strange faces would confront him, the questioning, cynical, doubting eyes. He wondered how he would react this time, such a long time since that initial campaign at the River Cinca.

As he left the building and proceeded down the street, the straight lines of the Calle de Alcala seemed to him, at that moment, like the future prospects of his life. Parallel lines of rails and houses limited the course of his fate, merging through perspective into a point. When he stopped, the distance would be the same. Only when he moved would that vortex recede in front of him, never to be obtained, never to be known.

★

Hilda knew the source of the kind of power now needed in Spain: vigorous youth, the power upon which creeds prey. In its happy sacrifices, little does youth heed the voice of future convenience, but rather, seeks death to form the seeds of martyrdom, those seeds from which ideas are born and creeds are spread. She was convinced that it was not so difficult to imbue the working, prostrate, desperate masses with the concept of world revolution if poverty was their environment. She had experienced poverty, had seen the flame flickering at the top of the ladder of Communism, had striven ever since to capture that elusive beacon. That mass, driven by the hoot of factory chimneys, the silent spectre of a time clock, and at breaking point through monotony, could be poured in a raging, unstoppable torrent if the leaders could only be found to channel that force. She knew, now, that those longed-for leaders would only be found among those who had time to concentrate upon thought, who had the surge of destruction ingrained in their very natures. These must be the ones that would destroy, to rebuild afterwards if necessary; but first must come destruction. They must crush, with the blow of a titan, the crumbling framework of the Christian civilisation. Now the pincers were open, and the clenched fist of her symbol must be the power that would close those pincers. And yet she knew that the hand was slipping, the groping fingers were being severed at their base, for they were not receiving the stream of life.

At the beginning she had felt that she could handle Dubrowsky, but she found she was becoming far more interested in him as a man than her purpose dictated.

She awoke, now, with a foggy brain, staring about the room in the grey light of early dawn. With groping fingers, her hand moved across the bed. Alone. Yet a certain disorder appeared about her. Empty champagne bottles, a broken glass upon the floor, a large red stain where spilled wine had seeped over the thick carpet.

With a grimace of distaste, she threw the sheets from her body and felt about on the floor for her slippers. Andre Dubrowsky! She wondered what had happened the night before. With an audible groan, she sought desperately to piece together the jigsaw puzzle. A puzzle all right, but a puzzle with certain large and important pieces missing. They had gone to the theatre: a musical, she remembered, and rather a dull one at that. Then to the Moulin Rouge for cocktails and a late dinner. After that? She didn't, she couldn't, remember. A blank, she had drawn a blank on the hours, that followed, and the feeling wasn't very pleasant. What had she said? She knew too well what she had done.

Suddenly she was glad that she was leaving Paris for a time, to recruit more followers from the outlying districts. Thank whatever gods might chance to be around for that. At least she wouldn't have to face Andre this day. With a sigh, she lifted the phone and called for a taxi.

Like the mists of the Seine, the endless passing of barges over its smooth surface; like spring and summer, autumn and winter; from Charleroi to Lille and from Lille to Lyon, and often to Antwerp, she wove her threads like the Arachnidae. Success had begun to smile upon her mission at last, yet Andre Dubrowsky still steered clear of the net, that impish smile at the corners of his eyes giving silent answer to her verbal reasoning.

'What a learned person you are,' he said when next they met. 'Why don't you become a professor at some university? You'd even look well in those awful black cassocks and ungainly, four-angled hats they're supposed to wear. Let's live and be merry, my dear. If I understand you right, you want me to join somewhere in something I know nothing about, and for that matter don't want to know anything. Well, perhaps your interest in me isn't quite the same as I had at first imagined.'

They were at Dubrowsky's studio, and champagne had been

flowing all the while. Reclining on a divan, her closely cropped hair tousled, and a provocative smile on her lips, she turned her finely chiselled features towards him and said, 'Andre, I thought you were a brave man.'

'Brave?' He laughed, and filled his glass to the brim again. 'My dear Hilda, bravery is for fools.'

'I'm not so sure,' she said, 'for fools are men I've been living and working with for these past three years then. You wouldn't sacrifice this stupid little studio and your small world of comforts for anything, would you?'

He leaned back and laced his hands behind his neck. 'Frankly, I've never been faced with that problem, and new things are not to my liking. The strange and the macabre have never appealed to me, except perhaps in women. In the case of women, strangeness is an asset.'

'You don't say?' She glared at him for an instant, and then settled back again with an impetuous gesture of her slim hand. 'Oh well, so much for that. The fact remains that if you'd follow me you could acquire power, such power as you've never imagined. You'd no longer be the pawn of critics and nagging dowagers.'

'I must say,' he grinned broadly, 'the latter aspect strikes my fancy and appeals to my better nature.'

'Be serious, Andre,' she said sharply. 'Do you know what it means to have *power*? You'll have the power to make and undo, to create or eliminate anything or anybody. At your slightest beck and call, hundreds will dance in the palm of your hand. Andre, you're an artist, so you can imagine the complacency for he who can mould bodies into a single unit, modelling them to his will. Finally you'll mould them to that will that's greater than life itself. For this thing doesn't belong to any one man, it belongs to all the world. This is the creed that will succeed when the steaming ruins of this misery will be broken embers under the heel of the conqueror.' She glanced up at him to confront a changed face.

A rigid black line arched those strange and changing eyes. Dubrowsky leaned over, and, grasping her arm, pulled her roughly to her feet, his powerful clutch bruising the bare skin.

'Daughter of Satan,' he said, 'do you know who my mother

was? She was a lady of St Petersburg long ago. Is that enough for you? I've seen through your little game from the very first day we met, you harvester of death. Once I thought of you as a woman, in spite of it all. I've preyed upon you as a mantis preys upon other insects, holding its victim away from its body. I've held you away from my heart. Wherever you've gone in this world, for you're much older than you appear, you've strewn sorrow and disgrace. For once you've failed to get your pound of flesh. And now, get out of this room, and never come back again. You've been taken for what you are!' With this, he unceremoniously pushed her out of the door and slammed it shut.

Uncontrollable sobs shook her frame. She had been laughed at, mocked and spurned. She had been used, for once, as she had used so many others.

Hours later, her hands behind her head, she stared into the blackness of her room. A hundred sounds came to her, wafted through the night: a creak – a door banged loudly – a horn in the distance – voices floating up from the street – laughter. Her mind did not focus upon the sounds. The mesh had been broken. For the first time she really doubted with all her being. She had been beaten at her own game, and with it came fear, the same fear she had known fleetingly in the past.

This time the cold gripped her very vitals, and icy chills around her heart smothered her in the weight of fear. From the chaos of her mind only one hand came forward, outstretched as a support. The hand was tapered and tanned, and it beckoned her back to a land she wished she had never known. In that land had begun the doubts, the black figures of remembrance, the shrouded forms of fear, to haunt her steps in the ever-descending path that she knew by instinct would lead her to death.

Edge of Doom

Which is the place where light dwells, and which is the place of darkness?

The Book of Job

'Comrade Hilda,' said Ricardo, eyeing her coldly, 'this isn't exactly a brigade you've formed in all these months.'

'It was the best I could do under the circumstances.'

'And what,' he said, 'were those circumstances? My reports show me that you've attended more cocktail parties than the number of men you've managed to enrol.'

'Things are extremely difficult in France,' she said lamely. 'Rest assured that cocktail parties are only a very necessary part of our little game.'

'You don't say. Well, perhaps you'd be interested to know that you've had every facility of money and assistance, and every door was opened to you ahead of time.'

'Those doors,' she said, 'have a peculiar habit of slamming shut whenever you approach them.'

'Excuses, excuses!' He thundered the words, rising to his feet and pacing back and forth. 'All I hear these days are excuses.'

'It's not a question of excuses,' she said. 'It's a question of being realistic. Things are not what they once were, you know.'

No, things were not as they had been, of that one thing she was certain. She felt tenseness about her; the walls were hemming her in. Now she knew the fear that she had seen in Schmidt's eyes, the tenor in his voice.

'Let's see now,' his voice droned on, as he seated himself and flipped through the pages of a voluminous book on his desk. 'You say we should be realistic. All right, let's be realistic, then. You've recruited a hundred and seventy-five men, out of whom only seventy-eight have crossed the border.' His bottle-green eyes, those changing eyes, looked at her as if she were not a human being at all, only a piece of machinery, a unit, a cogwheel that might have to be replaced. She had failed, and failure could mean only one thing. Ever since she had come to Spain, he was saying, she had made a disaster out of everything she had attempted for the Party. She had been told to use Juan Avila, and instead had allowed her ridiculous romanticism to control her will. It looked as if Juan had made use of her. Furthermore, she had decided she didn't like her life in Valencia, and so she had trumped up a fantastic charge against Juan Avila in order to advance her petty scheme. It had nearly cost him, Ricardo, his life. That charge remained unproven and had served only to further complicate matters. She had managed to get the Communist Party into a perfect turmoil, as if her small desires were of any significance whatever. From all this disastrous business she had been sent to Paris, where he had hoped she would somehow redeem herself and justify her place in the Party. Instead of justifying herself, she had returned almost empty handed. There was no room in the Party for inefficiency and stupid blundering. There was no place for that person who could not learn to rise above petty personal desires. She would go to the Hotel Colon until further orders were received, and she was to see no one.

He stopped and waved his hand at the doorway. The interview was at an end.

A bewildered Hilda left the office. What could she do? To whom could she turn? How could she stop this red-hot molten stream that, like lava erupted from a volcano, menaces with its slow and devastating force the village beneath? Darkness was encroaching, and the light was far away. That beacon at the top of the ladder had slipped from her grasp again, and she felt bewildered, lost in the maze of her mind.

She remembered that February night in 1924 when she had packed her few sorry belongings, leaving a letter for her father. Flickering lights had reflected on the wet surface of the street, and stormy rain clouds had trailed across the sky. It had been bleak and cold, and her cheap shoes had let in the dampness when she had walked only a short way. How had she felt on that day, so long ago now, when she set her face towards a new life, a new adventure that promised so much, but had really delivered so little?

Vienna. She remembered that her first stop had been Vienna, and the thrill of that first train ride seemed strangely clear. She had awakened, that day, to a drizzling morning and the flat lands had been left behind. The train ran between rolling hills that sharpened their profiles as they ascended. Later in the afternoon it steamed into that town of beauty and splendour, of grace and music, where art is felt more than seen. From the great parks and palaces, from the winding Danube to the beaming countryside around, it had been for her the one and only Vienna, once heart of a tremendous empire, seat of learning and political intrigue, where diplomats clashed wills over the lion's share of Europe. There slavery had been banned, and pacts of kings were brought to dust through treachery and greed. There every foreign invader had left his mark. Vienna had been, for her in that hour, like the great pyramids of Egypt, the temples of India, and all those historic marks whose skeletons may pass away, yet whose life throbs on for ever, even as the Danube was flowing down, taking with it the scenes of mountain grandeur, the songs of cities and the fragrance of roses from the southern plains.

So her new life had begun, a strange mingling of old ways with revolutionary ideals. And she had known moments of glory, times of power, and yet that glory and that power had somehow slipped from her clutching fingers, that glory she had sought had turned to ashes before her eyes, that power had melted away. How could she have been so foolish? She had allowed the numbing, paralysing force of love to overrule the clear dictates of her mind. And yet she could not really complain. She knew that now, when it was too late. Whatever life had meted out to her, whatever fate held in store, she would know that nothing could ever destroy her love for Juan Avila. But it was all too late, much too late. He was gone from her life, and she had driven him away by her incredible stupidity. How she wished he were with her now, his strong arms around her, his strong, protecting arms. She longed to hear his voice again, the tender words of endearment.

'Juan, Juan, what have I done?' she said, and was startled to discover that she had spoken aloud. Somehow she would have to take herself in hand, learn to control herself. Even now it might not be too late. Ricardo had said she would receive further orders. Perhaps she would have a chance to redeem herself, a chance for life.

But no, she needn't try to fool herself. She thought of the endless rolling of the sea, never an attractive thought before. Yet, beyond that sea there would be a chance, a hope. Hopeless! What escape could there be from this mighty organisation that sent its tentacles into every land and every city and town? She knew, better than anyone else, the final results of this movement of silent pawns towards the end of the last game of chess. The falling of the king would be but another name added to a black list.

★

Juan heard the drop of water as it fell upon the clay floor, as had its predecessors, forming a small cavity. Then another, filling it up. When the third came to add its volume to the first two, there was a splash and an overflow. The trickle of water ran down the slight incline, forming in its passing a line that wove crazily around, disappearing at last beneath a rock.

He had been watching this everyday phenomenon with fixed attention for the past half an hour. It soothed him to see such effortless comings and goings, such forming and transforming. He turned away, then, and levelled his field glasses over the brink of his dugout, focusing them out over the roaring new flood of the River Cinca below. 'They're very busy over there,' he said. 'Our orders still stand, however. We'll have to wait for them to make the first move, I suppose, and be chopped down like rats in a trap.'

A muted chorus of agreement arose behind him.

Earlier that morning a storm had struck without warning; sudden peals of thunder, which kept within their constricted grasp all the furies of greater tempests still unborn. Mountain gorges had been transformed into raging torrents, everything succumbing and changing. Where there was a dip, it had been filled to the brim. Where there had been a brink, there was now a chasm; where a rock, now a mound. Then there had followed the awesome thunder, followed by the sharp crack of the lightning flash, and over it all, echoes multiplied a thousand fold. The storm had abated as quickly as it had come, as if some childish whim had gripped the practical joker, and he had put aside his teasing for another time. Fresh and sweet had come the breeze, laden with the scents of countless flowers.

Cautiously Juan edged backwards, looking about him at the men who surrounded him. Some familiar faces were conspicuously absent, some voices missing.

Now again his roving eyes settled upon the persistent drops of water, that, intermittently and yet always with the same force, the same disintegration, formed into running erosion farther on. Each drop was forgotten, and yet its action, no matter how small, added up to the vast total that had formed, was forming, and would form the canyons, the rivers, and the seas over all the earth. There was a stream, too, of lives, dotted along the way, along the weary months since that day when Hilda had betrayed him, when, shrieking with laughter, the fates had dealt him the cards that had turned his life into a desolate region, where winds brought only the faintest whispers of laughter that once had been his, of beliefs that had tottered and fallen, only to rise in yet another place like bubbles in a cauldron, finally to disappear. There was one force that kept his mind in its rightful sphere: the desperate resolve to hold on to this shred of earth that was his for the moment, to claim for his pride at least this much of a victory. As time passed he had ever distanced himself from that creed, with its stern disciplines, that was to be followed only because it was, perhaps, the best, and thus would win. Doubt assailed his weary mind and heart. Throughout history, others faced the same staggering challenges when doubts of their own came through the open door of inevitable defeat. Surging through the mists that beclouded his memory, the readings, beliefs, the teachings of childhood that he had at one time taken to be true, seemed somehow truer now, at this moment, in the deep silences of his soul, in that unspoken reasoning that is seldom heard. His face twisted in a grim smile.

The stuttering of a machine gun, far down the line, brought him back to the world of reality. 'Comrades,' he said, 'it looks like another of their interminable foraging raids on our position.'

They did not answer, but in their sullen faces he could read the selfsame thought. Hours and days and weeks of fighting, of dry gullies and crumbling cliffs, of screaming shells and of ever-dwindling numbers. There was nothing to be said. They knew their positions; they knew their assignments. Death would be their companion again that night, and the sudden presence of water in the river would, apparently, not prevent the enemy from crossing the line.

★

Hilda, as she walked down the Rambla de Cataluna towards the Plaza de Cataluna where her hotel was located, could not avoid an occasional backward glance. Was she being followed already? Ridiculous, of course – only the overwrought imagination of an overly emotional moment. The click of her heels against the pavement, the dark, inscrutable faces of the men and women who passed by her, all registered in her mind, at this moment, as a confused jumble.

Where had she experienced this feeling of desolation before? When had she known such icy fear? Brussels, Belgium, and the curiously hatted police of that country. So young; she had been so very young then, and naive. Yet the Party had chosen to send her there to live among a colony of Spanish fruit sellers, to learn the language of Spain, to become acquainted with its customs. And now, curiously, snatches of those days came back to her. Belgium, and the interminable rain, with the flat countryside squared into a thousand hedges, fences and walls. Village after village merged into each other, while the roads had crisscrossed into the pattern of a madman's dream. Then came the hurry and scurry of a great railway station with which she was unfamiliar, and the streams of people. The organisation that she did not comprehend was thrown at the confused young girl. There were the luggage carriers and porters, ever anxious to seize her bags and disappear into some unknown region where she had to follow, not knowing why, except that her trunk was her own property and was being carted away. The curious flat French of the Belgian she under-stood, although it had seemed like a different language.

But the paralysing fear, the strangeness of it all, had soon faded away, and her Spanish became nearly perfect. Only the faintest lingering of a German accent had remained. In gay parties she had more than once been taken for a Spanish student who had lived many years in Belgium, though her long-limbed, slim body, blonde hair, and grey-blue eyes spelled her Germanic origin. Through her ever-growing experience, and her own cold logic, she had soon come upon the weak links that spread like a net throughout Europe and the world. She had felt, then, that it was her duty to extirpate them, step by step. Tighter and tighter had grown her ring around the confider, until the outer pressure burst and the being dissolved into another memory. The organisation had to win always, for nothing could come before the power that would one day absorb, through conviction of the masses, the rule of the entire world. And so had begun the endless chain, from one to the other. Then had come the inevitable rolling of time, the constant turning of the hourglass, filling the empty with the full. This had once been her life. With brilliance she had come, and with brilliance she had gone, and afterwards had been the greyness of forgetfulness, merging into the greyness of the weather. So long ago. A hundred lifetimes ago, and a hundred thousand deaths ago.

Hilda reached the entrance of the hotel, now a Communist Party headquarters, and was astounded to find the once beautiful building a shambles, while *milicianos* sprawled in the big arm-chairs, their feet upon tables or whatever might be handiest. Here were hard-faced women, some in their early teens, khaki overalls, and the inevitable red handkerchief tied at the throat. Others wore men's shirts, leaving little to the imagination.

As she walked through the tangled maze, she felt herself a foreigner amidst these people of blood and action, these people of passions that flooded forth and swept all in their wake. There was no outward show of her presence, only a furtive glance from a pair of drowsy eyes.

Any one of them could well be her shadow in days to come. Any one of them could eliminate her without a moment's hesitation.

And as the door of her room closed behind her, she locked it with shaking fingers, and leaned against it, a throbbing, dizzy numbness flooding her body. She felt as if she were on some endless desert, plodding aimlessly on, totally alone, the flat surface unwrinkled by any change. In the immensity that surrounded her, eyes looked down unchangeable and untouchable, waiting to see her drop. And yet another figure, coming from afar, beckoning to her, entreated her to have courage.

The forms and voices faded away, and the warm blood flowed back into her limbs. Juan Avila. Somehow she would have to find him, if he was still alive. He, alone, could save her, if he would. But what right had she to expect anything of him? She had falsely betrayed him, had accused him and had nearly cost him his life. Still, there was her love for him, and love, alone, could survive in a world that was falling in about her. Someway, somehow she had to convince him that she loved him more than life itself. But did she? Why was life so important to her of a sudden? Why was it so important that she flee this trap that yawned open for her? She had known all the while the risks involved, the possibilities of imminent death. And yet that possibility had seemed remote and distant, always attached to others, but never to herself. Maybe he would spurn her, laugh at her, as she had been mocked in Paris, but she had to take the chance. She had to reach him, plead with him, unburden that soul that for so many years had dreamt of a molten river, of grey shapes, and of sparks as of life flitting away.

Dark Valley

Yea, though I walk through the valley of the shadow of death, I will fear no evil, for Thou art with me.

The Ketubim of Judah

The dugout was shrouded in darkness. Pedro sat in a far corner, his rifle by his side, his back to the wall. A pigskin of wine lay nearby, and on a table rested the most cherished possession of the unit, the wireless, its light-green control panel seemingly filled with a thousand wriggling needles. The men were listening to a concert being given by the French post at Toulouse. *Against the rules,* thought Pedro, and reached for the pigskin of wine. Orders and rules and counter-orders! War and all the myriad confusions that accompanied it.

But the music wafted his imagination along newly created channels, for his days were filled with raucous commands, the stillness of the enemy nearby, the crashing thunder of attack or defence. Now the harmony reacted with greater force upon him than upon those who listen, surrounded by comfort. He sat with folded arms, a smile appearing at the corner of his mouth where a cigarette hung, lifeless and forgotten.

Pedro had become somewhat of an enigma to the men around him. They liked him spontaneously, and accepted him for what he was, but they knew very little about him. For him, the days that were gone seemed to have been forgotten, save that a look of pain occasionally crept into his grey eyes, and his ever-present friend, Pablo Maiquez, warned them against intruding into his private life.

He felt a warm glow from the wine spreading over him, and the relative comfort of the dugout assumed a new proportion. The distant rattle of machine guns was drowned by the persuasive strains of music, and war, for the moment, seemed far away. Only his friend Pablo knew, by long association, that, behind that inexpressive face, a lonely heart mourned for a brother whom he dearly loved, a brother who might well be facing him across the river at that very minute.

★

The road wound down to Balaguer, and Hilda, staring out from the cab of the truck, saw the craggy, hard hills, the coastal range of the north-east of Spain, not high, but jagged, as if some great beast of the reptilian age had lain there, his thorny back protruding as the silt of ages passed over him.

Not a cloud was in the sky, and all about was a world of colour, yellowish brown and white, the red roofs reflecting the morning light. To the west and the south, mountains, and to the north an open triangle. River Ebro. Hilda saw the greyish green of the olive trees and vineyards, unkempt and withered now, after more than two years of war. Fig trees were broken, and their branches strewn around where the weight of the unpicked fruit had destroyed the strength of the trees. Houses were crumbling, untenanted, with broken roofs and black, staring windows.

The driver of the truck had shared his food with her, and she felt that he was the first kind person she had met in a long time. He had asked no questions when she requested a ride at the control station of Pedralves. She had flashed her Communist Party card there, and an hour had slowly trickled by. Anguish and fear. Had she been missed? Surely by now they would have picked up her trail, and the guard did not seem to like the idea of a foreign Communist waiting for a truck or other passing vehicle. But, miraculously, her luck had held.

'Where are you headed, comrade?' had come the query as the driver opened the door of the truck and leaned out. 'Rather strange for one of you foreigners not to be riding around in a plush car.'

'My car broke down.'

'Oh?' he smiled grimly. 'Just inside Barcelona, I suppose. Well, let's leave it at that. In these troubled days we all have to help whenever we can. We all have troubles,' he added, 'and some of them are quite clearly of our own making, while some are plainly inherited. Well, all this talk isn't getting us on the way. Where are you headed?'

'Balaguer.'

'Now that's a coincidence,' he said as they were driving away. 'I'm heading there, too, and I hope you know what you're getting into. That place is bombed every day, if not twice a day. It's a centre for our communications, and is milling with troops, trucks, engineering outfits, and what have you. Supply stores are all over the place, so it's a sure target. It lies in the middle of those hills like coffee in a cup.' He laughed shortly. 'Coffee did I say? I've forgotten what it tastes like. I see by your red handkerchief that you're a Communist. Things are changing, aren't they?'

She didn't know how to size the man up. She had to be extremely cautious, for all men were her enemies now that she had come under the censure of the Party. She leaned her head back upon the seat and closed her eyes. Soon she was fast asleep, exhausted by the strain of the past days.

Endless hours. She slept, but woke with a start as the vehicle hit a rough spot in the road; dozed again, until the truck creaked to a stop. It was night.

The entrance to the busy quartermaster depot welcomed her. Here she could surely find some garrulous old sergeant who would tell her the whereabouts of Juan Avila. Perhaps there was a telephone she could use. Her smile greeted a grey-haired, weary looking man who sat behind his desk, almost buried under a pile of papers.

'Where can I find Juan Avila?'

He glanced at her, throwing up his hands in apparent disgust. 'And who is he? It's not sufficient that I have to send a hundred of this, five hundred of that, fifty of the other to points A, B and C, when all I have is twenty in all. Now I have to play detective. I suppose you're looking for a lover, and I think you're a girl, though I'd never know it by the haircut and the man's overalls. Anything can happen in these stupid days. Away with you. Ask the mayor of the city or something, anything.'

She struggled to remain calm. Leaning forward, she looked full into his face, using all the arts that nature had given her in order to enforce her petition. 'I saw by the newspaper that Captain Avila had been responsible for heroically halting a drive of the enemy across the flooded River Cinca. Surely you know his whereabouts now.'

The man ran a heavy hand through his hair in a futile gesture. 'Yes, yes, I know you're pretty. I suppose I'll have to help you find this humbug. Come along, and I'll take you to the telephone exchange. I have a friend there who might be able to help, and you can stay with my aunt on the outskirts of town. I'll leave the office in the clumsy hands of my corporal.'

The city was a shambles, caved-in houses sitting amidst their ruins, yet nobody seemed to pay any attention to the miserable beings that rummaged around their broken homes, amid charred pieces of clothing; here a smashed bed and there a broken chair, a dog or cat sitting disconsolately on the edge of what had once been a carpet. Old and worn faces looked with stony despair at the end of what had been the work of a lifetime.

'Get into that little room over there,' said the sergeant, pointing to a small nook beside the entrance of the building. 'I'll run on ahead and make the arrangements, and then come back for you. You'll be all right there for the moment, and besides, that used to be the place where the nuns taught the children when this was a school.' He paused and grinned vacantly at her. 'A fitting thing, hey? A frightened Communist hiding out in a room that once belonged to the Church.'

She stepped into the room, which smelled of decay, the funny little flowers of its tattered wallpaper looking ludicrous and out of place as it curled away from the walls.

Minutes later, the sergeant reappeared, closing the door behind him. 'The girl at the exchange has already advised Juan Avila of your presence here, and he's been told you wish to see him. It's better this way, much better, for you'd have had a hard time trying to contact him out there. He'll be down on his first free day.'

Thank God for that! God? That word was coming easily to her these days. *Remember, there is no God, there is no God!*

As he turned to open the door, the sergeant suddenly pushed her violently against the wall. A luxurious, camouflaged automobile had stopped before the building in a swirl of dust. The front door flew open and a black leather-jacketed stranger leapt out, a submachine gun in his hand. Hilda, peering out from behind the sheltering frame of the soldier, saw the man open the rear door. A dark face stared out from the interior, and two bottle-green eyes looked impassively about. She felt an acute pain in the region of her heart, and it seemed as if she had been turned inside out. Suddenly she was weak and cold sweat bathed her body.

Preceded by two men with submachine guns slung over their shoulders, heavy pistols on their hips, in through the entrance came Ricardo, her Nemesis. Behind him, his hands tied behind his back, came the changed and haggard-faced driver of the truck to Balaguer, and behind him another guard. The pack was closing in on her, and once they picked up her scent they would never abandon the chase. She had disobeyed orders. Escape! She must somehow escape, into the mountains, into a cave, anywhere! Any place where these ruthless, angry eyes could not follow, boring into her very soul.

Stillness prevailed after the measured tread had passed into the interior of the building. The sergeant turned to her. 'Come, and quickly. The corporal will lead them on a wild goose chase. It's not the same here as in Barcelona, and the nearer they get to the front the less power they'll have. Those are the jackals that bring down the dying, and not the tiger that brings down its prey.'

They neared a long, low rambling house and an old voice responded to his hammering on the door. '*Quien va?*'

'It is I, Carlos. Hurry up – *Tia.*'

A noise of bolts being drawn and the heavy door creaked open. The features of a very old woman greeted them. She was bent by age, her hands crossed in front of her, but her watery eyes looked complacently at life, and a hundred wrinkles surrounded a face that might once have been pretty. Wisps of white hair came through the yellowed handkerchief that framed the worn face, and a black, knitted shawl covered her shoulders.

'I want you to hide this girl,' said the sergeant.

'Ah, everybody seeks hiding these days,' she said. 'But this is the last place to hide a person. Everybody in town knows that I still pray to the Virgin of Montserrat that this war that has caused so much evil should soon pass.'

He interrupted angrily, anxiety registering in his voice. 'Yes, I know all that, but in the stall, the one down near the riverbed where the cow stayed that was taken away, it's empty now. There's an ammunition depot near there, and nobody would think of that as a likely hiding place.

'Yes, when someone is in need a person should help, our faith decrees. The faith of forgiveness, young lady. I can give you a bit of lettuce and some honey. That'll appease your hunger, for there is no food to be had in the town. Tomorrow night I'll bring you a little soup that I make from beans that are stolen for me from the depot.'

And so they walked unseen among the piles of rubble that were strewn about to a door that leaned crazily upon broken hinges, beckoning them with a lopsided smile into the dark interior of the stable.

'There are no blankets,' said the sergeant, 'and forget about smoking. The tiniest light will bring them in here post-haste. Hide in the loft if you hear anything moving around. And remember, sounds carry far.' With this, he left her.

With an audible sigh she lay back upon the hay. She felt suddenly so desperately tired. No matter what happened, first she would sleep, and perhaps things would seem more cheerful when she awoke. Like a great, black, velvet blanket falling upon a white spot, sleep enveloped her there.

★

It took some time for Pedro to realise that the red signal on the short-wave receiver was warning them of a communication. With a grimace of distaste he switched off the music.

'What the hell!' ejaculated Pablo.

'Can't you see we're being signalled from headquarters?'

Words filtered through the loudspeaker. 'Listen Butterfly, listen Butterfly. Here Station Three, here Station Three. Over.'

Pedro reached for the microphone and flipped the switch with his thumb. 'Connected. Over.'

Letters and numbers filled the air in an incredible jargon. Pablo sat at the table, jotting down the information on a worn pad, his pencil barely discernible in the half light.

With a sigh, Pedro sat back. 'I'll bet five to one it's an order for attack.'

'Prepare detail inform,' interceded Pablo. 'Suggest possible attack between hills seven-eight-two and nine-eight-one, south by south-west from the former. Well, there you have it. This is to be sent by tomorrow morning at five. Frankly, I think this message has been sent to mislead the enemy. Undoubtedly those damn Reds have the message, too, by this time and are busy decoding it.'

'Oh?' Pedro eyed him speculatively. 'And what then, smart one?'

'It's simple, really. We'll be asked to draw and concentrate the enemy in front of us so other forces might attack some place else. So,' and he laughed grimly, 'you can see that we'll have a nice, benevolent mission on our hands one of these days.'

The voice of the commanding officer cut into the conversation. Students seem to see things from many angles, he was saying, but those angles were of little value at the moment. Rather, they had to think about attacking the enemy, and not how and when and where and why. He made his way to a table and drew out a map of the region from a stack of papers and spread it open, drawing two crosses with a pencil. 'It's evident,' he said, 'that to gallop over the riverbed would be sheer folly. This flood in the river will not last for long, now that the cloudburst has passed. Therefore, we'll have to resort to some old and time-tested tactics. Perhaps they haven't been used here, but they've most certainly been followed in other days in this region. One troop will have to do the walking, and pass without being seen. That's easily said but not so easily done. We'll make a great show of preparation here, and descend in the approved military fashion to the line of fortifications that we've thrown together so scraggily next to the riverbed. We'll be thoroughly pounded by artillery and mortar fire, but they'll be getting their own peppering, too. The enemy have practically all their accompanying baggage and fire concentrated in that canyon behind them.'

'And who,' said Pedro, 'will be going on that pleasant little walk you spoke of?'

'All in good time,' said the officer. 'We'll pick thirty volunteers, the strongest and hardiest we have. That goes for the officer that leads them, too. Now, to get down to business. We're on a ledge here that slopes down gradually behind us. When the orders have been received, and darkness has fallen, the chosen men will march to the rear a good mile. Then they'll approach as cautiously as possible to the brink at this spot here on the map.' He stabbed determinedly at the black cross with the blunt end of the pencil. 'This area is known to all of us, for it's been reconnoitred more than once. It ought to be as familiar as the palm of your hand. In any case, from that point on our other company is immovably entrenched, and the valley steepens so that it is only a narrow break between these two crosses. That's the place to come through. The Reds have never dared to approach through there, for it's so mined that a rabbit couldn't make his way across without being blown to bits. However, there's a path that can only be tight-roped one by one. Of course, once the river is crossed, there will be enemy mines to contend with. The artillery will concentrate all their fire on that immediate region as well as the enemy trenches. At that place the cliffs sort of turn inwards into a dried-up watercourse. There's bound to be a Red sentry there with a telephone. Too, the enemy machine guns will be found on those cliffs, and they can rake the entire valley with perfect precision. A pleasant little outing, hey?'

'And who,' grunted Pablo, 'is to lead this little parade?'

'Pedro, of course. Who else?'

'What?' Pablo snorted. 'Well, now, that's one dirty shame. I can outrun and out-walk this poor fellow any day. What's he supposed to do, heave rocks around or carry furniture?'

Pedro's heavy hand fell affectionately on his friend's shoulder. 'Thanks, but if the Fates will it, I'll gladly accept it. Nature seems to have adapted me better than most to resist. So be it.'

★

Far up in the sky Hilda heard, through her sleep-laden brain, the drone of far away motors. And in the sky eager eyes scanned a map with many notations written upon it. Along a dry creek bed, little squares were drawn with red ink. Far below, shimmering mountains seemed to drop away into a great cauldron. Not a light could be seen. A stream of blue flashes came from the darkness below, harmlessly passing to the left of the formation.

She sat up in the stygian darkness of the stable, her ears straining to catch the oncoming and ever-increasing sound. Around her were a hundred night noises: a patter of small feet, the creaking of a timber, the chirping of crickets. Pulling her knees up under her chin, she clasped her ankles. She realised, of a sudden, that she was shivering, though the night was not cold. A musty smell was everywhere. She wondered what time it was.

First, a thudding crash, far away towards the road from which she had come. Everywhere, machine guns released their staccato sounds. Amidst them came the deeper boom of anti-aircraft guns. An inferno had developed where only silence had prevailed a few short moments before. Crashes now, making the earth tremble, were behind her, but to her instant horror they were coming closer. She distinctly perceived the hideous shriek of the missiles of death – and then she felt as if a great hand had thrown her into a far corner. Everything was falling around her. Darkness.

Through a dense fog of different colours, yet always with a red background, a haze of confused thoughts appeared, snatches, as if from a broken film, flickering over an imaginary screen. She saw a small girl running beside a tall lady with no discernible features. A doll lay broken in the gutter, and she was trying to pick it up, but they would not let her.

More debris and more explosions! Darkness once again.

And a face appeared before her now, old and tired and wrinkled. As if from far away a voice whispered gently, 'Poor girl, no home, no friends, no family. *Dios mio.* So many people killed in this war, so many families destroyed. What drives people to do these things?'

And from the broken form, an answering whisper. 'I can't feel anything.'

The old woman tried to pull the heavy beams from the body that was half-buried in bricks, tiles and masonry. Her frail strength was not enough. Seating herself, she brushed away the dust that clung to Hilda's face. 'I had a daughter once, about your age,' she said. 'She's disappeared. I'm ignorant of many things, and you're from a foreign country. I don't know your creed or way of thinking but by the red handkerchief you wear you pretend to be a Communist. You must have been – once – but now you're not. They're after you, otherwise you wouldn't have been hiding here. Ah, death is near you, my child, but as I am old it's near me too.'

Hilda's beautiful grey eyes opened, and in them was an expression of the unknown, that deep unknown that she had tried to reason about, had tried to deny. 'Could you raise me just a little?' she said. 'Yes, that's better. Tell Juan Avila, whom I've so much harmed, that my wish is that he should forgive me. I tried to suppress the only feeling that can uplift the human spirit, love for our fellow beings. I love him – do you hear? I love him now, but I was too stupid to acknowledge it. Too late. Too late. All the sufferings I've endured these past two years have convinced me at the edge of darkness. I bow to the creed of love.' She breathed a low, deep sigh, the great eyes closing on the anxious face that bent over her. 'Let me lie back down – let me rest – rest.'

Extending her shaking hand over Hilda's head, the old woman stroked the golden hair with gentle strokes, her fingertips caressing the pale cheek. 'Poor girl. And what of your father and mother?'

A tear trickled out from under the closed eyelids. A shudder passed through the broken form – and a body lay where life had been.

Kneeling, the woman placed her stained handkerchief over the still face. Her gnarled hands made the sign of the cross, and, with closed eyes, she prayed for the victim of fate. Across the still air came the chorus of a marching unit, the surging notes of the Communist *Internationale*.

> *Arriba parias de la Tierra,*
> *En pie famelica legion…*

Rolling, impressive and sonorous. Life went on, to fight and destroy. Death lay, quiet and forgotten, and over it all, an old woman whispered her prayers.

The Wayfarer

In our watching we have watched for a nation that could not save us. They hunt our steps. We cannot go in our streets. Our end is near, our days are fulfilled; for our end is come.

The Book of Lamentations

A thin crescent, high up in the sky, served to deepen the shadows even more. Pedro could scarcely see the ground ahead of him. Worming his body forward, he cautiously retraced a path he had reconnoitred that same afternoon, followed by the men. The front seemed strangely quiet, broken only now and then by the sharp crack of a sniper taking his toll.

This was the only passage through the densely mined field. He glanced at the luminous face of his watch. Two minutes to spare, and they had reached the riverbed. Soon this deathly silence would be shattered by the sound of explosions.

He deployed the men by squads under the overhanging brink of the river's edge. If they sent up flares, at least they would be safe for the time being. Then, from far away, came four distinct thuds. Wave after wave of shrieking missiles rocketed over, transforming the world into heaving, flying chaos. Explosions everywhere. A tremendous concussion rocked the earth, flattening them to the ground. The signal. The minefields had been exploded, thank God.

As had been prearranged, the men disappeared into the dust and gloom. Was it his imagination, or could he hear a distinct rumble along the ground? It sounded as if a herd of cattle were being driven across the riverbed. Probably more gunnery farther up the river. He would have to act, and quickly, for soon the artillery would be blasting this place to rubble.

He ran into the narrow, steep ravine, knowing that any opposition would have been taken care of by the advance guard.

Everything was illuminated under the barrage of artillery, a lurid red glow, with yellowish black, billowing clouds enveloping the entire area.

Racing along the narrow ravine, he realised, by sheer instinct, that he was behind the enemy's position. This would be the worst moment of all.

★

'Well now,' said Juan Avila, 'that's a nice little piece of news. There's to be an imminent attack, and this night, too, of all times, when you can't see a damn thing. Too bad the water had to drain out of that river so fast. Double the watch, for there's not a sound out there. The Legion is cooking up something, and tell those that guard the ravine to be extra careful.'

He leaned his elbows over the parapet and rested comfortably against it. Above him was the black void of the sky, with here and there a star hanging, as though some capricious jeweller had studded black velvet with diamonds of different sizes. He remembered that night, leaving the massive portals of the desecrated church. Somehow he had felt that in that hour he had regained his lost youth, that carefree youth that he had practically forgotten. Had he really been the pilot of his own ship of being? He wondered. Mankind, back once again to its primeval state, where food and rest and sleep were the only obsessions. Hilda Krantz. The only woman he had ever loved. And yet she had betrayed him. How and why was this possible? To his mind there came anew the vision of the old and bent woman saying to him, 'Such a shame you arrived too late, my son. She wanted so very much to see you. She said to tell you that she always loved you, but that fate played its little game.'

All gone now, in days not so long, but to him it seemed for ever. Was it possible that there was nothing left of that wonderful brain and captivating personality but a lot of broken bones scattered around by rats? Still, he knew in that dark hour that as long as his brain had the capacity to remember and to reconstruct moments, seeing once again the happy smile flashing across that face otherwise so wilfully serene, she had not really gone for ever.

He tilted back his head and stared up at the immensity of space above him. For thousands of years and in the thousands of years to come, others had asked and would ask the same soul-searching question. And he saw himself in the school; saw those first few frantic actions: springing upon the fence, brawling in the streets, fleeing through the gathering gloom. Yet Nemesis had decreed that he and his brother should oppose each other almost from the cradle. His father had known the course he was setting for himself. And yet he had only sought to channel the age-old hatred through a creed that began by levelling economy and granting equality to all. But in striving to reach that goal there seemed to be formed, in return, an autocracy more rigid and unyielding than any power he had ever dreamed existed. Where was spiritual peace, the contentment of mankind with its surroundings and activities? Juan had known that peace when playing with his brother, when listening with bated breath to the stories told by his mother, when looking into Hilda's grey eyes when first they met, sharing the incommunicable intensity of their ideas: peace of mind and heart, and all from the concept of love – not in the satisfying of carnal lusts, in the calming of instinctive passions.

Four distinct thuds came to his ears, now, followed immediately by the shrieking of shells. Pandemonium broke loose about him: behind, in front, below, on top of him. Shells were falling everywhere. Thick, yellowish-black clouds enveloped him, and a great explosion sounded far up the river. The minefield, he supposed.

From then on, all was madness and insanity. They had opened fire behind him now, and he was being attacked in the rearguard. Orders shouted out. Counter-attack, and try to envelop those weaker forces. Shoot the way through. The boom of hand grenades augmented the raging storm about him. Taking a last, hurried look over the parapet, he breathed a sigh of relief. Someone had acted intelligently for a change. The riverbed was no longer white. Instead, a brown, ever-growing torrent was gripping the bushes, the rocks with hungry, thrusting fingers. He smiled a grim, hard smile. With this flood the doom of the attackers was sealed. He had thought about that dam for a long time, but the wisdom of not having blown it up was only too apparent now.

Dawn appeared as the barrage of artillery slowly slackened. A haggard and worn Juan crawled wearily from an explosion cone and took toll of the battlefield. A deathlike silence suddenly prevailed. Of his company, something like a troop remained. Of the attackers, none. Around each of the attacking groups sprawled figures, the dust settling down upon them as if to hide their pain-wracked faces. And on the far side, a greater number of victims of man-made hell lay about in grotesque attitudes.

A groan from one of the bodies, and something in the build of the man, the great shoulders, the black hair, caused Juan to leap forward. Pedro. The world was spinning around him. Nothing mattered, for his eyes were focused only upon that face that death had marked for its own. Plucking feverishly at his canteen, he forced some drops of water through the clenched teeth.

The eyes opened and stared blankly into his. 'You!' came the gasping word. 'You! Traitor to your family!'

'Be quiet,' said Juan, desperation colouring his voice. 'You must rest.'

'Rest?' He coughed, flecks of reddened foam dotting his lips. 'Yes, I'll rest, but only – only after I've told you that your way has led to hell – straight down to hell.' The lips closed, his eyes rolled backward in their sockets, and a rattling, gurgling sound came from the crimson-stained chest.

Juan arose, and through a mist that seemed to him to exist everywhere about, there came a voice, as if from a hundred miles away, asking a question – insisting. Brushing a shaking hand across his eyes, Juan answered, 'My brother.'

As the released slaves of Saladin, as the beaten warriors of the second crusade, as all those who suffer for the final conquering of a creed, so Juan Avila found himself on the stairway of his life. Behind were dark and passionate shadows; interwoven with them were the flames of destruction and the cries of the accused. About him was the sure knowledge of inevitable defeat of his cause, for the enemy was growing stronger every day. Personalities had dwindled away and no longer existed, for his mental process was obscured by fear. Only abject terror remained. And yet, at the end of the long stairway, shining like a beacon from the last step, was the shape that for two thousand years had assembled around itself compassion, beauty, love and forgiveness. He would somehow live through this awful hell, would somehow find his way out of this tangled maze of darkness and chaos. The shadow of the cross fell now across his tortured soul, even as it had fallen across his body in that distant church so long ago. He would yet live to redeem himself, to make his reason for living clear to himself.

Standing there over the twisted body of his brother, the words of a long-forgotten prayer flooded his being. 'Holy Mary, Mother of God, pray for us sinners, now and at the hour of our death…'

Appendix: Memoir
(or how writing a book converted me)

In 1952, while a ministerial student at the Presbyterian seminary in San Anselmo, California, I had an epiphany that changed my career and my personal religion, among other things.

The epiphany was channelled through the person of a young man from Spain, whose stepfather's assassination had triggered the horrific Spanish Civil War that in turn presaged the Second World War.

The Spaniard's name was William Pedraza. His mother was the Baroness Jacques de Borchgrave who was living in Grass Valley, California, having returned to her homeland following the murder of her husband, the Belgian Ambassador to Spain.

Pedraza was a teacher at the San Rafael Military Academy in the California city of the same name. I was also a teacher at that school, while attending nearby San Francisco Theological Seminary from 1952 through 1953.

Though I had, as a sailor, taken part in the Second World War, I had not an inkling of the roles played by international communism and Germany's National Socialism in the Spanish conflagration that consumed over one million lives, including 4184 Roman Catholic clergy and countless numbers of nuns and monks. Fifty years later, on 28 October 2005, seven of those priests and one nun were beatified as martyrs for refusing to renounce their faith. Late night conversations with Pedraza convinced me that his was a story that desperately needed to be told. This was especially true considering that communism, following the demise of Hitlerism, remained the only dangerous threat to world peace.

Out of those Pedraza-initiated marathon conversations, and some meetings with the Baroness, came a book that was finally published with the help and encouragement of legendary Oscar-winning MGM screenwriter Frances Marion, who was the first to tell me I knew how to write.

Though the story of a young Spanish communist who re-discovers his Catholic faith received what can only be described as rave reviews by people like Bishop Sheen, Ronald Reagan, various Catholic organisations and the media, the book sank into oblivion after two editions were produced. An effort by famed Catholic director Leo McCarey to turn *Wayfarers of Fate* into a film following his William Holden opus *Satan Never Sleeps* failed for lack of funding and McCarey's premature death.

Never having been to Spain, much of the highly-detailed physical descriptions, that one critic called 'descriptive narrative all too real', had to come from the lips of Pedraza. That same critic, one Patricia Harding, reminded me in May 2006 that I had written an anti-war novel when she wrote that it 'certainly captures the chaos, the horrors and the desolation of war – graphically tragic and a human tragedy.'

Reagan, on the other hand, said he intended to recommend copies to 'some of our liberal producers, just to watch them squirm'. It was Reagan who persuaded Leo McCarey to option the book for a film, by convincing his best friend, William Holden (the best man at Reagan's wedding) to pitch the book to McCarey as the perfect follow-up to his pro-Catholic film *Satan Never Sleeps* in which Holden had starred.

Walter Winchell, with whom I would one day work on the occult aspects of the Robert Kennedy assassination, told me that I was wasting my 'talent' at the seminary because he thought I would make a good reporter.

As it happened, he was a bit of a prophet because, while writing the book, I left the seminary and was seriously contemplating Catholicism. Actually, I had been baptised Catholic in Foley, Alabama, but by the time I was seven years old, my family had become Methodists, still later becoming Presbyterians.

That switch to Protestantism came about because my parents had an unpleasant disagreement with the local priest over funeral arrangements for my older brother, killed by a train as he was going back to his Civilian Conservation Corps post in Wisconsin. I never did find out what caused my parents to abandon the faith and they refused to talk about it to me or anyone else in the family.

Hence my many siblings were shocked when, in God's time, my footsteps followed those of Juan Avila, the hero of *Wayfarers of Fate* back to the long-abandoned faith of my childhood.

Meanwhile, one critic for the respected *Marin County Independent Journal* opined that my labour of love over a three-year period produced a first novel that was 'delicate, dedicated, sensitive, explosive – (that) had the stamp of greatness about it – uncommon, useful, vivid – I read it without laying it down. It has meaning for America and should be read by millions'; words that sounded pretty good to a twenty-five-year-old.

Needless to say, the 'millions' were an illusion, though the praise would have been nearly enough to convince me to switch from fledgling minister to full-time writer. But it was another line in that same 1956 review that apparently caused Winchell to urge me to become a newsman. I found out later that the line was 'It is as fresh as tomorrow's paper and as old as time.' Frankly, I preferred the reviewer's words: 'shedding welcome light into a dark chamber – filled with compassion', especially the last word, since I was still idealistic. But I still never thought it was an anti-war novel.

Fifty years flew past. I took Winchell's advice, became a reporter at the *LA Examiner* and the *Anaheim Bulletin*, as well as the *National Educator*. A series of books followed, including a small one on the murder of RFK (that I recently discovered is selling used on the internet for $97!). Then came *Bitter Harvest*, about the farm labour war, which was serialised in many papers, and *The Child Seducers*, a book that I wrote based on a newspaper series I had written on the sex-education battle in Anaheim. Meanwhile, I was promoted to writing a daily 'School and Family' column while producing another book, *The Conspirators – Men Against God*. All this frenetic activity led to my fifteen minutes of international TV and radio fame.

In 1977 (by then secretary of my council at Queen of Angels Catholic church in Riverside, California) I had a second epiphany and used my small savings and money from sale of a horse, a truck and some land to start a cancer organisation, naming it the Cancer Federation.

Thirty years later, that organisation is a sizeable national charity that, in addition to funding research and scholarships, produces a magazine and various books (including several of mine, for which I receive no remuneration).

In 2005, a young man who operates our office computer put my name into the internet and, lo and behold, all my literary output, including serialisations of some books, came pouring forth. What a shock!

Missing, however, was *Wayfarers*. Since I did not have a copy, we decided to give it a try and I was stunned to discover five internet bookstores selling used copies ranging in price from $75 to $1000. The *Inland Empire Radio News* site said the book had 'touched the hearts of many'. That was music to my ears, especially since, on 15 June 2006 the book was back in bookstores in America.

That should give some hope to my fellow golden-agers, especially since my alma mater in Oregon, Pacific University, has just informed me that the book is now in their library's permanent collection. That is nice, since they totally ignored it the first time around.

This present interest on Pacific's part might be partially explained by the fact that over the years, my charity has donated a couple of hundred thousand dollars to the school. Am I too cynical?

In any case, I played out, in my own life's journey, many of the same impulses that shaped Juan Avila's life. True, I never was a communist, but I did find myself involved in living in a 'Students in Industry' project in 1951, that the FBI later described as a communist front, much to my consternation. Just as the hero of my book found his way out of the shadows to his childhood faith, so the book's research and production impelled me to abandon a life of Protestantism for a return to Rome, to the amazed perplexity of many who thought they had me figured out.

The last line of *Wayfarers* sums it up. Originally, the final line, uttered by Juan on the battlefield as his world collapses about him, was the 'Our Father'. The new edition, though, ends with what I believe a Catholic would be more likely to say: 'Holy Mary, Mother of God, pray for us sinners, now and at the hour of our death...'; those words summing up not only my hero's battlefield conversion, but perhaps my recognition of my own mortality, years later.

I have often wondered how profoundly different my life would have been if I had not been impelled to write *Wayfarers of Fate*. But then, perhaps that title applies more to me than to any of the novel's characters.

John Steinbacher